Dark Mirror

of

The World's Desire

"Say, thou Evil, must I indeed steal the beauty of another to win him whom I love?" Meriamun asked.

"This must thou do," said the Evil, "or lose him in Helen's arms."

Then she doubted no more, but lifted the shining Evil and held it to her. With a dreadful laugh it twined itself about her, and lo! it shrank to the shape of a girdling, double-headed snake of gold with eyes of ruby flame. And as it shrank, Meriamun watched herself in the mirror. And as she watched, her face grew as the face of death—ashen and hollow—then slowly burned into life again. But all her loveliness was now changed. Her dark locks changed to locks of gold . . . her deep eyes changed to eyes of blue . . . the glory of her pride changed to the sweetness of Helen's smile.

Now she would go forth—heavy with her sin, but her heart alight as with a flame—to win Odysseus the Wanderer to her arms . . . no matter what the cost!

Also by H. Rider Haggard
Published by Ballantine Books:

PEOPLE OF THE MIST

WHEN THE WORLD SHOOK

WISDOM'S DAUGHTER

THE WORLD'S DESIRE

H. Rider Haggard
and
Andrew Lang

A Del Rey Book

BALLANTINE BOOKS • NEW YORK

A Del Rey Book
Published by Ballantine Books

ISBN 0-345-27218-8

Manufactured in the United States of America

First Ballantine Books Edition: January 1972
Second Printing: December 1977

Cover art by Michael Herring

TO

W. B. RICHMOND, A.R.A.

CONTENTS

BOOK I

BOOK II

BOOK III

THE WORLD'S
DESIRE

Come with us, ye whose hearts are set
On this, the Present to forget;
Come read the things whereof ye know
They were not, and could not be so!
The murmur of the fallen creeds,
Like winds among wind-shaken reeds
Along the banks of holy Nile,
Shall echo in your ears the while;
The fables of the North and South
Shall mingle in a modern mouth;
The fancies of the West and East
Shall flock and flit about the feast
Like doves that cooed, with waving wing,
The banquets of the Cyprian king.
Old shapes of song that do not die
Shall haunt the halls of memory,
And though the Bow shall prelude clear
Shrill as the song of Gunnar's spear,
There answer sobs from lute and lyre
That murmured of The World's Desire.

.   .   .   .   .

There lives no man but he hath seen
The World's Desire, the fairy queen.
None but hath seen her to his cost,
Not one but loves what he has lost.
None is there but hath heard her sing
Divinely through his wandering ;
Not one but he hath followed far
The portent of the Bleeding Star ;
Not one but he hath chanced to wake,
Dreamed of the Star and found the Snake.
Yet, through his dreams a wandering fire.
Still, still she flits, THE WORLD'S DESIRE !

BOOK I

1. THE SILENT ISLE

Across the wide backs of the waves, beneath the mountains, and between the islands, a ship came stealing from the dark into the dusk, and from the dusk into the dawn. The ship had but one mast, one broad brown sail with a star embroidered on it in gold; her stem and stern were built high, and curved like a bird's beak; her prow was painted scarlet, and she was driven by oars as well as by the western wind.

A man stood alone on the half-deck at the bows, a man who looked always forward, through the night, and the twilight, and the clear morning. He was of no great stature, but broad-breasted and very wide-shouldered, with many signs of strength. He had blue eyes, and dark curled locks falling beneath a red cap such as sailors wear, and over a purple cloak, fastened with a brooch of gold. There were threads of silver in his curls, and his beard was flecked with white. His whole heart was following his eyes, watching first for the blaze of the island beacons out of the darkness, and, later, for the smoke rising from the far-off hills. But he watched in vain; there was neither light nor smoke on the gray peak that lay clear against a field of yellow sky.

There was no smoke, no fire, no sound of voices, nor cry of birds. The isle was deadly still.

As they neared the coast, and neither heard nor saw a

sign of life, the man's face fell. The gladness went out of his eyes, his features grew older with anxiety and doubt, and with longing for tidings of his home.

No man ever loved his home more than he, for this was Odysseus, the son of Laertes—whom some call Ulysses—returned from his unsung second wandering. The whole world has heard the tale of his first voyage, how he was tossed for ten years on the sea after the taking of Troy, how he reached home at last, alone and disguised as a beggar; how he found violence in his house, how he slew his foes in his own hall, and won his wife again. But even in his own country he was not permitted to rest, for there was a curse upon him and a labour to be accomplished. He must wander again till he reached the land of men who had never tasted salt, nor ever heard of the salt sea. There he must sacrifice to the Sea-God, and then, at last, set his face homewards. Now he had endured that curse, he had fulfilled the prophecy, he had angered, by misadventure, the Goddess who was his friend, and after adventures that have never yet been told, he had arrived within a bowshot of Ithaca.

He came from strange countries, from the Gates of the Sun and the White Rock, from the Passing Place of Souls and the people of Dreams.

But he found his own isle more still and strange by far. The realm of Dreams was not so dumb, the Gates of the Sun were not so still, as the shores of the familiar island beneath the rising dawn.

This story, whereof the substance was set out long ago by Rei, the instructed Egyptian priest, tells what he found there, and the tale of the last adventures of Odysseus, Laertes' son.

The ship ran on and won the well-known haven, sheltered from wind by two headlands of sheer cliff. There she sailed straight in, till the leaves of the broad olive tree at the head of the inlet were tangled in her cordage. Then the Wanderer, without once looking back, or saying one word of farewell to his crew, caught a bough of the olive tree with his hand, and swung himself ashore. Here he kneeled, and kissed the earth, and, covering his head within his cloak, he prayed that he might find his house at peace, his wife dear and true, and his son worthy of him.

But not one word of his prayer was to be granted. The Gods give and take, but on the earth the Gods cannot restore.

When he rose from his knees he glanced back across the waters, but there was now no ship in the haven, nor any sign of a sail upon the seas.

And still the land was silent; not even the wild birds cried a welcome.

The sun was hardly up, men were scarce awake, the Wanderer said to himself; and he set a stout heart to the steep path leading up the hill, over the wolds, and across the ridge of rock that divides the two masses of the island. Up he climbed, purposing, as of old, to seek the house of his faithful servant, the swineherd, and learn from him the tidings of his home. On the brow of a hill he stopped to rest, and looked down on the house of the servant. But the strong oak palisade was broken, no smoke came from the hole in the thatched roof, and, as he approached, the dogs did not run barking, as sheep-dogs do, at the stranger. The very path to the house was overgrown, and dumb with grass; even a dog's keen ears could scarcely have heard a footstep.

The door of the swineherd's hut was open, but all was dark within. The spiders had woven a glittering web across the empty blackness, a sign that for many days no man had entered. Then the Wanderer shouted twice, and thrice, but the only answer was an echo from the hill. He went in, hoping to find food, or perhaps a spark of fire sheltered under the dry leaves. But all was vacant and cold as death.

The Wanderer came forth into the warm sunlight, set his face to the hill again, and went on his way to the city of Ithaca.

He saw the sea from the hill-top glittering as of yore, but there were no brown sails of fisher-boats on the sea. All the land that should now have waved with the white corn was green with tangled weeds. Half-way down the rugged path was a grove of alders, and the basin into which water flowed from the old fountain of the Nymphs. But no maidens were there with their pitchers; the basin was broken, and green with mould; the water slipped through the crevices and hurried to the sea. There were no offerings of wayfarers, rags and pebbles, by the well; and on the altar of the Nymphs the flame had long been cold. The very ashes were covered with grass, and a branch of ivy had hidden the stone of sacrifice.

On the Wanderer pressed with a heavy heart; now the high roof of his own hall and the wide fenced courts were within his sight, and he hurried forward to know the worst.

Too soon he saw that the roofs were smokeless, and all the court was deep in weeds. Where the altar of Zeus had stood in the midst of the court there was now no altar, but a great, gray mound, not of earth, but of white dust mixed with black. Over this mound the coarse grass pricked up scantily, like thin hair on a leprosy.

Then the Wanderer shuddered, for out of the gray mound peeped the charred black bones of the dead. He drew near, and, lo! the whole heap was of nothing else than the ashes of men and women. Death had been busy here: here many people had perished of a pestilence. They had all been consumed on one funeral fire, while they who laid them there must have fled, for there was no sign of living man. The doors gaped open, and none entered, and none came forth. The house was dead, like the people who had dwelt in it.

Then the Wanderer paused where once the old hound Argos had welcomed him and had died in that welcome. There, unwelcomed, he stood, leaning on his staff. Then a sudden ray of the sun fell on something that glittered in the heap, and he touched it with the end of the staff he had in his hand. It slid jingling from the heap; it was a bone of a fore-arm, and that which glittered on it was a half-molten ring of gold. On the gold these characters were engraved:

ΙΚΜΑΛΙΟΣ ΜΕΠΟΙΕΣΕΝ.

(Icmalios made me.)

At the sight of the armlet the Wanderer fell on the earth, grovelling among the ashes of the pyre, for he knew the gold ring which he had brought from Ephyre long ago, for a gift to his wife Penelope. This was the bracelet of the bride of his youth, and here, a mockery and a terror, were those kind arms in which he had lain. Then his strength was shaken with sobbing, and his hands clutched blindly before him, and he gathered dust and cast it upon his head till the dark locks were defiled with the ashes of his dearest, and he longed to die.

There he lay, biting his hands for sorrow, and for wrath against God and Fate. There he lay while the sun in the heavens smote him, and he knew it not; while the wind of the sunset stirred in his hair, and he stirred not. He could not even shed one tear, for this was the sorest of all the sorrows that he had known on the waves of the sea, or on land among the wars of men.

The sun fell and the ways were darkened. Slowly the eastern sky grew silver with the moon. A nightfowl's voice was heard from afar, it drew nearer; then through the shadow of the pyre the black wings fluttered into the light, and the carrion bird fixed its talons and its beak on the Wanderer's neck. Then he moved at length, tossed up an arm, and caught the bird of darkness by the neck, and broke it, and dashed it on the ground. His sick heart was mad with the little sudden pain, and he clutched for the knife in his girdle that he might slay himself, but he was unarmed. At last he rose, muttering, and stood in the moonlight, like a lion in some ruinous palace of forgotten kings. He was faint with hunger and weak with long lamenting, as he stepped within his own doors. There he paused on that high threshold of stone where once he had sat in the disguise of a beggar, that very threshold whence, on another day, he had shot the shafts of doom among the wooers of his wife and the wasters of his home. But now his wife was dead: all his voyaging was ended here, and all his wars were vain. In the white light the house of his kingship was no more than the ghost of a home, dreadful, unfamiliar, empty of warmth and love and light. The tables were fallen here and there through the long hall; mouldering bones, from the funeral feast, and shattered cups and dishes lay in one confusion; the ivory chairs were broken, and on the walls the moonbeams glistened now and again from points of steel and blades of bronze, though many swords were dark with rust.

But there, in its gleaming case, lay one thing friendly and familiar. There lay the Bow of Eurytus, the bow for which great Heracles had slain his own host in his halls; the dreadful bow that no mortal man but the Wanderer could bend. He was never used to carry this precious bow with him on shipboard, when he went to the wars, but treasured it at home, the memorial of a dear friend foully slain. So now, when the voices of dog, and slave, and child, and wife were mute, there yet came out of the stillness a word of welcome to the Wanderer. For this bow, which had thrilled in the grip of a god, and had scattered the shafts of the vengeance of Heracles, was wondrously made and magical. A spirit dwelt within it which knew of things to come, which boded the battle from afar, and therefore always before the slaying of men the bow sang strangely through the night. The voice of it was thin and shrill, a ringing and a singing of the string of the bow. While the Wanderer stood and looked on his weapon, hark! the bow began to thrill! The sound was faint at first, a thin note, but as he listened the voice of it in that silence grew clear, strong, angry, and triumphant. In his ears and to his heart it seemed that the wordless chant rang thus—

> Keen and low
> Doth the arrow sing
> The Song of the Bow,
> The sound of the string.
> The shafts cry shrill:
> Let us forth again,
> Let us feed our fill
> On the flesh of men.

Greedy and fleet
  Do we fly from far,
Like the birds that meet
  For the feast of war,
Till the air of fight
  With our wings be stirred,
As it whirrs from the flight
  Of the ravening bird.
Like the flakes that drift
  On the snow-wind's breath,
Many and swift,
  And winged for death—
Greedy and fleet,
  Do we speed from far,
Like the birds that meet
  On the bridge of war.
Fleet as ghosts that wail,
  When the dart strikes true,
Do the swift shafts hail,
  Till they drink warm dew.
Keen and low
  Do the gray shafts sing
The Song of the Bow,
  The sound of the string.

This was the message of Death, and this was the first sound that had broken the stillness of his home.

At the welcome of this music which spoke to his heart—this music he had heard so many a time—the Wanderer knew that there was war at hand. He knew that the wings of his arrows should be swift to fly, and their beaks of bronze were whetted to drink the blood of men. He put out his hand and took the bow, and tried the string, and it answered shrill as the song of the swallow.

Then at length, when he heard the bowstring twang to his touch, the fountains of his sorrow were unsealed; tears came like soft rains on a frozen land, and the Wanderer wept.

When he had his fill of weeping, he rose, for hunger drove him—hunger that is of all things the most shameless, being stronger far than sorrow, or love, or any other desire. The Wanderer found his way through the narrow door behind the daïs, and stumbling now and again over fallen fragments of the home which he himself had built, he went to the inner, secret storehouse. Even *he* could scarcely find the door, for saplings of trees had grown up about it; yet he found it at last. Within the holy well the water was yet babbling and shining in the moonlight over the silver sands; and here, too, there was store of mouldering grain, for the house had been abundantly rich when the great plague fell upon the people while he was far away. So he found food to satisfy his hunger, after a sort, and next he gathered together out of his treasure-chest the beautiful golden armour of unhappy Paris, son of Priam, the false love of fair Helen. These arms had been taken at the sack of Troy, and had lain long in the treasury of Menelaus in Sparta; but on a day he had given them to Odysseus, the dearest of all his guests. The Wanderer clad himself in this golden gear, and took the sword called 'Euryalus's Gift,' a bronze blade with a silver hilt, and a sheath of ivory, which a stranger had given him in a far-off land. Already the love of life had come back to him, now that he had eaten and drunk, and had heard the Song of the Bow, the Slayer of Men. He lived yet, and hope lived in him though his house was desolate, and his wedded wife was dead, and there was none to give him tidings of his one child, Telemachus. Even so life beat strong in his heart, and his hands would keep his head if any sea-robbers had come to the city of Ithaca and made their home there, like hawks in the forsaken nest of an eagle of the sea. So he clad himself in his armour, and chose out two spears from a stand of lances, and cleaned them, and girt about his shoulders a quiver full of shafts, and took in hand his great bow, the Bow of Eurytus, which no other man could bend.

Then he went forth from the ruined house into the moonlight, went forth for the last time; for never again did the high roof echo to the footstep of its lord. Long has the grass grown over it, and the sea-wind wailed!

2. THE VISION OF THE
WORLD'S DESIRE

The fragrant night was clear and still, the silence scarce broken by the lapping of the waves, as the Wanderer went down from his fallen home to the city on the sea, walking warily, and watching for any light from the houses of the people. But they were all as dark as his own, many of them roofless and ruined, for, after the plague, an earthquake had smitten the city. There were gaping chasms in the road, here and there, and through rifts in the walls of the houses the moon shone strangely, making ragged shadows. At last the Wanderer reached the Temple of Athene, the Goddess of War; but the roof had fallen in, the pillars were overset, and the scent of wild thyme growing in the broken pavement rose where he walked. Yet, as he stood by the door of the fane, where he had burned so many a sacrifice, at length he spied a light blazing from the windows of a great chapel by the sea. It was the Temple of Aphrodite, the Queen of Love, and from the open door a sweet savour of incense and a golden blaze rushed forth till they were lost in the silver of the moonshine and in the salt smell of the sea. Thither the Wanderer went slowly, for his limbs were swaying with weariness, and he was half in a dream. Yet he hid himself cunningly in the shadow of a long avenue of myrtles, for he guessed that sea-robbers were keeping revel in the forsaken shrine. But he heard no sound of singing and no tread of dancing feet within the fane of the Goddess of Love; the sacred

9

plot of the goddess and her chapels were silent. He hearkened awhile, and watched, till at last he took courage, drew near the doors, and entered the holy place. But in the tall, bronze braziers there were no faggots burning, nor were there torches lighted in the hands of the golden men and maids, the images that stand within the fane of Aphrodite. Yet, if he did not dream, nor take moonlight for fire, the temple was bathed in showers of gold by a splendour of flame. None might see its centre nor its fountain; it sprang neither from the altar nor the statue of the goddess, but was everywhere imminent, a glory not of this world, a fire untended and unlit. And the painted walls with the stories of the loves of men and gods, and the carven pillars and the beams, and the roof of green, were bright with flaming fire!

At this the Wanderer was afraid, knowing that an Immortal was at hand; for the comings and the goings of the gods were attended, as he had seen, by this wonderful light of unearthly fire. So he bowed his head, and hid his face as he sat by the altar in the holiest of the holy shrine, and with his right hand he grasped the horns of the altar. As he sat there, perchance he woke, and perchance he slept. However it was, it seemed to him that soon there came a murmuring and a whispering of the myrtle leaves and laurels, and a sound in the tops of the pines, and then his face was fanned by a breath more cold than the wind that wakes the dawn. At the touch of this breath the Wanderer shuddered, and the hair on his flesh stood up, so cold was the strange wind.

There was silence; and he heard a voice, and he knew that it was the voice of no mortal, but of a goddess. For the speech of goddesses was not strange in his ears; he knew the clarion cry of Athene, the Queen of Wisdom and of War; and the winning words of Circe, the Daughter of the Sun, and the sweet song of Calypso's voice as she wove with her golden shuttle at the loom. But now the words came sweeter than the moaning of doves, more soft than sleep. So came the golden voice, whether he woke or whether he dreamed.

'Odysseus, thou knowest me not, nor am I thy lady, nor

hast thou ever been my servant! Where is she, the Queen of the Air, Athene, and why comest *thou* here as a suppliant at the knees of the daughter of Dione?'

He answered nothing, but he bowed his head in deeper sorrow.

The voice spake again:

'Behold, thy house is desolate; thy hearth is cold. The wild hare breeds on thy hearthstone, and the nightbird roosts beneath thy roof-tree. Thou hast neither child nor wife nor native land, and *she* hath forsaken thee—thy Lady Athene. Many a time didst thou sacrifice to her the thighs of kine and sheep, but didst thou ever give so much as a pair of doves to *me*? Hath she left thee, as the Dawn forsook Tithonus, because there are now threads of silver in the darkness of thy hair? Is the wise goddess fickle as a nymph of the woodland or the wells? Doth she love a man only for the bloom of his youth? Nay, I know not; but this I know, that on thee, Odysseus, old age will soon be hastening—old age that is pitiless, and ruinous, and weary, and weak—age that cometh on all men, and that is hateful to the Gods. Therefore, Odysseus, ere yet it be too late, I would bow even thee to my will, and hold thee for my thrall. For I am she who conquers all things living: Gods and beasts and men. And hast thou thought that thou only shalt escape Aphrodite? Thou that hast never loved as I would have men love; thou that hast never obeyed me for an hour, nor ever known the joy and the sorrow that are mine to give? For thou didst but endure the caresses of Circe, the Daughter of the Sun, and thou wert aweary in the arms of Calypso, and the Sea King's daughter came never to her longing. As for her who is thy dear wife Penelope, thou didst love her with a loyal heart, but never with a heart of fire. Nay, she was but thy companion, thy house-wife, and the mother of thy child. She was mingled with all thy memories of the land thou lovest, and so thou gavest her a little love. But she is dead; and thy child too is no more; and thy very country is as the ashes of a forsaken hearth where once was a camp of men. What have all thy wars and wanderings won for thee, all thy labours, and all the adventures thou hast achieved?

For what didst thou seek among the living and the dead? Thou soughtest that which all men seek—thou soughtest *The World's Desire*. They find it not, nor hast thou found it, Odysseus; and thy friends are dead; thy land is dead; nothing lives but Hope. But the life that lies before thee is new, without a remnant of the old days, except for the bitterness of longing and remembrance. Out of this new life, and the unborn hours, wilt thou not give, what never before thou gavest, one hour to me, to be my servant?'

The voice, as it seemed, grew softer and came nearer, till the Wanderer heard it whisper in his very ear, and with the voice came a divine fragrance. The breath of her who spoke seemed to touch his neck; the immortal tresses of the Goddess were mingled with the dark curls of his hair.

The voice spake again:

'Nay, Odysseus, didst thou not once give me one little hour? Fear, not, for thou shalt not see me at this time, but lift thy head and look on The World's Desire!'

Then the Wanderer lifted his head, and he saw, as it were in a picture or in a mirror of bronze, the vision of a girl. She was more than mortal tall, and though still in the first flower of youth, and almost a child in years, she seemed fair as a goddess, and so beautiful that Aphrodite herself may perchance have envied this loveliness. She was slim and gracious as a young shoot of a palm tree, and her eyes were fearless and innocent as a child's. On her head she bore a shining urn of bronze, as if she were bringing water from the wells, and behind her was the foliage of a plane tree. Then the Wanderer knew her, and saw her once again as he had seen her, when in his boyhood he had journeyed to the Court of her father, King Tyndareus. For, as he entered Sparta, and came down the hill Taygetus, and as his chariot wheels flashed through the ford of Eurotas, he had met her there on her way from the river. There, in his youth, his eyes had gazed on the loveliness of Helen, and his heart had been filled with the desire of the fairest of women, and like all the princes of Achaia he had sought her hand in marriage. But Helen was given to another man, to Menelaus, Atreus' son, of an evil house, that the knees of many might be loosened in death, and that there might be a song in the ears of men in after time.

As he beheld the vision of young Helen, the Wanderer too grew young again. But as he gazed with the eyes and loved with the first love of a boy, she melted like a mist, and out of the mist came another vision. He saw himself, disguised as a beggar, beaten and bruised, yet seated in a long hall bright with gold, while a woman bathed his feet, and anointed his head with oil. And the face of the woman was the face of the maiden, and even more beautiful, but sad with grief and with an ancient shame. Then he remembered how once he had stolen into Troy town from the camp of the Achæans, and how he had crept in a beggar's rags within the house of Priam to spy upon the Trojans, and how Helen, the fairest of women, had bathed him, and anointed him with oil, and suffered him to go in peace, all for the memory of the love that was between them of old. As he gazed, that picture faded and melted in the mist, and again he bowed his head, and kneeled by the golden altar of the Goddess, crying:

'Where beneath the sunlight dwells the golden Helen?' For now he had only one desire: to look on Helen again before he died.

Then the voice of the Goddess seemed to whisper in his ear:

'Did I not say truth, Odysseus? Wast not thou my servant for one hour, and did not Love save thee in the city of the Trojans on that night when even Wisdom was of no avail?'

He answered: 'Yea, O Queen!'

'Behold, then,' said the voice, 'I would again have mercy and be kind to thee, for if I aid thee not thou hast no more life left among men. Home, and kindred, and native land thou hast none; and, but for me, thou must devour thine own heart and be lonely till thou diest. Therefore I breathe into thy heart a sweet forgetfulness of every sorrow, and I breathe love into thee for her who was thy first love in the beginning of thy days.

'For Helen is living yet upon the earth. And I will send thee on the quest of Helen, and thou shalt again take joy in war and wandering. Thou shalt find her in a strange land, among a strange people, in a strife of gods and men; and the wisest and bravest of men shall sleep at last in the arms of the fairest of women. But learn this, Odysseus; thou must set thy heart on no other woman, but only on Helen.

'And I give thee a sign to know her by in a land of magic, and among women that deal in sorceries.

'*On the breast of Helen a jewel shines, a great starstone, the gift I gave her on her wedding-night when she was bride to Menelaus. From that stone fall red drops like blood, and they drip on her vestment, and there vanish, and do not stain it.*

'By the Star of Love shalt thou know her; by the star shalt thou swear to her; and if thou knowest not the portent of the Bleeding Star, or if thou breakest that oath, never in this life, Odysseus, shalt thou win the golden Helen! And thine own death shall come from the water— the swiftest death—that the saying of the dead prophet may be fulfilled. Yet first shalt thou lie in the arms of the golden Helen.'

The Wanderer answered:

'Queen, how may this be, for I am alone on a sea-girt isle, and I have no ship and no companions to speed me over the great gulf of the sea?'

Then the voice answered:

'Fear not! the gods can bring to pass even greater things than these. Go from my house, and lie down to sleep in my holy ground, within the noise of the wash of the waves. There sleep, and take thy rest! Thy strength shall come back to thee, and before the setting of the new sun thou shalt be sailing on the path to The World's Desire. But first drink from the chalice on my altar. Fare thee well!'

The voice died into silence, like the dying of music. The Wanderer awoke and lifted his head, but the light had faded, and the temple was gray in the first waking of the dawn. Yet there, on the altar where no cup had been, stood a deep chalice of gold, full of red wine to the brim. This the Wanderer lifted and drained—a draught of Nepenthe, the magic cup that puts trouble out of mind. As he drank, a wave of sweet hope went over his heart, and buried far below it the sorrow of remembrance, and the trouble of the past, and the longing desire for loves that were no more.

With a light step he went forth like a younger man, taking the two spears in his hand, and the bow upon his back, and he lay down beneath a great rock that looked toward the deep, and there he slept.

3. THE SLAYING OF THE SIDONIANS

Morning broke in the East. A new day dawned upon the silent sea, and on the world of light and sound. The sunrise topped the hill at last, and fell upon the golden raiment of the Wanderer where he slept, making it blaze like living fire. As the sun touched him, the prow of a black ship stole swiftly round the headland, for the oarsmen drove her well with the oars. Any man who saw her would have known her to be a vessel of the merchants of Sidon—the most cunning people and the greediest of gain —for on her prow were two big-headed shapes of dwarfs, with gaping mouths and knotted limbs. Such gods as those were worshipped by the Sidonians. She was now returning from Albion, an isle beyond the pillars of Heracles and the gates of the great sea, where much store of tin is found; and she had rich merchandise on board. On the half-deck beside the steersman was the captain, a thin, keen-eyed sailor, who looked shoreward and saw the sun blaze on the golden armour of the Wanderer. They were so far off that he could not see clearly what it was that glittered yellow, but all that glittered yellow was a lure for him, and gold drew him on as iron draws the hands of heroes. So he bade the helmsman steer straight in, for the sea was deep below the rock, and there they all saw a man lying asleep in golden armour. They whispered together, laughing silently, and then sprang ashore, taking with them a rope of twisted ox-hide, a hawser of the ship, and

16

a strong cable of byblus, the papyrus plant. On these ropes they cast a loop and a running knot, a lasso for throwing, so that they might capture the man in safety from a distance. With these in their hands they crept up the cliff, for their purpose was to noose the man in golden armour, and drag him on board their vessel, and carry him to the mouth of the river of Egypt, and there sell him for a slave to the King. For the Sidonians, who were greedy of everything, loved nothing better than to catch free men and women, who might be purchased, by mere force or guile, and then be sold again for gold and silver and cattle. Many kings' sons had thus been captured by them, and had seen the day of slavery in Babylon, or Tyre, or Egyptian Thebes, and had died sadly, far from the Argive land.

So the Sidonians went round warily, and, creeping in silence over the short grass and thyme towards the Wanderer, were soon as near him as a child could throw a stone. Like shepherds who seek to net a sleeping lion, they came cunningly; yet not so cunningly but that the Wanderer heard them through his dreams, and turned and sat up, looking around him half awake. But as he woke the noose fell about his neck and over his arms, and they drew it hard, and threw him on his back. Before they could touch him he was on his feet again, crying his war-cry terribly, the cry that shook the towers of Ilium, and he rushed upon them, clutching at his sword hilt. The men who were nearest him and had hold of the rope let it fall from their hands and fled, but the others swung behind him, and dragged with all their force. If his arms had been free so that he might draw his sword, it would have gone ill with them, many as they were, for the Sidonians have no stomach for sword blades; but his arms were held in the noose. Yet they did not easily master him; but, as those who had fled came back, and they all laid hands on the rope together, they overpowered him by main force at last, and hauled him, step by step, till he stumbled on a rock and fell. Then they rushed at him, and threw themselves all upon his body, and bound him with ropes in cunning sailor knots. But the booty was dearly won, and they did not all return alive; for he crushed one man with his knees till the breath left him, and the thigh of another he broke with a blow of his foot.

But at last his strength was spent, and they had him like a bird in a snare; so, by might and main, they bore him to their ship, and thew him down on the fore-deck of the vessel. There they mocked him, though they were half afraid; for even now he was terrible. Then they hauled up the sail again and sat down to the oars. The wind blew fair for the mouth of the Nile and the slave-market of Egypt. The wind was fair, and their hearts were light, for they had been among the first of their people to deal with the wild tribes of the island Albion, and had bought tin and gold for African sea shells and rude glass beads from Egypt. And now, near the very end of their adventure, they had caught a man whose armour and whose body were worth a king's ransom. It was a lucky voyage, they said, and the wind was fair!

The rest of the journey was long, but in well-known waters. They passed by Cephalonia and the rock of Ægilips, and wooded Zacynthus, and Samê, and of all those isles he was the lord, whom they were now selling into captivity. But he lay still, breathing heavily, and he stirred but once—that was when they neared Zacynthus. Then he strained his head round with a mighty strain, and he saw the sun go down upon the heights of rocky Ithaca, for that last time of all.

So the swift ship ran along the coast, slipping by forgotten towns. Past the Echinean isles, and the Elian shore, and pleasant Eirene they sped, and it was dusk ere they reached Dorion. Deep night had fallen when they ran by Pylos; and the light of the fires in the hall of Pisistratus, the son of Nestor the Old, shone out across the sandy sea-coast and the sea. But when they were come near Malea, the southernmost point of land, where two seas meet, there the storm snatched them, and drove them ever southwards, beyond Crete, towards the mouth of the Nile. They scudded long before the storm-wind, losing their reckoning, and rushing by island temples that showed like ghosts through the mist, and past havens which they could not win. On they fled, and the men would gladly have lightened the ship by casting the cargo overboard; but the captain watched the hatches with a sword and two bronze-tipped spears in his hand. He would sink or swim with the ship; he would go down with his treasure, or reach Sidon, the City of Flowers, and build a white house among the palms by the waters of Bostren, and never try the sea again.

So he swore; and he would not let them cast the Wanderer overboard, as they desired, because he had brought bad luck. 'He shall bring a good price in Tanis,' cried the captain. And at last the storm abated, and the Sidonians took heart, and were glad like men escaped from death; so they sacrificed and poured forth wine before the dwarf-gods on the prow of their vessel, and burned incense on their little altar. In their mirth, and to mock the Wanderer, they hung his sword and his shield against the mast, and his quiver and his bow they arrayed in the fashion of a trophy; and they mocked him, believing that he knew no word of their speech. But he knew it well, as he knew the speech of the people of Egypt; for he had seen the cities of many men, and had spoken with captains and mercenaries from many a land in the great wars.

The Sidonians, however, jibed and spoke freely before him, saying how they were bound for the rich city of Tanis, on the banks of the River of Egypt, and how the captain was minded to pay his toll to Pharaoh with the body and the armour of the Wanderer. That he might seem the comelier, and a gift more fit for a king, the sailors slackened his bonds a little, and brought him dried meat and wine, and he ate till his strength returned to him. Then he entreated them by signs to loosen the cord that bound his legs; for indeed his limbs were dead through the strength of the bonds, and his armour was eating into his flesh. At his prayer they took some pity of him and loosened his bonds again, and he lay upon his back, moving his legs to and fro till his strength came back.

So they sailed southward ever, through smooth waters and past the islands that lie like water-lilies in the midland sea. Many a strange sight they saw: vessels bearing slaves, whose sighing might be heard above the sighing of wind and water—young men and maidens of Ionia and Achaia, stolen by slave-traders into bondage; now they would touch at the white havens of a peaceful city; and again they would watch a smoke on the sea-line all day, rising black into the heavens; but by nightfall the smoke would change to a great roaring fire from the beacons of a beleaguered island town; the fire would blaze on the masts of the ships of the besiegers, and show blood-red on their sails, and glitter on the gilded shields that lined the bulwarks of the ships. But the Sidonians sped on till, one night, they anchored off a little isle that lies over against the mouth of the Nile. Beneath this isle they moored the ship, and slept, most of them, ashore.

Then the Wanderer began to plot a way to escape, though the enterprise seemed desperate enough. He was lying in the darkness of the hold, sleepless and sore with his bonds, while his guard watched under an awning in the moonlight on the deck. They dreamed so little of his escaping that they visited him only by watches, now and again; and, as it chanced, the man whose turn it was to see that all was well fell asleep. Many a thought went through the prisoner's mind, and now it seemed to him that the vision of the Goddess was only a vision of sleep, which came, as they said, through the false Gates of Ivory, and not through the Gates of Horn. So he was to live in slavery after all, a king no longer, but a captive, toiling in the Egyptian mines of Sinai, or a soldier at a palace gate, till he died. Thus he brooded, till out of the stillness came a thin, faint, thrilling sound from the bow that hung against the mast over his head, the bow that he never thought to string again. There was a noise of a singing of the bow and of the string, and the wordless song shaped itself thus in the heart of the Wanderer:

> Lo! the hour is nigh
>   And the time to smite,
> When the foe shall fly
>   From the arrow's flight!
> Let the bronze bite deep!

Let the war-birds fly
Upon them that sleep
    And are ripe to die!
Shrill and low
    Do the gray shafts sing
The Song of the Bow,
    The sound of the string!

Then the low music died into the silence, and the Wanderer knew that the next sun would not set on the day of slavery, and that his revenge was near. His bonds would be no barrier to his vengeance; they would break like burnt tow, he knew, in the fire of his anger. Long since, in his old days of wandering, Calypso, his love, had taught him in the summer leisure of her seagirt isle how to tie knots that no man could untie, and to undo all the knots that men can bind. He remembered this lesson in the night when the bow sang of war. So he thought no more of sleeping, but cunningly and swiftly unknotted all the cords and the bonds which bound him to a bar of iron in the hold. He might have escaped now, perhaps, if he had stolen on deck without waking the guards, dived thence and swam under water towards the island, where he might have hidden himself in the bush. But he desired revenge no less than freedom, and had set his heart on coming in a ship of his own, and with all the great treasure of the Sidonians, before the Egyptian King.

With this in his mind, he did not throw off the cords, but let them lie on his arms and legs and about his body, as if they were still tied fast. But he fought against sleep, lest in moving when he woke he might reveal the trick, and be bound again. So he lay and waited, and in the morning the sailors came on board, and mocked at him again. In his mirth one of the men took a dish of meat and of lentils, and set it a little out of the Wanderer's reach as he lay bound, and said in the Phœnician tongue:

'Mighty lord, art thou some god of Javan' (for so the Sidonians called the Achæans), 'and wilt thou deign to taste our sacrifice? Is not the savour sweet in the nostrils of my lord? Why will he not put forth his hand to touch our offering?'

Then the heart of Odysseus muttered sullenly within him, in wrath at the insolence of the man. But he constrained himself and smiled, and said:

'Wilt thou not bring the mess a very little nearer, my friend, that I may smell the sweet incense of the sacrifice?'

They were amazed when they heard him speak in their own tongue; but he who held the dish brought it nearer, like a man that angers a dog, now offering the meat, and now taking it away.

So soon as the man was within reach, the Wanderer sprang out, the loosened bonds falling at his feet, and smote the sailor beneath the ear with his clenched fist. The blow was so fierce, for all his anger went into it, that it crushed the bone, and drove the man against the mast of the ship so that the strong mast shook. Where he fell, there he lay, his feet kicking the floor of the hold in his death-pain.

Then the Wanderer snatched from the mast his bow and his short sword, slung the quiver about his shoulders, and ran on to the raised decking of the prow.

The bulwarks of the deck were high, and the vessel was narrow, and before the sailors could stir for amazement the Wanderer had taken his stand behind the little altar and the dwarf-gods. Here he stood with an arrow on the string, and the bow drawn to his ear, looking about him terribly.

Now panic and dread came on the Sidonians when they saw him standing thus, and one of the sailors cried:

'Alas! what god have we taken and bound? Our ship may not contain him. Surely he is Resef Mikal, the God of the Bow, whom they of Javan call Apollo. Nay, let us land him on the isle and come not to blows with him, but entreat his mercy, lest he rouse the waves and the winds against us.'

But the captain of the ship of the Sidonians cried:

'Not so, ye knaves! Have at him, for he is no god, but a mortal man; and his armour is worth many a yoke of oxen!'

Then he bade some of them climb the decking at the further end of the ship, and throw spears at him thence;

and he called others to bring up one of the long spears and charge him with that. Now these were huge pikes, that were wielded by five or six men at once, and no armour could withstand them; they were used in the fights to drive back boarders, and to ward off attacks on ships which were beached on shore in the sieges of towns.

The men whom the captain appointed little liked the task, for the long spears were laid on tressels along the bulwarks, and to reach them and unship them it was needful to come within range of the bow. But the sailors on the further deck threw all their spears at once, while five men leaped on the deck where the Wanderer stood. He loosed the bowstring and the shaft sped on its way; again he drew and loosed, and now two of them had fallen beneath his arrows, and one was struck by a chance blow from a spear thrown from the further deck, and the other two leaped back into the hold.

Then the Wanderer shouted from the high decking of the prow in the speech of the Sidonians:

'Ye dogs, ye have sailed on your latest sea-faring, and never again shall ye bring the hour of slavery on any man.'

So he cried, and the sailors gathered together in the hold, and took counsel how they should deal with him. But meanwhile the bow was not silent, and of those on the hinder deck who were casting spears, one dropped and the others quickly fled to their fellows below, for on the deck they had no cover.

The sun was now well risen, and shone on the Wanderer's golden mail, as he stood alone on the decking, with his bow drawn. The sun shone, there was silence, the ship swung to her anchor; and still he waited, looking down, his arrow pointing at the level of the deck to shoot at the first head which rose above the planking. Suddenly there came a rush of men on to the further decking, and certain of them tore the shields that lined the bulwarks from their pins, and threw them down to those who were below, while others cast a shower of spears at the Wanderer. Some of the spears he avoided; others leaped back from his mail; others stood fast in the altar and in the bodies of the dwarf-gods; while he answered with an arrow that did not miss its aim. But his eyes were always watching most keenly the hatches nearest him, whence a gangway ran down to the lower part of the ship, where the oarsmen sat; for only thence could they make a rush on him. As he watched and drew an arrow from the quiver on his shoulder, he felt, as it were, a shadow between him and the deck. He glanced up quickly, and there, on the yard above his head, a man, who had climbed the mast from behind, was creeping down to drop on him from above. Then the Wanderer snatched a short spear and cast it at the man. The spear sped quicker than a thought, and pinned his two hands to the yard so that he hung there helpless, shrieking to his friends. But the arrows of the Wanderer kept raining on the men who stood on the further deck, and presently some of them, too, leaped down in terror, crying that he was a god and not a man, while others threw themselves into the sea, and swam for the island.

Then the Wanderer himself waited no longer, seeing them all amazed, but he drew his sword and leaped down among them with a cry like a sea-eagle swooping on seamews in the crevice of a rock. To right and left he smote with the short sword, making a havoc and sparing none, for the sword ravened in his hand. And some fell over the benches and oars, but such of the sailors as could flee rushed up the gangway into the further deck, and thence sprang overboard, while those who had not the luck to flee fell where they stood, and scarcely struck a blow. Only the captain of the ship, knowing that all was lost, turned and threw a spear in the Wanderer's face. But he watched the flash of the bronze and stooped his head, so that the spear struck only the golden helm and pierced it through, but scarcely grazed his head. Now the Wanderer sprang on the Sidonian captain, and smote him with the flat of his sword so that he fell senseless on the deck, and then he bound him hand and foot with cords as he himself had been bound, and made him fast to the iron bar in the hold. Next he gathered up the dead in his mighty arms, and set them against the bulwarks of the fore-deck—

harvesting the fruits of War. Above the deck the man who had crept along the yard was hanging by his two hands which the spear had pinned together to the yard.

'Art thou there, friend?' cried the Wanderer, mocking him. 'Hast thou chosen to stay with me rather than go with thy friends, or seek new service? Nay, then, as thou art so staunch, abide there and keep a good look-out for the river mouth and the market where thou shalt sell me for a great price.' So he spoke, but the man was already dead of pain and fear. Then the Wanderer unbuckled his golden armour, which clanged upon the deck, and drew fresh water from the hold to cleanse himself, for he was stained like a lion that has devoured an ox. Next, with a golden comb he combed his long dark curls, and he gathered his arrows out of the bodies of the dead, and out of the thwarts and the sides of the ship, cleansed them, and laid them back in the quiver. When all this was ended he put on his armour again; but strong as he was, he could not tear the spear from the helm without breaking the gold; so he snapped the shaft and put on the helmet with the point of the javelin still fixed firm in the crest, as Fate would have it so, and this was the beginning of his sorrows. Next he ate meat and bread, and drank wine, and poured forth some of the wine before his gods. Lastly he dragged up the heavy stone with which the ship was moored, a stone heavier far, they say, than two other men could lift. He took the tiller in his hand; the steady north wind, the Etesian wind, kept blowing in the sails, and he steered straight southward for the mouths of the Nile.

4. THE BLOOD-RED SEA

A hard fight it had been and a long, and the Wanderer was weary. He took the tiller of the ship in his hand, and steered for the South and for the noonday sun, which was now at his highest in the heavens. But suddenly the bright light of the sky was darkened and the air was filled with the rush, and the murmur, and the winnowing of innumerable wings. It was as if all the birds that have their homes and seek their food in the great salt marsh of Cayster had risen from the South and had flown over sea in one hour, for the heaven was darkened with their flight, and loud with the call of cranes and the whistling cry of the wild ducks. So dark was the thick mass of flying fowl, that a flight of swans shone snowy against the black cloud of their wings. At the view of them the Wanderer caught his bow eagerly into his hand and set an arrow on the string, and, taking a careful aim at the white wedge of birds, he shot a wild swan through the breast as it swept high over the mast. Then, with all the speed of its rush, the wild white swan flashed down like lightning into the sea behind the ship. The Wanderer watched its fall, when, lo! the water where the dead swan fell splashed up as red as blood and all afoam! The long silver wings and snowy plumage floated on the surface flecked with blood-red stains, and the Wanderer marvelled as he bent over the bulwarks and gazed steadily upon the sea. Then he saw that the wide sea round the ship was covered, as far as the eye could reach, as it were with a blood-red scum. Hither and thither the red stain was tossed like foam, yet beneath, where the deep wave divided, the Wanderer saw that the streams of the sea were gray and green below the crimson dye. As he watched he saw, too, that the red froth was drifted always onward from the South and from the mouth of the River of Egypt, for behind the wake of the ship it was most red of all, though he had not marked it while the battle raged. But in front the colour grew thin, as if the stain that the river washed down was all but spent. In his heart the Wanderer thought, as any man must have deemed, that on the banks of the River of Egypt there had been some battle of great nations, and that the War God had raged furiously, wherefore the holy river as it ran forth stained all the sacred sea. Where war was, there was his home, no other home had he now, and all the more eagerly he steered right on to see what the Gods would send him. The flight of birds was over and past; it was two hours after noon, the light was high in the heaven, when, as he gazed, another shadow fell on him, for the sun in mid-heaven grew small, and red as blood. Slowly a mist rose up over it from the South, a mist that was thin but as black as night. Beyond, to the southward, there was a bank of cloud like a mountain wall, steep, and polished, and black, tipped along the ragged crest with fire, and opening ever and again with flashes of intolerable splendour, while the bases were scrawled over with lightning like a written scroll. Never had the Wanderer in all his voyaging on the sea and on the great River Oceanus that girdles the earth, and severs the dead from the living men—never had he beheld such a darkness. Presently he came as it were within the jaws of it, dark as a wolf's mouth, so dark that he might not see the corpses on the deck, nor the mast, nor the dead man swinging from the yard, nor the captain of the Phœnicians who groaned aloud below, praying to his gods. But in the wake of the ship there was one break of clear blue sky on the horizon, in which the little isle where he had slain the Sidonians might be discerned far off, as bright and white as ivory.

Now, though he knew it not, the gates of his own world

were closing behind the Wanderer for ever. To the North, whence he came, lay the clear sky, and the sunny capes and isles, and the airy mountains of the Argive lands, white with the temples of familiar Gods. But in face of him, to the South, whither he went, was a cloud of darkness and a land of darkness itself. There were things to befall more marvellous than are told in any tale; there was to be a war of the peoples, and of the Gods, the True Gods and the False, and there he should find the last embraces of Love, the False Love and the True.

Foreboding somewhat of the perils that lay in front, the Wanderer was tempted to shift his course and sail back to the sunlight. But he was one that had never turned his hand from the plough, nor his foot from the path, and he thought that now his path was foreordained. So he lashed the tiller with a rope, and groped his way with his hands along the deck till he reached the altar of the dwarf-gods, where the embers of the sacrifice still were glowing faintly. Then with his sword he cut some spear-shafts and broken arrows into white chips, and with them he filled a little brazier, and taking the seed of fire from the altar set light to it from beneath. Presently the wood blazed up through the noonday night, and the fire flickered and flared on the faces of the dead men that lay about the deck, rolling to larboard and to starboard, as the vessel lurched, and the flame shone red on the golden armour of the Wanderer.

Of all his voyages this was the strangest sea-faring, he cruising alone, with a company of the dead, deep into a darkness without measure or bound, to a land that might not be descried. Strange gusts of sudden wind blew him hither and thither. The breeze would rise in a moment from any quarter, and die as suddenly as it rose, and another wind would chase it over the chopping seas. He knew not if he sailed South or North, he knew not how time passed, for there was no sight of the sun. It was night without a dawn. Yet his heart was glad, as if he had been a boy again, for the old sorrows were forgotten, so potent was the draught of the chalice of the Goddess, and so keen was the delight of battle.

'Endure, my heart,' he cried, as often he had cried

before, 'a worse thing than this thou hast endured,' and he
caught up a lyre of the dead Sidonians, and sang:—

> Though the light of the sun be hidden,
>   Though his race be run,
> Though we sail in a sea forbidden
>   To the golden sun;
> Though we wander alone, unknowing,—
>   Oh, heart of mine,—
> The path of the strange sea-going,
>   On the blood-red brine:
> Yet endure! We shall not be shaken
>   By things worse than these;
> We have 'scaped, when our friends were taken,
>   On the unsailed seas;
> Worse deaths have we faced and fled from,
>   In the Cyclops' den,
> When the floor of his cave ran red from
>   The blood of men;
> Worse griefs we have known undaunted,
>   Worse fates have fled;
> When the Isle that our long love haunted
>   Lay waste and dead!

So he was chanting when he descried, faint and far off,
a red glow cast up along the darkness like sunset on the
sky of the Under-world. For this light he steered, and
soon he saw two tall pillars of flame blazing beside each
other, with a narrow space of night between them. He
helmed the ship towards these, and when he came near
them they were like two mighty mountains of wood burning far into heaven, and each was lofty as the pyre that
blazes over men slain in some red war, and each pile
roared and flared above a steep crag of smooth black
basalt, and between the burning mounds of fire lay the
flame-flecked water of a haven.

The ship neared the haven and the Wanderer saw,
moving like fireflies through the night, the lanterns in the
prows of boats, and from one of the boats a sailor hailed
him in the speech of the people of Egypt, asking him if he
desired a pilot.

'Yea,' he shouted. The boat drew near, and the pilot

came aboard, a torch in his hand; but when his eyes fell on the dead men in the ship, and the horror hanging from the yard, and the captain bound to the iron bar, and above all, on the golden armour of the hero, and on the spear-point fast in his helm, and on his terrible face, he shrank back in dread, as if the God Osiris himself, in the Ship of Death, had reached the harbour. But the Wanderer bade him have no fear, telling him that he came with much wealth and with a great gift for the Pharaoh. The pilot, therefore, plucked up heart, and took the helm, and between the two great hills of blazing fire the vessel glided into the smooth waters of the River of Egypt, the flames glittering on the Wanderer's mail as he stood by the mast and chanted the Song of the Bow.

Then, by the counsel of the pilot, the vessel was steered up the river towards the Temple of Heracles in Tanis, where there is a sanctuary for strangers, and where no man may harm them. But first, the dead Sidonians were cast overboard into the great river, for the dead bodies of men are an abomination to the Egyptians. And as each body struck the water the Wanderer saw a hateful sight, for the face of the river was lashed into foam by the sudden leaping and rushing of huge four-footed fish, or so the Wanderer deemed them. The sound of the heavy plunging of the great water-beasts, as they darted forth on the prey, smiting at each other with their tails, and the gnashing of their jaws when they bit too eagerly, and only harmed the air, and the leap of a greedy sharp snout from the waves, even before the dead man cast from the ship had quite touched the water—these things were horrible to see and hear through the blackness and by the firelight. A River of Death it seemed, haunted by the horrors that are said to prey upon the souls and bodies of the Dead. For the first time the heart of the Wanderer died within him, at the horror of the darkness and of this dread river and of the water-beasts that dwelt within it. Then he remembered how the birds had fled in terror from this place, and he bethought him of the blood-red sea.

When the dead men were all cast overboard and the river was once more still, the Wanderer spoke, sick at heart, and inquired of the pilot why the sea had run so red, and whether war was in the land, and why there was night over all that country. The fellow answered that there was no war, but peace, yet the land was strangely plagued with frogs and locusts and lice in all their coasts, the sacred River Sihor running red for three whole days, and now, at last, for this the third day, darkness over all the world. But as to the cause of these curses the pilot knew nothing, being a plain man. Only the story went among the people that the Gods were angry with Khem (as they call Egypt), which indeed was easy to see, for those things could come only from the Gods. But why they were angered the pilot knew not, still it was commonly thought that the Divine Hathor, the Goddess of Love, was wroth because of the worship given in Tanis to one they called THE STRANGE HATHOR, a goddess or a woman of wonderful beauty, whose Temple was in Tanis. Concerning her the pilot said that many years ago, some thirty years, she had first appeared in the country, coming none knew whence, and had been worshipped in Tanis, and had again departed as mysteriously as she came. But now she had once more chosen to appear visible to men, strangely, and to dwell in her temple; and the men who beheld her could do nothing but worship her for her beauty. Whether she was a mortal woman or a goddess the pilot did not know, only he thought that she who dwells in Atarhechis, Hathor of Khem, the Queen of Love, was angry with the strange Hathor, and had sent the darkness and the plagues to punish them who worshipped her. The people of the seaboard also murmured that it would be well to pray the Strange Hathor to depart out of their coasts, if she were a goddess; and if she were a woman to stone her with stones. But the people of Tanis vowed that they would rather die, one and all, than do aught but adore the incomparable beauty of their strange Goddess. Others again, held that two wizards, leaders of certain slaves of a strange race, wanderers from the desert, settled in Tanis, whom they called the Apura, caused all these sorrows by art-magic. As if, forsooth, said the pilot, those barbarian slaves were more powerful than all the priests of Egypt.

But for his part, the pilot knew nothing, only that if the Divine Hathor were angry with the people of Tanis it was hard that she must plague all the land of Khem.

So the pilot murmured, and his tale was none of the shortest; but even as he spoke the darkness grew less dark and the cloud lifted a little so that the shores of the river might be seen in a green light like the light of Hadez, and presently the night was rolled up like a veil, and it was living noonday in the land of Khem. Then all the noise of life broke forth in one moment, the kine lowing, the wind swaying the feathery palms, the fish splashing in the stream, men crying to each other from the river banks, and the voice of multitudes of people in every red temple praising Ra, their great God, whose dwelling is the sun. The Wanderer, too, praised his own Gods, and gave thanks to Apollo, and to Helios Hyperion, and to Aphrodite. And in the end the pilot brought the ship to the quay of a great city, and there a crew of oarsmen was hired, and they sped rejoicing in the sunlight, through a canal dug by the hands of men, to Tanis and the Sanctuary of Heracles, the Safety of Strangers. There the ship was moored, there the Wanderer rested, having a good welcome from the shaven priests of the temple.

5. MERIAMUN THE QUEEN

Strange news flies fast. It was not long before the Pharaoh, who then was with his Court in Tanis, the newly rebuilded city, heard how there had come to Khem a man like a god, wearing golden armour, and cruising alone in a ship of the dead. In these years the white barbarians of the sea and of the isles were wont to land in Egypt, to ravage the fields, carry women captive, and fly again in their ships. But not one of them had dared to sail in the armour of the Aquaiusha, as the Egyptians named the Achæans, right up the river to the city of Pharaoh. The King, therefore, was amazed at the story, and when he heard that the stranger had taken sanctuary in the Temple of Heracles, he sent instantly for his chief counsellor. This was his Master Builder, who bore a high title in the land, an ancient priest named Rei. He had served through the long reign of the King's father, the divine Rameses the Second, and he was beloved both of Meneptah and of Meriamun his Queen. Him the King charged to visit the Sanctuary and bring the stranger before him. So Rei called for his mule, and rode down to the Temple of Heracles beyond the walls.

When Rei came thither, a priest went before him and led him to the chamber where the warrior chanced to be eating the lily bread of the land, and drinking the wine of the Delta. He rose as Rei entered, and he was still clad in his golden armour, for as yet he had not any change of

33

raiment. Beside him, on a bronze tripod, lay his helmet, the Achæan helmet, with its two horns and with the bronze spear-point still fast in the gold.

The eyes of Rei the Priest fell on the helmet, and he gazed so strangely at it that he scarcely heard the Wanderer's salutation. At length he answered courteously, but always his eyes wandered back to the broken spear-point.

'Is this thine, my son?' he asked, taking it in his hand, while his voice trembled.

'It is my own,' said the Wanderer, 'though the spear-head in it was lent me of late, in return for arrows not a few and certain sword-strokes,' and he smiled.

The ancient priest bade the Temple servants retire, and as they went they heard him murmuring a prayer.

'The Dead spoke truth,' he muttered, still gazing from the helmet in his hand to the Wanderer; 'ay, the Dead speak seldom, but they never lie.'

'My son, thou hast eaten and drunk,' then said Rei the Priest and Master Builder, 'and may an old man ask whence thou camest, where is thy native city, and who are thy parents?'

'I come from Alybas,' answered the Wanderer, for his own name was too widely known, and he loved an artful tale. 'I come from Alybas; I am the son of Apheidas, son of Polypemon, and my own name is Eperitus.'

'And wherefore comest thou here alone in a ship of dead men, and with more treasure than a king's ransom?'

'It was men of Sidon who laboured and died for all that cargo,' said the Wanderer; 'they voyaged far for it, and toiled hard, but they lost it in an hour. For they were not content with what they had, but made me a prisoner as I lay asleep on the coast of Crete. But the Gods gave me the upper hand of them, and I bring their captain, and much white metal and many swords and cups and beautiful woven stuffs, as a gift to your King. And for thy courtesy, come with me, and choose a gift for thyself.'

Then he led the old man to the treasure-chambers of the Temple, which was rich in the offerings of many travellers, gold and turquoise and frankincense from Sinai and Punt, great horns of carved ivory from the unknown

East and the South; bowls and baths of silver from the Khita, who were the allies of Egypt. But amidst all the wealth, the stranger's cargo made a goodly show, and the old priest's eyes glittered as he looked at it.

'Take thy choice, I pray thee,' said the Wanderer, 'the spoils of foemen are the share of friends.'

The priest would have refused, but the Wanderer saw that he looked ever at a bowl of transparent amber, from the far-off Northern seas, that was embossed with curious figures of men and gods, and huge fishes, such as are unknown in the Midland waters. The Wanderer put it into the hands of Rei.

'Thou shalt keep this,' he said, 'and pledge me in wine from it when I am gone, in memory of a friend and a guest.'

Rei took the bowl, and thanked him, holding it up to the light to admire the golden colour.

'We are always children,' he said, smiling gravely. 'See an old child whom thou hast made happy with a toy. But we are men too soon again; the King bids thee come with me before him. And, my son, if thou wouldst please me more than by any gift, I pray thee pluck that spear-head from thy helmet before thou comest into the presence of the Queen.'

'Pardon me,' said the Wanderer. 'I would not harm my helmet by tearing it roughly out, and I have no smith's tools here. The spear-point, my father, is a witness to the truth of my tale, and for one day more, or two, I must wear it.'

Rei sighed, bowed his head, folded his hands, and prayed to his God Amen, saying:

'O Amen, in whose hand is the end of a matter, lighten the burden of these sorrows, and let the vision be easy of accomplishment, and I pray thee, O Amen, let thy hand be light on thy daughter Meriamun, the Lady of Khem.'

Then the old man led the Wanderer out, and bade the priests make ready a chariot for him; and so they went through Tanis to the Court of Meneptah. Behind them followed the priests, carrying gifts that the Wanderer had chosen from the treasures of the Sidonians, and the miserable captain of the Sidonians was dragged along after them, bound to the hinder part of a chariot. Through the gazing crowd they all passed on to the Hall of Audience, where, between the great pillars, sat Pharaoh on his golden throne. Beside him, at his right hand, was Meriamun, the beautiful Queen, who looked at the priests with weary eyes, as if at a matter in which she had no concern. They came in and beat the earth with their brows before the King. First came the officers, leading the captain of the Sidonians for a gift to Pharaoh, and the King smiled graciously and accepted the slave.

Then came others, bearing the cups of gold fashioned like the heads of lions and rams, and the swords with pictures of wars and huntings etched on their blades in many-coloured gold, and the necklets of amber from the North, which the Wanderer had chosen as gifts for Pharaoh's Queen and Pharaoh. He had silks, too, embroidered in gold, the needlework of Sidonian women, and all these the Queen Meriamun touched to show her acceptance of them, and smiled graciously and wearily. But the covetous Sidonian groaned, when he saw his wealth departing from him, the gains for which he had hazarded his life in unsailed seas. Lastly, Pharaoh bade them lead the Wanderer in before his presence, and he came unhelmeted, in all his splendour, the goodliest man that had ever been seen in Khem. He was of no great height, but very great of girth, and of strength unmatched, and with the face of one who had seen what few have seen and lived. The beauty of youth was gone from him, but his face had the comeliness of a warrior tried on sea and land; the eyes were of a valour invincible, and no woman could see him but she longed to be his love.

As he entered murmurs of amazement passed over all the company, and all eyes were fixed on him, save only the weary and wandering eyes of the listless Meriamun. But when she chanced to lift her face, and gaze on him, they who watch the looks of kings and queens saw her turn gray as the dead, and clutch with her hand at her side. Pharaoh himself saw this though he was not quick to mark what passed, and he asked her if anything ailed her, but she answered:—

'Nay, only methinks the air is sick with heat and perfume. Greet thou this stranger.' But beneath her robe her fingers were fretting all the while at the golden fringes of her throne.

'Welcome, thou Wanderer,' cried Pharaoh, in a deep and heavy voice, 'welcome! By what name art thou named, and where dwell thy people, and what is thy native land?'

Bowing low before Pharaoh, the Wanderer answered, with a feigned tale, that his name was Eperitus of Alybas, the son of Apheidas. The rest of the story, and how he had been taken by the Sidonians, and how he had smitten them on the seas, he told as he had told it to Rei. And he displayed his helmet with the spear-point fast in it. But when she saw this Meriamun rose to her feet as if she would be gone, and then fell back into her seat even paler than before.

'The Queen, help the Queen, she faints,' cried Rei the Priest, whose eyes had never left her face. One of her ladies, a beautiful woman, ran to her, knelt before her, and chafed her hands, till she came to herself, and sat up with angry eyes.

'Let be!' she said, 'and let the slave who tends the incense be beaten on the feet. Nay, I will remain here, I will not to my chamber. Let be!' and her lady drew back afraid.

Then Pharaoh bade men lead the Sidonian out, and slay him in the market-place for his treachery; but the man, whose name was Kurri, threw himself at the feet of the Wanderer, praying for his life. The Wanderer was merciful, when the rage of battle was over, and his blood was cool.

'A boon, O Pharaoh Meneptah,' he cried. 'Spare me this man! He saved my own life when the crew would have cast me overboard. Let me pay my debt.'

'Let him be spared, as thou wilt have it so,' spoke Pharaoh, 'but revenge dogs the feet of foolish mercy, and many debts are paid ere all is done.'

Thus it chanced that Kurri was given to Meriamun to be her jeweller and to work for her in gold and silver. To the Wanderer was allotted a chamber in the Royal Palace, for the Pharaoh trusted that he would be a leader of his Guard, and took great pleasure in his beauty and his strength.

As he left the Hall of Audience with Rei, the Queen Meriamun lifted her eyes again, and looked on him long, and her ivory face flushed rosy, like the ivory that the Sidonians dye red for the trappings of the horses of kings. But the Wanderer marked both the sudden fear and the blush of Meriamun, and, beautiful as she was, he liked it ill, and his heart foreboded evil. When he was alone with Rei, therefore, he spoke to him of this, and prayed the old man to tell him if he could guess at all the meaning of the Queen.

'For to me,' he said, 'it was as if the Lady knew my face, and even as if she feared it; but I never saw her like in all my wanderings. Beautiful she is, and yet—but it is ill speaking in their own land of kings and queens!'

At first, when the Wanderer spoke thus, Rei put it by, smiling. But the Wanderer, seeing that he was troubled, and remembering how he had prayed him to pluck the spear-point from his helmet, pressed him hard with questions. Thus, partly out of weariness, and partly for love of him, and also because a secret had long been burning in his heart, the old man took the Wanderer into his own room in the Palace, and there he told him all the story of Meriamun the Queen.

6. THE STORY OF MERIAMUN

Rei, the Priest of Amen, the Master Builder, began his story unwillingly enough, and slowly, but soon he took pleasure in telling it as old men do, and in sharing the burden of a secret.

'The Queen is fair,' he said; 'thou hast seen no fairer in all thy voyagings?'

'She is fair indeed,' answered the Wanderer. 'I pray that she be well-mated and happy on her throne?'

'That is what I will tell thee of, though my life may be the price of the tale,' said Rei. 'But a lighter heart is well worth an old man's cheap risk, and thou may'st help me and her, when thou knowest all. Pharaoh Meneptah, her lord, the King, is the son of the divine Rameses, the ever-living Pharaoh, child of the Sun, who dwelleth in Osiris.'

'Thou meanest that he is dead?' asked the Wanderer.

'He dwelleth with Osiris,' said the Priest, 'and the Queen Meriamun was his daughter by another bed.'

'A brother wed a sister!' exclaimed the Wanderer.

'It is the custom of our Royal House, from the days of the Timeless Kings, the children of Horus. An old custom.'

'The ways of his hosts are good in the eyes of a stranger,' said the Wanderer, courteously.

'It is an old custom, and a sacred,' said Rei, 'but women, the custom-makers, are often custom-breakers.

39

And of all women, Meriamun least loves to be obedient, even to the dead. And yet she had obeyed, and it came about thus. Her brother Meneptah—who now is Pharaoh —the Prince of Kush while her divine father lived, had many half-sisters, but Meriamun was the fairest of them all. She is beautiful, a Moon-child the common people called her, and wise, and she does not know the face of fear. And thus it chanced that she learned, what even our Royal women rarely learn, all the ancient secret wisdom of this ancient land. Except Queen Taia of old, no woman has known what Meriamun knows, what I have taught her—I and another counsellor.'

He paused here, and his mind seemed to turn on unhappy things.

'I have taught her from her childhood,' he went on— 'would that I had been her only familiar—and, after her divine father and mother, she loved me more than any, for she loved few. But of all whom she did not love she loved her Royal brother least. He is slow of speech, and she is quick. She is fearless and he has no heart for war. From her childhood she scorned him, mocked him, and mastered him with her tongue. She even learned to excel him in the chariot races—therefore it was that the King his father made him but a General of the Foot Soldiers—and in guessing riddles, which our people love, she delighted to conquer him. The victory was easy enough, for the divine Prince is heavy-witted; but Meriamun was never tired of girding at him. Plainly, even as a little child she grudged that he should come to wield the scourge of power, and wear the double crown, while she should live in idleness, and hunger for command.'

'It is strange, then, that of all his sisters, if one must be Queen, he should have chosen her,' said the Wanderer.

'Strange, and it happened strangely. The Prince's father, the divine Rameses, had willed the marriage. The Prince hated it no less than Meriamun, but the will of a father is the will of the Gods. In one sport the divine Prince excelled, in the Game of Pieces, an old game in Khem. It is no pastime for women, but even at this Meriamun was determined to master her brother. She bade me carve her a new set of the pieces fashioned with the heads of cats, and shaped from the hard wood of Azebi.[1] I carved them with my own hands, and night by night she played with me, who have some name for skill at the sport.

'One sunset it chanced that her brother came in from hunting the lion in the Libyan hills. He was in an evil humour, for he had found no lions, and he caused the huntsmen to be stretched out, and beaten with rods. Then he called for wine, and drank deep at the Palace gate, and the deeper he drank the darker grew his humour.

'He was going to his own Court in the Palace, striking with a whip at his hounds, when he chanced to turn and see Meriamun. She was sitting where those three great palm-trees are, and was playing at pieces with me in the cool of the day. There she sat in the shadow, clad in white and purple, and with the red gold of the snake of royalty in the blackness of her hair. There she sat as beautiful as the Hathor, the Queen of Love; or as the Lady Isis when she played at pieces in Amenti with the ancient King. Nay, an old man may say it, there never was but one woman more fair than Meriamun, if a woman she be, she whom our people call the *Strange Hathor*.'

Now the Wanderer bethought him of the tale of the pilot, but he said nothing, and Rei went on.

'The Prince saw her, and his anger sought for something new to break itself on. Up he came, and I rose before him, and bowed myself. But Meriamun fell indolently back in her chair of ivory, and with a sweep of her slim hand she disordered the pieces, and bade her waiting woman, the lady Hataska, gather up the board, and carry all away. But Hataska's eyes were secretly watching the Prince.

' "Greeting, Princess, our Royal sister," said Meneptah. "What art thou doing with these?" and he pointed with his chariot whip at the cat-headed pieces. "This is no woman's game, these pieces are not soft hearts of men to be moved on the board by love. This game needs wit! Get thee to thy broidery, for there thou may'st excel."

[1]Cyprus.

' "Greeting, Prince, our Royal brother," said Meria-mun. "I laugh to hear thee speak of a game that needs wit. Thy hunting has not prospered, so get thee to the banquet board, for there, I hear, the Gods have granted thee to excel."

' "It is little to say," answered the Prince, throwing himself into a chair whence I had risen, "it is little to say, but at the game of pieces I have wit enough to give thee a temple, a priest and five bowmen, and yet win,"—for these, O Wanderer, are the names of some of the pieces.

' "I take the challenge," cried Meriamun, for now she had brought him where she wanted; "but I will take no odds. Here is my wager. I will play thee three games, and stake the sacred circlet upon my brow, against the Royal uraeus on thine, and the winner shall wear both."

' "Nay, nay, Lady," I was bold to say, "this were too high a stake."

' "High or low, I accept the wager," answered the Prince. "This sister of mine has mocked me too long. She shall find that her woman's wit cannot match me at my own game, and that my father's son, the Royal Prince of Kush and the Pharaoh who shall be, is more than the equal of a girl. I hold thy wage, Meriamun!"

' "Go then, Prince," she cried, "and after sunset meet me in my antechamber. Bring a scribe to score the games; Rei shall be the judge, and hold the stakes. But beware of the golden Cup of Pasht! Drain it not to-night, lest I win a love game, though we do not play for love!"

'The Prince went scowling away, and Meriamun laughed, but I foresaw mischief. The stakes were too high, the match was too strange, but Meriamun would not listen to me, for she was very wilful.

'The sun fell, and two hours after the Royal Prince of Kush came with his scribe, and found Meriamun with the board of squares before her, in her antechamber.

'He sat down without a word, then he asked, who should first take the field.

' "Wait," she said, "first let us set the stakes," and lifting from her brow the golden snake of royalty, she shook her soft hair loose, and gave the coronet to me. "If I lose," she said, "never may I wear the uraeus crown."

' "That shalt thou never while I draw breath," answered the Prince, as he too lifted the symbol of his royalty from his head and gave it to me. There was a difference between the circlets, the coronet of Meriamun was crowned with one crested snake, that of the divine Prince was crowned with twain.

' "Ay, Meneptah," she said, 'but perchance Osiris, God of the Dead, waits thee, for surely he loves those too great and good for earth. Take thou the field and to the play." At her words of evil omen, he frowned. But he took the field and readily, for he knew the game well.

'She moved in answer heedlessly enough, and afterwards she played at random and carelessly, pushing the pieces about with little skill. And so he won this first game quickly, and crying, *"Pharaoh is dead,"* swept the pieces from the board. "See how I better thee," he went on in mockery. "Thine is a woman's game; all attack and no defence."

' "Boast not yet, Meneptah," she said. "There are still two sets to play. See, the board is set and I take the field."

'This time the game went differently, for the Prince could scarce make prisoner of a single piece save of one temple and two bowmen only, and presently it was the turn of Meriamun to cry *"Pharaoh is dead,"* and to sweep the pieces from the board. This time Meneptah did not boast but scowled, while I set the board and the scribe wrote down the game upon his tablets. Now it was the Prince's turn to take the field.

' "In the name of the holy Thoth," he cried, to whom I vow great gifts of victory."

' "In the name of holy Pasht," she made answer, "to whom I make daily prayer." For, being a maid, she swore by the Goddess of Chastity, and being Meriamun, by the Goddess of Vengeance.

' " 'Tis fitting thou should'st vow by her of the Cat's Head," he said, sneering.

' "Yes; very fitting," she answered, "for perchance she'll lend me her claws. Play thou, Prince Meneptah."

'And he played, and so well that for a while the game went against her. But at length, when they had struggled long, and Meriamun had lost the most of her pieces, a light came into her face as though she had found what she sought. And while the Prince called for wine and drank, she lay back in her chair and looked upon the board. Then she moved so shrewdly and upon so deep a plan that he fell into the trap that she had laid for him, and could never escape. In vain he vowed gifts to the holy Thoth, and promised such a temple as there was none in Khem.

' "Thoth hears thee not; he is the God of lettered men," said Meriamun, mocking him. Then he cursed and drank more wine.

' "Fools seek wit in wine, but only wise men find it," quoth she again. 'Behold, Royal brother, *Pharaoh is dead,* and I have won the match, and beaten thee at thine own game. Rei, my servant, give me that circlet; nay, not my own, the double one, which the divine Prince wagered. So I set it on my brow, for it is mine, Meneptah. In this, as in all things else, I have conquered thee."

'And she rose, and standing full in the light of the lamps, the Royal uraeus on her brow, she mocked him, bidding him come do homage to her who had won his crown, and stretching forth her small hand for him to kiss it. And so wondrous was her beauty that the divine Prince of Kush ceased to call upon the evil Gods because of his ill fortune, and stood gazing on her.

' "By Ptah, but thou art fair," he cried, "and I pardon my father at last for willing thee to be my Queen!"

' "But I will never pardon him," said Meriamun.

'Now the Prince had drunk much wine.

' "Thou shalt be my Queen," he said, "and for earnest I will kiss thee. This, at the least, being the strongest, I can do." And ere she could escape him, he passed his arm about her and seized her by the girdle, and kissed her on the lips and let her go.

'Meriamun grew white as the dead. By her side there hung a dagger. Swiftly she drew it, and swiftly struck at his heart, so that had he not shrunk from the steel surely he had been slain; and she cried as she struck, "Thus, Prince, I pay thy kisses back."

'But as it chanced, she only pierced his arm, and before she could strike again I had seized her by the hand.

' "Thou serpent," said the Prince, pale with rage and fear. "I tell thee I will kiss thee yet, whether thou wilt or not, and thou shalt pay for this."

'But she laughed softly now that her anger was spent, and I led him forth to seek a physician, who should bind up his wound. And when he was gone, I returned, and spoke to her, wringing my hands.

' "Oh, Royal Lady, what hast thou done? Thou knowest well that thy divine father destines thee to wed the Prince of Kush whom but now thou didst smite so fiercely."

' "Nay, Rei, I will none of him—the dull clod, who is called the son of Pharaoh. Moreover, he is my half-brother, and it is not meet that I should wed my brother. for nature cries aloud against the custom of the land."

' "Nevertheless, Lady, it *is* the custom of thy Royal house, and thy father's will. Thus the Gods, thine ancestors, were wed; Isis to Osiris. Thus great Thothmes and Amenemhat did and decreed, and all their forefathers and all their seed. Oh, bethink thee—I speak it for thine ear, for I love thee as mine own daughter—bethink thee, for thou canst not escape, that Pharaoh's bed is the step to Pharaoh's throne. Thou lovest power; here is the gate of power, and mayhap upon a time the master of the gate shall be gone and thou shalt sit in the gate alone."

' "Ah, Rei, now thou speakest like the counsellor of those who would be kings. Oh, did I not hate him with this hatred! And yet can I rule him. Why, 'twas no chance game that we played this night: the future lay upon the board. See, his diadem is upon my brow! At first he won, for I chose that he should win. Well, so mayhap it shall be; mayhap I shall give myself to him—hating him the while. And then the next game; that shall be for life and love and all things dear, and I shall win it, and mine shall be the uraeus crest, and mine shall be the double crown of ancient Khem, and I shall rule like Hatshepu, the great

Queen of old, for I am strong, and to the strong is victory."

' "Yes," I made answer, "but, Lady, see thou that the Gods turn not thy strength to weakness; thou art too passionate to be all strength, and in a woman's heart passion is the door by which King Folly enters. Today thou hatest, beware, lest to-morrow thou should'st love."

' "Love," she said, gazing scornfully; "Meriamun loves not till she find a man worthy of her love."

' "Ay, and then——?"

"And then she loves to all destruction, and woe to them who cross her path. Rei, farewell."

'Then suddenly she spoke to me in another tongue, that few know save her and me, and that none can read save her and me, a dead tongue of a dead people, the people of that ancient City of the Rock, whence all our fathers came.[2]

' "I go," she said, and I trembled as she spoke, for no man speaks in this language when he has any good thought in his heart. "I go to seek the counsel of That thou knowest," and she touched the golden snake which she had won.

'Then I threw myself on the earth at her feet, and clasped her knees, crying, "My daughter, my daughter, sin not this great sin. Nay, for all the kingdoms of the world, wake not That which sleepeth, nor warm again into life That which is a-cold."

'But she only nodded, and put me from her,'—and the old man's face grew pale as he spoke.

---

[2]Probably the mysterious and indecipherable ancient books, which were occasionally excavated in old Egypt, were written in this dead language of a more ancient and now forgotten people. Such was the book discovered at Coptos, in the sanctuary there, by a priest of the Goddess. 'The whole earth was dark, but the moon shone all about the Book.' A scribe of the period of the Ramessids mentions another indecipherable ancient writing. 'Thou tellest me thou understandest no word of it, good or bad. There is, as it were, a wall about it that none may climb. Thou art instructed, yet thou knowest it not; this makes me afraid.' Birch, *Zeitschrift*, 1871, pp. 61-64. *Papyrus Anastasi* I, pl. X. 1.8, pl. X. 1.4. Maspero, *Hist. Anc.*, pp. 66-67.

'What meant she?' said the Wanderer.

Rei hid his face in his hands, and for a space he was silent.

'Nay, wake not *thou* That which sleepeth, Wanderer,' he said, at length. 'My tongue is sealed. I tell thee more than I would tell another. Do not ask,—but hark! They come again! Now my Ra and Pasht and Amen curse them; may the red swine's mouth of Set gnaw upon them in Amenti; may the Fish of Sebek flesh his teeth of stone in them for ever, and feed and feed again!'

'Why dost thou curse thus, Rei, and who are they that go by?' said the Wanderer. 'I hear their tramping and their song.'

Indeed there came a light noise of many shuffling feet, pattering outside the Palace wall, and the words of a song rang out triumphantly:

The Lord our God He doth sign and wonder,
   Tokens He shows in the land of Khem,
He hath shattered the pride of the Kings asunder
   And casteth His shoe o'er the Gods of them!
He hath brought forth frogs in their holy places,
   He hath sprinkled the dust upon crown and hem,
He hath hated their kings and hath darkened their faces;
   Wonders He works in the land of Khem.

'These are the accursed blaspheming conjurors and slaves, the Apura,' said Rei, as the music and the tramping died away. 'Their magic is greater than the lore even of us who are instructed, for their leader was one of ourselves, a shaven priest, and knows our wisdom. Never do they march and sing thus but evil comes of it. Ere day dawn we shall have news of them. May the Gods destroy them, they are gone for the hour. It were well if Meriamun the Queen would let them go for ever, as they desire, to their death in the desert, but she hardens the King's heart.'

7. THE QUEEN'S VISION

There was silence without at last; the clamour and the tread of the Apura were hushed in the distance, dying far away, and Rei grew calm, when he heard no longer the wild song, and the clashing of the timbrels.

'I must tell thee, Eperitus,' he said, 'how the matter ended between the divine Prince and Meriamun. She bowed her pride before her father and her brother: her father's will was hers; she seemed to let her secret sleep, and she set her own price on her hand. In everything she must be the equal of Pharaoh—that was her price; and in all the temples and all the cities she was to be solemnly proclaimed joint heir with him of the Upper and Lower Land. The bargain was struck and the price was paid. After that night over the game of pieces Meriamun was changed. Thenceforth she did not mock at the Prince, she made herself gentle and submissive to his will.

'So the time drew on till at length in the beginning of the month of the rising of the waters came the day of her bridal. With a mighty pomp was Pharaoh's daughter wedded to Pharaoh's son. But her hand was cold as she stood at the altar, cold as the hand of one who sleeps in Osiris. Proudly and coldly she sat in the golden chariot passing in and out the great gates of Tanis. Only when she listened and heard the acclaiming thousands shout *Meriamun* so loudly that the cry of *Meneptah* was lost in the echoes of her name—then only did she smile.

48

'Cold, too, she sat in her white robes at the feast that Pharaoh made, and she never looked at the husband by her side, though he looked kindly on her.

'The feast was long, but it ended at last, and then came the music and the singers, but Meriamun, making excuse, rose and went out, attended by her ladies. And I also, weary and sad at heart, passed thence to my own chamber and busied myself with the instruments of my art, for, stranger, I build the houses of Gods and kings.

'Presently, as I sat, there came a knocking at the door, and a woman entered wrapped in a heavy cloak. She put aside the cloak, and before me was Meriamun in all her bridal robes.

' "Heed me not, Rei," she said, "I am yet free for an hour; and I would watch thee at thy labour. Nay, it is my humour; gainsay me not, for I love well to look at that wrinkled face of thine, scored by the cunning chisel of thy knowledge and thy years. So from a child have I watched thee tracing the shapes of mighty temples that shall endure when ourselves, and perchance the very Gods we worship, have long since ceased to be. Ah, Rei, thou wise man, thine is the better part, for thou buildest in cold enduring stone and attirest thy walls as thy fancy bids thee. But I—I build in the dust of human hearts, and my will is written in their dust. When I am dead, raise me a tomb more beautiful than ever has been known, and write upon the portal, *Here, in the last temple of her pride, dwells that tired builder, Meriamun, the Queen.*"

'Thus she talked wildly in words with little reason.

' "Nay, speak not so," I said, "for is it not thy bridal night? What dost thou here at such a time?"

' "What do I here? Surely I come to be a child again! See, Rei, in all wide Khem there is no woman so shamed, so lost, so utterly undone as is tonight the Royal Meriamun, whom thou lovest. I am lower than she who plies the street for bread, for the loftier the spirit the greater is the fall. I am sold into shame, and power is my price. Oh, cursed be the fate of woman who only by her beauty can be great. Oh, cursed by that ancient Counsellor thou wottest of, and cursed by I who wakened That which slept, and warmed That which was a-cold in my breath and in my breast! And cursed be this sin to which he led me! Spurn me, Rei; strike me on the cheek, spit upon me, on Meriamun, the Royal harlot who sells herself to win a crown. Oh, I hate him, hate him, and I will pay him in shame for shame—him, the clown in king's attire. See here,"—and from he robe she drew a white flower that was known to her and me—"twice to-day have I been minded with this deadly blossom to make an end of me, and of all my shame, and all my empty greed of glory. But this thought has held my hand: I, Meriamun, will live to look across his grave and break his images, and beat out the writings of his name from every temple wall in Khem, as they beat out the hated name of Hatshepu. I——" and suddenly she burst into a rain of tears; she who was not wont to weep.

'"Nay, touch me not," she said. "They were but tears of anger. Meriamun is mistress of her Fate, not Fate of Meriamun. And now, my lord awaits me, and I must be gone. Kiss me on the brow, old friend, whilst yet I am the Meriamun thou knowest, and then kiss me no more for ever. At the least this is well for thee, for when Meriamun is Queen of Khem thou shalt be first in all the land, and stand on the footsteps of my throne. Farewell." And she gathered up her raiment and cast her white flower of death in the flame of the brazier, and was gone, leaving me yet sadder at heart. For now I knew that she was not as other women are, but greater for good or evil.

'On the morrow night I sat again at my task, and again there came a knocking at the door, and again a woman entered and threw aside her wrappings. It was Meriamun. She was pale and stern, and as I rose she waved me back.

'"Has, then, the Prince—thy husband——," I stammered.

'"Speak not to me of the Prince, Rei, my servant," she made answer. "Yesternight I spoke to thee wildly, my mind was overwrought; let it be forgotten—a wife am I, a happy wife;" and she smiled so strangely that I shrunk back from her.

' "Now to my errand. I have dreamed a dream, a troublous dream, and thou art wise and instructed, therefore I pray thee interpret my vision. I slept and dreamed of a man, and in my dream I loved him more than I can tell. For my heart beat to his heart, and in the light of him I lived, and all my soul was his, and I knew that I loved him for ever. And Pharaoh was my husband; but, in my dream, I loved him not. Now there came a woman rising out of the sea, more beautiful than I, with a beauty fairer and more changeful than the dawn upon the mountains; and she, too, loved this godlike man, and he loved her. Then we strove together for his love, matching beauty against beauty, and wit against wit, and magic against magic. Now one conquered, and now the other; but in the end the victory was mine, and I went arrayed as for a marriage bed—and I clasped a corpse.

' "I woke, and again I slept, and saw myself wearing another garb, and speaking another tongue. Before me was the man I loved, and there, too, was the woman, wrapped about with beauty, and I was changed, and yet I was the very Meriamun thou seest. And once more we struggled for the mastery and for this man's love, and in that day she conquered me.

' "I slept, and again I woke, and in another land than Khem—a strange land, and yet methought I knew it from long ago. There I dwelt among the graves, and dark faces were about me, and I wore That thou knowest for a girdle. And the tombs of the rock wherein we dwelt were scored with the writings of a dead tongue—the tongue of that land whence our fathers came. We were all changed, yet the same, and once more the woman and I struggled for the mastery, and though I seemed to conquer, yet a sea of fire came over me, and I woke and I slept again.

' "Then confusion was piled upon confusion, nor can my memory hold all that came to pass. For this game played itself afresh in lands, and lives, and tongues without number. Only the last bout and the winner were not revealed to me.

' "And in my dream I cried aloud to the protecting Gods to escape out of the dream, and I sought for light that I might see whence these things were. Then, as in a vision, the Past opened up its gates. It seemed that upon a time, thousand, thousand ages agone, I and this man of my dream had arisen from nothingness and looked in each other's eyes, and loved with a love unspeakable, and vowed a vow that shall endure from time to time and world to world. For we were not mortal then, but partook of the nature of the Gods, being more fair and great than any of human kind, and our happiness was the happiness of Heaven. But in our great joy we hearkened to the Voice of That thou knowest, of that Thing, Rei, with which, against thy counsel, I have but lately dealt. The kiss of our love awakened That which slept, the fire of our love warmed That which was a-cold! We defied the holy Gods, worshipping them not, but rather each the other, for we knew that as the Gods we were eternal. And the Gods were angered against us and drew us up into their presence. And while we trembled they spake as with a voice:

' " 'Ye twain who are one life, each completing each, because with your kisses ye have wakened That which slept, and with the fire of our love have warmed That which was a-cold: because ye have forgotten them that gave you life and love and joy: hearken to your Doom!

' " 'From Two be ye made *Three,* and through all Time strive ye to be twain again. Pass from this Holy Place down to the Hell of Earth, and though ye be immortal put on the garments of mortality. Pass on from Life to Life, live and love and hate and seem to die: have acquaintance with every lot, and in your blind forgetfulness, being one and being equal, work each other's woe according to the law of Earth, and for your love's sake sin and be shamed, perish and re-arise, appear to conquer and be conquered, pursuing your threefold destiny, which is one destiny, till the hours of punishment are outworn, and, at the word of Fate, the unaltering circle meets, and the veil of blindness falls from your eyes, and, as a scroll, your folly is un-rolled, and the hid purpose of your sorrow is accomplished and once more ye are Twain and One.'

' "Then, as we trembled, clinging each to each, again the great Voice spoke:

' " 'Ye twain who are One—let That to which ye have hearkened divide you and enfold you! Be ye Three!'

' "And as the Voice spoke I was torn with agony, and strength went out of me, and there, by him I loved, stood the woman of my dream crowned with every glory and adorned with the Star. And we were three. And between him and me, yet enfolding him and me, writhed that Thing thou wottest of. And he whom I loved turned to look upon the fair woman, wondering, and she smiled and stretched out her arms towards him as one who would take that which is her own, and, Rei, in that hour, though it was but a dream, I knew the mortal pain of jealousy, and awoke trembling. And now read thou this vision, Rei, thou who art learned in the interpretation of dreams and in the ways of sleep."

' "Oh, Lady," I made answer, "this thing is too high for me, I cannot interpret it; but where thou art, there may I be to help thee."

' "I know thy love," she said, "but in thy words is little light. So—so—let it pass! It was but a dream, and if indeed it came from the Under World, why, it was from no helpful God, but rather from Set, the Tormentor; or from Pasht, the Terrible, who throws the creeping shadow of her doom upon the mirror of my sleep. For that which is decreed will surely come to pass! I am blown like the dust by the breath of Fate; now to rest upon the Temple's loftiest tops, now to be trodden underfoot of slaves, and now to be swallowed by the bitter deep, and in season thence rolled forth again. I love not this lord of mine, who shall be Pharaoh, and never may *he* come whom I shall love. 'Tis well that I love him not, for to love is to be a slave. When the heart is cold then the hand is strong, and I am fain to be the Queen leading Pharaoh by the beard, the first of all the ancient land of Khem; for I was not born to serve. Nay, while I may, I rule, awaiting the end of rule. Look forth, Rei, and see how the rays from Mother Isis' throne flood all the courts and all the city's streets and break in light upon the water's breast. So shall the Moon-child's fame flood all this land of Khem. What matters it, if ere the morn Isis must pass to her dominion of the Dead, and the voice of Meriamun be hushed within a sepulchre?"'

'So she spoke and went thence, and on her face was no bride's smile, but rather such a gaze as that with which the great sphinx, Horemku, looks out across the desert sands.'

'A strange Queen, Rei,' said the Wanderer, as he paused, 'but what have I to make in this tale of a bride and her mad dreams?'

'More than thou shalt desire,' said Rei; 'but let us come to the end, and thou shalt hear thy part in the Fate.'

8. THE KA, THE BAI, AND THE KHOU

'The Divine Pharaoh Rameses died and was gathered to Osiris. With these hands I closed his coffin and set him in his splendid tomb, where he shall rest unharmed for ever till the day of the awakening. And Meriamun and Meneptah reigned in Khem. But to Pharaoh she was very cold, though he did her will in everything, and they had but one child, so that in a while he wearied of her loveliness.

'But hers was the master-mind, and she ruled Pharaoh as she ruled all else.

'For me, my lot was bettered; she talked much with me, and advanced me to great dignity, so that I was the first Master Builder in Khem, and Commander of the legion of Amen.

'Now it chanced that Meriamun made a feast, where she entertained Pharaoh, and Hataska sat beside him. She was the first lady about the Queen's person, a beautiful but insolent woman, who had gained Pharaoh's favour for the hour. Now wine worked so with the King that he toyed openly with the lady Hataska's hand, but Meriamun the Queen took no note, though Hataska, who had also drunk of the warm wine of the Lower Land, grew insolent, as was her wont. She quaffed deep from her cup of gold, and bade a slave bear it to the Queen, crying, "Pledge me, my sister."

'The meaning of her message was plain to all who heard; this waiting lady openly declared herself wife to

Pharaoh and an equal of the Queen. Now Meriamun cared nothing for Pharaoh's love, but for power she did care, and she frowned, while a light shone in her dark eyes; yet she took the cup and touched it with her lips.

'Presently she lifted her own cup in turn and toyed with it, then made pretence to drink, and said softly to the King's paramour, who had pledged her:

' "Pledge me in answer, Hataska, my servant, for soon, methinks, thou shalt be greater than the Queen."

'Now this foolish woman read her saying wrong, and took the golden cup from the eunuch who bore it.

"With a little nod to the Queen, and a wave of her slim hand, Hataska drank, and instantly, with a great cry, she fell dead across the board. Then, while all the company sat in terror, neither daring to be silent nor to speak, and while Meriamun smiled scornfully on the dark head lying low among the roses on the board, Pharaoh leaped up, mad with wrath, and called to the guards to seize the Queen. But she waved them back, and, speaking in a slow, cold voice, she said:

' "Dare not to touch Khemi's anointed Queen lest your fate be as *her* fate. For thee, Meneptah, forget not thy marriage oath. What, am I Queen, and shall thy wantons throw their insolence in my teeth and name me their sister? Not so, for if my eyes be blind yet are my ears open. Peace, she is rightly served—choose thou a lowlier mistress!"

'And Pharaoh made no answer, for he feared her with an ever-growing fear. But she, sinking back in her seat of state, played with the gold kepher on her breast, and watched them bear the body forth to the House of Osiris. One by one all the company made obeisance and passed thence, glad to be gone, till at the last there were left only Pharaoh and Meriamun the Queen, and myself—Rei the Priest—for all were much afraid. Then Pharaoh spoke, looking neither at her nor at me, and half in fear, half in anger.

' "Thou hateful woman, accursed be the day when first I looked upon thy beauty. Thou hast conquered me, but beware, for I am still Pharaoh and thy Lord. Cross my

purpose once again, and, by Him who sleeps at Philæ, I
will discrown thee and give thy body to the tormentors,
and set thy soul loose to follow her whom thou hast
slain."

'Then Meriamun answered proudly:

' "Pharaoh, be warned: lift but one finger against my
majesty and thou art doomed. Thou canst not slay me,
but I can over-match thee, and I swear by the same oath!
By Him who sleeps at Philæ, lift but a hand against me,
ay, harbour one thought of treachery, and thou diest. Not
lightly can I be deceived, for I have messengers that thou
canst not hear. Something, Royal Meneptah, do I know of
the magic of that Queen Taia who was before me. Now
listen—do this one thing and all shall be well. Go on thy
path and leave me to follow mine. Queen I am, Queen I
will remain, and in all matters of the State mine must be
an equal voice though it is thine that speaks. And, for the
rest, we are apart henceforth, for thou fearest me, and,
Meneptah, I love not thee, nor any man."

' "As thou hast spoken, so be it," quoth Pharaoh, for
his heart sank, and his fear came back upon him. "Evil
was the day when first we met, and this is the price of my
desire. Henceforth we are apart in bed and board, but in
the council we are still one, for our ends are one. I know
thy power, Meriamun, thou gifted of the evil Gods; thou
needest not fear that I shall seek to slay thee, for a spear
cast against the heavens returns on him who threw it. Rei,
my servant, thou wert witness to our oaths; hear now their
undoing. Meriamun, the Queen of ancient Khem, thou art
no more wife of mine. Farewell."

'And he went heavily and stricken with fear.

' "Nay," she said, gazing after him, "no more am I
Meneptah's wife, but still am I Khemi's dreaded Queen.
Oh, thou old priest, I am aweary. See what a lot is mine,
who have all things but love, and yet am sick of all! I
longed for power, and power is mine, and what is power?
It is a rod wherewith we beat the air that straightway closes
on the stroke. Yes, I tire of my loveless days and of this
dull round of common things. Oh, for one hour of love
and in that hour to die! Oh that the future would lift its

veil and disclose the face of time to be! Say, Rei! Wilt thou be bold and dare a deed?" And she clasped me by the sleeve and whispered in my ear, in the dead tongue known to her and me—"Her I slew—thou sawest———"

' "Ay, Queen, I saw—what of her? 'Twas ill done."

' "Nay, 'twas rightly done and well done. But thou knowest she is not yet cold, nor for a while will be, and I have the art to drag her spirit back ere she be cold, from where she is, and to force knowledge from its lips—for being an Osiris all the future is open to her in this hour."

' "Nay, nay," I cried. "It is unholy—not lightly may we disturb the dead, lest the Guardian Gods be moved to anger."

' "Yet will I do it, Rei. If thou dost fear, come not. But I go. I am fain for knowledge, and thus only may I win it. If I die in the dread endeavour, write this of Meriamun the Queen: That in seeking the to-be—she found it!"

' "Nay, Royal Lady," I answered, "thou shalt not go alone. I too have some skill in magic, and perchance can ward evil from thee. So, if indeed thou wilt dare this dreadful thing, behold now, as ever, I am thy servant."

' "It is well. See, now, the body will this night be laid in the sanctuary of the Temple of Osiris that is near the great gates, as is the custom, to await the coming of the embalmers. Come ere she be colder than my heart, come with me, Rei, to the house of the Lord of the Dead!"

'She passed to her chamber, wrapped herself about in a dark robe, and hurried with me to the Temple doors, where we were challenged by the guards.

' "Who passes? In the name of the Holy Osiris speak."

' "Rei, the Master Builder and the anointed Priest, and with him another," I made answer. "Open."

' "Nay, I open not. There is one within who may not be wakened."

' "Who, then, is within?"

' "She whom the Queen slew."

' "The Queen sends one who would look on her she slew."

'Then the priest gazed on the hooded form beside me and started back, crying, "A token, noble Rei."

'I held up the Royal signet, and, bowing, he opened. Being come within the Temple I lit the tapers that had been prepared. Then by their feeble light we passed through the outer hall till we came to the curtains that veil the sanctury of the Holy Place, and here I quenched the tapers; for no fire must enter there, save that which burns upon the altar of the dead. But through the curtains came rays of light.

' "Open!" said Meriamun, and I opened, and hand in hand we passed in. On the altar that is in the place the flame burnt brightly. The chamber is not wide and great, for this is the smallest of the temples of Tanis, but yet so large that the light could not reach its walls nor pierce the overhanging gloom, and by much gazing scarcely could we discover the outline of the graven shapes of the Holy Gods that are upon the walls. But the light fell clear upon the great statue of the Osiris that was seated behind the altar fashioned in the black stone of Syene, wound about with the corpse-cloths, wearing on his head the crown of the Upper Land, and holding in his hands the crook of divinity and the awful scourge of punishment. the light shone all about the white and dreadful shape that was placed upon his holy knees, the naked shape of lost Hataska who this night had died at the hand of Meriamun. There she bowed her head against the sacred breast, her long hair streaming down on either side, her arms tied across her heart, and her eyes, whence the hues of life had scarcely faded, widely staring at the darkness of the shrine. For at Tanis to this day it is the custom for a night to place those of high birth or office who die suddenly upon the knees of the statue of Osiris.

' "See," I said to the Queen, speaking low, for the weight of the haunted place sank into my heart, "see how she who scarce an hour ago was but a lovely wanton hath by thine act been clad in majesty greater than all the glory of the earth. Bethink thee, wilt thou dare indeed to summon back the spirit to the body whence thou hast set it free? Not easily, O Queen, may it be done for all thy magic, and if perchance she answereth thee, it may well be that the terror of her words shall utterly o'erwhelm us."

' "Nay," she made answer. "I am instructed. I fear not. I know by what name to call the Khou that hovers on the threshold of the Double Hall of Truth, and how to send it back to its own place. I fear not, but if perchance thou fearest, Rei, depart hence and leave me to the task alone."

' "Nay," I said. "I also am instructed, and I go not. But I say to thee this is unholy."

'Then Meriamun spake no more—but lifting up her hands she held them heavenwards, and so for a while she stood, her face fixed, as was the face of dead Hataska. Then, as must be done, I drew the circle round us and round the altar and the statue of Osiris and that which sat upon his knee. With my staff I drew it, and standing therein I said the holy words which should ward away the evil things that come near in such an hour.

'Now, Meriamun threw a certain powder into the flame upon the altar. Thrice she threw the powder, and as she threw it a ball of flame rose from the altar and floated away, each time that she threw did the ball of fire rise; and this it was needful to do, for by fire only may the dead be manifest, and therefore was a globe of fire given to each of the three shapes that together make the threefold spirit of the dead. And when the three globes of fire had melted into air, passing over the head of the statue of Osiris, thrice did Meriamun cry aloud:

' *"Hataska! Hataska! Hataska!*

' "By the dreadful Name I summon thee.

' "I summon thee from the threshold of the Double Hall.

' "I summon thee from the Gates of Judgment.

' "I summon thee from the door of Doom.

' "By the link of life and death that is between thee and me, I bid thee come from where thou art and make answer to that which I shall ask of thee."

'She ceased, but no answer came. Still the cold Osiris smiled, and still the body on his knee sat with open eyes gazing into nothingness.

' "Not thus easily," I whispered, "may this dreadful thing be done. Thou art instructed in the Word of Fear. If thou darest, let it pass thy lips, or let us be gone."

' "Nay, it shall be spoken," she said—and thus she wrought. Passing to the statue she hid her head within her cloak and with both hands grasped the feet of the slain Hataska.

'Seeing this I also crouched upon the floor and hid my face, for it is death to hear that Word with an uncovered face.

'Then in so soft a whisper that scarce had its breath stirred a feather on her lips, Meriamun spoke the Word of Fear which may not be written, whose sound has power to pass all space and open the ears of the dead who dwell in Amenti. Softly she said it, but in a shout of thunder it was caught up and echoed from her lips, and down the eternal halls it seemed to rush on the feet of storm and the wings of wind, so that the roof rocked and the deep foundations of the temple quivered like a wind-stirred tree.

' "Unveil, ye mortals!" cried a dreadful voice, "and look upon the sight of fear that ye have dared to summon."

'And I rose and cast my cloak from about my face and gazed, then sank down in terror. For round about the circle that I had drawn pressed all the multitude of the dead; countless as the desert sands they pressed, gazing with awful eyes upon us twain. And the fire that was on the altar died away, but yet was there light, for it shone from those dead eyes, and in the eyes of lost Hataska there was light.

'And ever the faces changed, never for one beat of time did they cease to change. For as we gazed upon a face it would melt, even to the eyes, and round these same eyes again would gather but no more the same. And like the sloping sides of pyramids were the faces set about us from the ground to the Temple roof—and on us were fixed their glowing eyes.

'And I, Rei, being instructed, knew that to suffer myself to be overcome with terror was death, as it was death to pass without the circle. So in my heart I called upon Osiris, Lord of the Dead, to protect us, and even as I named the ineffable name, lo! all the thousand thousand faces bent themselves in adoration and then, turning, looked each upon the other even as though each spake to each, and changed, and swiftly changed.

' "Meriamun," I said, gathering up my strength, "fear not, but beware!"

' "Nay, wherefore should I fear," she answered, "because the veil of sense is torn, and for an hour we see those who are ever about our path and whose eyes watch our most secret thought continually? I fear not." And she stepped boldly, even to the edge of the circle, and cried:

' "All hail, ye Sahus, spirits of the awful dead, among whom I also shall be numbered."

'And as she came the changing faces shrunk away, leaving a space before her. And in the space there grew two arms, mighty and black, that stretched themselves towards her, until there was not the length of three grains of wheat betwixt the clutching fingers and her breast.

'But Meriamun only laughed and drew back a space.

' "Not so, thou Enemy," she said, "this circle thou may'st not break; it is too strong for thee. But to the work. Hataska, once again by the link of life and death I summon thee—and this time thou must come, thou who wast a wanton and now art 'greater than the Queen.' "

'And as she spoke, from the dead form of the woman on Osiris' knee there issued forth another form and stood before us, as a snake issues from its slough. And as was the dead Hataska so was this form, feature for feature, look for look, and limb for limb. But still the corpse rested upon Osiris' knee, for this was but the *Ka* that stood before us.

'And thus spoke the voice of Hataska in the lips of the Ka:

' "What wouldest thou with me who am no more of thy company, O thou by whose hand my body did perish? Why troublest thou me?"

'And Meriamun made answer: "I would this of thee, that thou shouldest declare unto me the future, even in the presence of this great company. Speak, I command thee."

'And the Ka said: "Nay, Meriamun, that I cannot do, for I am but the Ka—the Dweller in the Tomb, the guardian of what was Hataska whom thou didst slay, whom I must watch through all the days of death till resurrection is. Of the future I know naught; seek thou that which knows."

' "Stand thou on one side," quoth the Queen, and the Dweller in the Tomb obeyed.

'Then once more she called upon Hataska and there came a sound of rushing wings. And behold, on the head of the statue of Osiris sat a great bird, feathered as it were with gold. But the bird had the head of a woman, and the face was fashioned as the face of Hataska. And thus it spoke, that was the *Bai*:

' "What wouldest thou with me, Meriamun, who am no more of thy company, Why dost thou draw me from the Under World, thou by whose hand my body did perish?"

'And Meriamun said: "This I would of thee that thou shouldest declare unto me the future. Speak, I command thee."

'And the Bai said: "Nay, Meriamun, that I cannot do. I am but the Bai of her who was Hataska, and I fly from Death to Life and Life to Death, till the hour of awakening is. Of the future I know naught; seek thou that which knows."

' "Rest thou where thou art," quoth the Queen, and there it rested, awful to see.

'Then once more Meriamun called upon Hataska, bidding her hear the summons where she was.

'And behold the eyes of the Dead One that was upon the knee of Osiris glowed, and glowed the eyes of the Dweller in the Tomb, and of the winged Messenger who sat above. And then there was a sound as the sound of wind, and from above, cleaving the darkness, descended a Tongue of Flame and rested on the brow of the dead Hataska. And the eyes of all the thousand thousand spirits turned and gazed upon the Tongue of Flame. And then dead Hataska spoke—though her lips moved not, yet she spoke. And this she said:

' "What wouldest thou with me, Meriamun, who am no more of thy company? Why dost thou dare to trouble me, thou by whose hand my body did perish, drawing me from the threshold of the Double Hall of Truth, back to the Over World?"

'And Meriamun the Queen said, "Oh, thou *Khou,* for this purpose have I called thee. I am aweary of my days and I fain would learn the future. The future fain would I learn, but the forked tongue of That which sleeps tells me no word, and the lips of That which is a-cold are dumb! Tell me, then, thou, I charge thee by the word that has power to open the lips of the dead, thou who in all things art instructed, what shall be the burden of my days?"

'And the dread Khou made answer: "Love shall be the burden of thy days, and Death shall be the burden of thy love. Behold one draws near from out the North whom thou hast loved, whom thou shalt love from life to life, till all things are accomplished. Bethink thee of a dream that thou dreamedst as thou didst lie on Pharaoh's bed, and read its riddle. Meriamun, thou art great and thy name is known upon the earth, and in Amenti is thy name known. High is thy fate, and through blood and sorrow shalt thou find it. I have spoken, let me hence."

' "It is well," the Queen made answer. "But not yet mayest thou go hence. First I command thee, by the word of dread and by the link of life and death, declare unto me if here upon the earth and in this life I shall possess him whom I shall love?"

' "In sin and craft and sorrow, Meriamun, thou shalt possess him; in shame and jealous agony he shall be taken from thee by one who is stronger than thou, though thou art strong; by one more beautiful than thou, though thou art beautiful; and ruin thou shalt give him for his guerdon, and ruin of the heart shalt thou harvest for thy portion. But for this time she shall escape thee, whose footsteps march with thine, and with his who shall be thine and hers. Nevertheless, in a day to come thou shalt pay her back measure for measure, and evil for evil. I have spoken. Let me hence."

' "Not yet, O Khou—not yet. I have still to learn. Show me the face of her who is mine enemy, and the face of him who is my love."

' "Thrice mayest thou speak to me, O thou greatly

daring," answered the dread Khou, "and thrice I may make reply, and then farewell till I meet thee on the threshold of the hall whence thou hast drawn me. Look now on the face of that Hataska whom thou slewest."

'And we looked, and behold the face of dead Hataska changed, and changed the face of the Double, the Ka that stood on one side, and the face of the great bird, the *Bai*, that spread his wings about the head of Osiris. And they grew beautiful, yes, most exceeding beautiful so that it cannot be told, and the beauty was that of a woman asleep. Then lo, there hung above Hataska, as it were, the shadow of one who watched her sleeping. And his face we saw not, for, O thou Wanderer, it was hidden by the visor of a golden two-horned helm, and in that helm stood fast *the bronze point of a broken spear!* But he was clad in the armour of the people of the Northern Sea, the Aquaiusha, and his hair fell dark about his shoulders like the petals of the hyacinth flower.

' "Behold thine enemy and behold thy love! Farewell," said the dread Khou, speaking though dead Hataska's lips, and as the words died the sight of beauty faded and the Tongue of Flame shot upwards and was lost, and once more the eyes of the thousand thousand dead turned and looked upon each other, even as though their lips whispered each to each.

'But for a while Meriamun stood silent, as one amazed. Then, awaking, she waved her hand and cried, "Begone, thou *Bai!* Begone, thou *Ka!*"

'And the great bird whereof the face was as the face of Hataska spread his golden wings and passed away to his own place, and the Ka that was in the semblance of Hataska drew near to the dead one's knees, and passed back into her from whom she came. And all the thousand thousand faces melted though the fiery eyes still gazed upon us.

'Then Meriamun covered her head and once more spoke the awful Word, and I also covered up my head. But, as must be done, this second time she called the Word aloud, and yet though she called it loud, it came but as a tiny whisper from her lips. Nevertheless, at the sound of it, once more was the Temple shaken as by a storm.

'Then Meriamun unveiled, and behold, again the fire burned upon the altar, and on the knees of the Osiris sat Hataska, cold and still in death, and round them was emptiness and silence.

'But Meriamun grasped me by the arm, and she spoke faintly:

' "Now that all is done, I greatly fear for that which has been, and that which shall be. Lead me hence, O Rei, son of Pames, for I can no more."

'And so with a heavy heart I led her forth, who of all sorceresses is the very greatest. Behold, thou Wanderer, wherefore the Queen was troubled at the coming of the man in the armour of the North, in whose two-horned golden helm stands fast the point of a broken spear.'

BOOK II

1. THE PROPHETS OF THE APURA

'These things are not without the Gods,' said the Wanderer, who was called Eperitus, when he had heard all the tale of Rei the Priest, son of Pames, the Head Architect, the Commander of the Legion of Amen. Then he sat silent for a while, and at last raised his eyes and looked upon the old man.

'Thou hast told a strange tale, Rei. Over many a sea have I wandered, and in many a land I have sojourned. I have seen the ways of many peoples, and have heard the voices of the immortal Gods. Dreams have come to me and marvels have compassed me about. It has been laid upon me to go down into Hades, that land which thou namest Amenti, and to look on the tribes of the Dead; but never till now have I known so strange a thing. For mark thou, when first I beheld this fair Queen of thine I thought she looked upon me strangely, as one who knew my face. And now, Rei, if thou speakest truth, *she* deems that she has met me in the ways of night and magic. Say, then, who was the man of the vision of the Queen, the man with dark and curling locks, clad in golden armour after the fashion of the Achæans whom ye name the Aquaiusha, wearing on his head a golden helm, wherein was fixed a broken spear?'

'Before me sits such a man,' said Rei, 'or perchance it is a God that my eyes behold.'

'No God am I,' quoth the Wanderer, smiling, 'though

the Sidonians deemed me nothing less when the black bow twanged and the swift shafts flew. Read me the riddle, thou that art instructed.'

Now the aged Priest looked upon the ground, then turned his eyes upward, and with muttering lips prayed to Thoth, the God of Wisdom. And when he had made an end of prayer he spoke.

'*Thou* art the man,' he said. 'Out of the sea thou hast come to bring the doom of love on the Lady Meriamun and on thyself the doom of death. This I know, but of the rest I know nothing. Now, I pray thee, oh thou who comest in the armour of the North, thou whose face is clothed in beauty, and who art of all men the mightiest and hast of all men the sweetest and most guileful tongue, go back, go back into the sea whence thou camest, and the lands whence thou hast wandered.'

'Not thus easily may men escape their doom,' quoth the Wanderer. 'My death may come, as come it must; but know this, Rei, I do not seek the love of Meriamun.'

'Then it well may chance that thou shalt find it, for ever those who seek love lose, and those who seek not find.'

'I am come to seek another love,' said the Wanderer, 'and I seek her till I die.'

'Then I pray the Gods that thou mayest find her, and that Khem may thus be saved from sorrow. But here in Egypt there is no woman so fair as Meriamun, and thou must seek farther as quickly as may be. And now, Eperitus, behold I must away to do service in the Temple of the Holy Amen, for I am his High Priest. But I am commanded by Pharaoh first to bring thee to the feast at the Palace.'

Then he led the Wanderer from his chamber and brought him by a side entrance to the great Palace of the Pharaoh at Tanis, near the Temple of Ptah. And first he took him to a chamber that had been made ready for him in the Palace, a beautiful chamber, richly painted with beast-headed Gods and furnished with ivory chairs, and couches of ebony and silver, and with a gilded bed.

Then the Wanderer went into the shining baths, and dark-eyed girls bathed him and anointed him with fragrant oil, and crowned him with lotus flowers. When they had bathed him they bade him lay aside his golden armour and his bow and the quiver full of arrows, but this the Wanderer would not do, for as he laid the black bow down it thrilled with a thin sound of war. So Rei led him, armed as he was, to a certain antechamber, and there he left him, saying that he would return again when the feast was done. Trumpets blared as the Wanderer waited, drums rolled, and through the wide thrown curtains swept the lovely Meriamun and the divine Pharaoh Meneptah, with many lords and ladies of the Court, all crowned with roses and with lotus blooms.

The Queen was decked in Royal attire, her shining limbs were veiled in broidered silk; about her shoulders was a purple robe, and round her neck and arms were rings of well-wrought gold. She was stately and splendid to see, with pale brows and beautiful disdainful eyes where dreams seemed to sleep beneath the shadow of her eyelashes. On she swept in all her state and pride of beauty, and behind her came the Pharaoh. He was a tall man, but ill-made and heavy-browed, and to the Wanderer it seemed that he was heavy-hearted too, and that care and terror of evil to come were always in his mind.

Meriamun looked up swiftly.

'Greeting, Stranger,' she said. 'Thou comest in warlike guise to grace our feast.'

'Methought, Royal Lady,' he made answer, 'that anon when I would have laid it by, this bow of mine sang to me of present war. Therefore I am come armed—even to thy feast.'

'Has thy bow such foresight, Eperitus?' said the Queen. 'I have heard but once of such a weapon, and that in a minstrel's tale. He came to our Court with his lyre from the Northern Sea, and he sang of the Bow of Odysseus.'

'Minstrel or not, thou dost well to come armed, Wanderer,' said the Pharaoh; 'for if thy bow sings, my own heart mutters much to me of war to be.'

'Follow me, Wanderer, however it fall out,' said the Queen.

So he followed her and the Pharaoh till they came to a

splendid hall, carven round with images of fighting and feasting. Here, on the painted walls, Ramses Miamun drove the thousands of the Khita before his single valour; here men hunted wild-fowl through the marshes with a great cat for their hound. Never had the Wanderer beheld such a hall since he supped with the Sea King of the fairy isle. On the daïs, raised above the rest, sat the Pharaoh, and by him sat Meriamun the Queen, and by the Queen sat the Wanderer in the golden armour of Paris, and he leaned the black bow against his ivory chair.

Now the feast went on and men ate and drank. The Queen spoke little, but she watched the Wanderer beneath the lids of her deep-fringed eyes.

Suddenly, as they feasted and grew merry, the doors at the end of the chamber were thrown wide, the Guards fell back in fear, and behold, at the end of the hall, stood two men. Their faces were tawny, dry, wasted with desert wandering; their noses were hooked like eagle's beaks, and their eyes were yellow as the eyes of lions. They were clad in rough skins of beasts, girdled about their waists with leathern thongs, and fiercely they lifted their naked arms, and waved their wands of cedar. Both men were old, one was white-bearded, the other was shaven smooth like the priests of Egypt. As they lifted the rods on high the Guards shrank like beaten hounds, and all the guests hid their faces, save Meriamun and the Wanderer alone. Even Pharaoh dared not look on them, but he murmured angrily in his beard:

'By the name of Osiris,' he said, 'here be those Soothsayers of the Apura once again. Now Death waits on those who let them pass the doors.'

Then one of the two men, he who was shaven like a priest, cried with a great voice:

'Pharaoh! Pharaoh! Pharaoh! Hearken to the word of Jahveh. Wilt thou let the people go?'

'I will not let them go,' he answered.

Pharaoh! Pharaoh! Pharaoh! Hearken to the word of Jahveh. If thou wilt not let the people go, then shall all the first-born of Khem, of the Prince and the slave, of the ox and the ass, be smitten of Jahveh. Wilt thou let the people go?'

Now Pharaoh hearkened, and those who were at the feast rose and cried with a loud voice:

'O Pharaoh, let the people go! Great woes are fallen upon Khem because of the Apura. O Pharaoh, let the people go!'

Now Pharaoh's heart was softened and he was minded to let them go, but Meriamun turned to him and said:

'Thou shalt not let the people go. It is not these slaves, nor the God of these slaves, who bring the plagues on Khem, but it is that strange Goddess, the False Hathor, who dwells here in the city of Tanis. Be not so fearful—ever hadst thou a coward heart. Drive the False Hathor hence if thou wilt, but hold these slaves to their bondage. I still have cities that must be built, and yon slaves shall build them.'

Then the Paraoh cried: 'Hence! I bid you. Hence, and to-morrow shall your people be laden with a double burden and their backs shall be red with stripes. I will not let the people go!'

Then the two men cried aloud, and pointing upward with their staffs they vanished from the hall, and none dared to lay hands on them, but those who sat at the feast murmured much.

Now the Wanderer marvelled why Pharaoh did not command the Guards to cut down these unbidden guests, who spoiled his festival. The Queen Meriamun saw the wonder in his eyes and turned to him.

'Know thou, Eperitus,' she said, 'that great plagues have come of late on this land of ours—plagues of lice and frogs and flies and darkness, and the changing of pure waters to blood. And these things our Lord the Pharaoh deems have been brought upon us by the curse of yonder magicians, conjurers and priests among certain slaves who work in the land at the building of our cities. But I know well that the curses come on us from Hathor, the Lady of Love, because of that woman who hath set herself up here in Tanis, and is worshipped as the Hathor.'

'Why then, O Queen,' said the Wanderer, 'is this false

Goddess suffered to abide in your fair city? for, as I know well, the immortal Gods are ever angered with those who turn from their worship to bow before strange altars.'

'Why is she suffered? Nay, ask of Pharaoh my Lord. Methinks it is because her beauty is more than the beauty of women, so the men say who have looked on it, but I have not seen it, for only those men see it who go to worship at her shrine, and then from afar. It is not meet that the Queen of all the Lands should worship at the shrine of a strange woman, come—like thyself, Eperitus—from none knows where: if indeed she be a woman and not a fiend from the Under World. But if thou wouldest learn more, ask my Lord the Pharaoh, for he knows the Shrine of the False Hathor, and he knows who guard it, and what is it that bars the way.'

Now the Wanderer turned to Pharaoh saying: 'O Pharaoh, may I know the truth of this mystery?'

Then Meneptah looked up, and there was doubt and trouble on his heavy face.

'I will tell thee readily, thou Wanderer, for perchance such a man as thou, who hast travelled in many lands and seen the faces of many Gods, may understand the tale, and may help me. In the days of my father, the holy Rameses Miamun, the keepers of the Temple of the Divine Hathor awoke, and lo! in the Sanctuary of the temple was a woman in the garb of the Aquaiusha, who was Beauty's self. But when they looked upon her, none could tell the semblance of her beauty, for to one she seemed dark and to the other fair, and to each man of them she showed a diverse loveliness. She smiled upon them, and sang most sweetly, and love entered their hearts, so that it seemed to each man that she only was his Heart's Desire. But when any man would have come nearer and embraced her, there was that about her which drove him back, and if he strove again, behold, he fell down dead. So at last they subdued their hearts, and desired her no more, but worshipped her as the Hathor come to earth, and made offerings of food and drink to her, and prayers. So three years passed, and at the end of the third year the keepers of the temple looked and the Hathor was gone.

Nothing remained of her but a memory. Yet there were some who said that this memory was dearer than all else that the world has to give.

'Twenty more seasons went by, and I set upon the throne of my father, and was Lord of the Double Crown. And, on a day, a messenger came running and cried:

' "Now is Hathor come back to Khem, now is Hathor come back to Khem, and, as of old, none may draw near her beauty!" Then I went to see, and lo! before the Temple of Hathor a great multitude was gathered, and there on the pylon brow stood the Hathor's self shining with changeful beauty like the Dawn. And as of old she sang sweet songs, and, to each man who heard, her voice was the voice of his own beloved, living and lost to him, or dead and lost. Now every man has such a grave in his heart as that whence Hathor seems to rise in changeful beauty. Month by month she sings thus, one day in every month, and many a man has sought to win her and her favour, but in the doorways are they who meet him and press him back; and if he still struggles on, there comes a clang of swords and he falls dead, but no wound is found on him. And, Wanderer, this is truth, for I myself have striven and have been pressed back by that which guards her. But I alone of men who have looked on her and heard her, strove not a second time, and so saved myself alive.'

'Thou alone of men lovest life more than the World's Desire!' said the Queen. 'Thou hast ever sickened for the love of this strange Witch, but thy life thou lovest even better than her beauty, and thou dost not dare attempt again the adventure of her embrace. Know, Eperitus, that this sorrow is come upon the land, that all men love yonder witch and rave of her, and to each she wears a different face and sings in another voice. When she stands upon the pylon tower, then thou wilt see the madness with which she has smitten them. For they will weep and pray and tear their hair. Then they will rush through the temple courts and up to the temple doors, and be thrust back again by that which guards her. But some will yet strive madly on, and thou wilt hear the clash of arms and they will fall dead before thee. Accursed is the land, I tell thee, Wanderer; because of that Phantom it is accursed. For it is she who brings these woes on Khem; from her, not from our slaves and their mad conjurers, come plagues, I say, and all evil things. And till a man be found who may pass her guard, and come face to face with the witch and slay her, plagues and woes and evil things shall be the daily bread of Khem. Perchance, Wanderer, thou art such a man,' and she looked on him strangely. 'Yet is so, this is my counsel, that thou go not up against her, lest thou also be bewitched, and a great man be lost to us.'

Now the Wanderer turned the matter over in his heart and made answer:

'Perchance, Lady, my strength and the favour of the Gods might serve me in such a quest. But methinks that this woman is meeter for words of love and the kisses of men than to be slain with the sharp sword, if, indeed, she be not of the number of the immortals.'

Now Meriamun flushed and frowned.

'It is not fitting so to talk before me,' she said. 'Of this be sure, that if the Witch may be come at, she shall be slain and given to Osiris for a bride.'

Now the Wanderer saw that the Lady Meriamun was jealous of the beauty and renown and love of her who dwelt in the temple, and was called the Strange Hathor, and he held his peace, for he knew when to be silent.

2. THE NIGHT OF DREAD

The feast dragged slowly on, for Fear was of the company. The men and women were silent, and when they drank, it was as if one had poured a little oil on a dying fire. Life flamed up in them for a moment, their laughter came like the crackling of thorns, and then they were silent again. Meanwhile the Wanderer drank little, waiting to see what should come. But the Queen was watching him whom already her heart desired, and she only of all the company had pleasure in this banquet. Suddenly a side-door opened behind the daïs, there was a stir in the hall, each guest turning his head fearfully, for all expected some evil tidings. But it was only the entrance of those who bear about in the feasts of Egypt an effigy of the Dead, the likeness of a mummy carved in wood, and who cry: 'Drink, O King, and be glad, thou shalt soon be even as he! Drink, and be glad.' The stiff, swathed figure, with its folded hands and gilded face, was brought before the Pharaoh, and Meneptah, who had sat long in sullen brooding silence, started when he looked on it. Then he broke into an angry laugh.

'We have little need of thee to-night,' he cried, as he saluted the symbol of Osiris. 'Death is near enough, we want not thy silent preaching. Death, Death is near!'

He fell back in his gilded chair, and let the cup drop from his hand, gnawing his beard.

'Art thou a man?' spoke Meriamun, in a low clear

voice; 'are you men, and yet afraid of what comes to all? Is it only to-night that we first hear the name of Death? Remember the great Men-kau-ra, remember the old Pharaoh who built the Pyramid of Hir. He was just and kind, and he feared the Gods, and for his reward they showed him Death, coming on him in six short years. Did he scowl and tremble, like all of you to-night, who are scared by the threats of slaves? Nay, he outwitted the Gods, he made night into day, he lived out twice his years, with revel and love and wine in the lamp-lit groves of persea trees. Come, my guests, let us be merry, if it be but for an hour. Drink, and be brave!'

'For once thou speakest well,' said the King. 'Drink and forget; the Gods who give Death give wine,' and his angry eyes ranged through the hall, to seek some occasion of mirth and scorn.

'Thou Wanderer!' he said suddenly. 'Thou drinkest not: I have watched thee as the cups go round; what, man, thou comest from the North, the sun of thy pale land has not heat enough to foster the vine. Thou seemest cold, and a drinker of water; why wilt thou be cold before thine hour? Come, pledge me in the red wine of Khem. Bring forth the cup of Pasht!' he cried to them who waited, 'bring forth the cup of Pasht, the King drinks!'

Then the chief butler of Pharaoh went to the treasure-house, and came again, bearing a huge golden cup, fashioned in the form of a lion's head, and holding twelve measures of wine. It was an ancient cup, sacred to Pasht, and a gift of the Rutennu to Thothmes, the greatest of that name.

'Fill it full of unmixed wine!' cried the King. 'Dost thou grow pale at the sight of the cup, thou Wanderer from the North? I pledge thee, pledge thou me!'

'Nay, King,' said the Wanderer, 'I have tasted wine of Ismarus before to-day, and I have drunk with a wild host, the one-eyed Man Eater!' For his heart was angered by the King and he forgot his wisdom, but the Queen marked the saying.

'Then pledge me in the cup of Pasht!' quoth the King.

'I pray thee, pardon me,' said the Wanderer, 'for wine

makes wise men foolish and strong men weak, and to-night methinks we shall need our wits and our strength.'

'Craven!' cried the King, 'give me the bowl. I drink to thy better courage, Wanderer,' and lifting the great golden cup, he stood up and drank it, and then dropped staggering into his chair, his head fallen on his breast.

'I may not refuse a King's challenge, though it is ill to contend with our hosts,' said the Wanderer, turning somewhat pale, for he was in anger. 'Give me the bowl!'

He took the cup, and held it high; then pouring a little forth to his Gods, he said, in a clear voice, for he was stirred to anger beyond his wont:

I drink to the Strange Hathor!

He spoke, and drained the mighty cup, and set it down on the board, and even as he laid down the cup, and as the Queen looked at him with eyes of wrath, there came from the bow beside his seat a faint shrill sound, a ringing and a singing of the bow, a noise of running strings and a sound as of rushing arrows.

The warrior heard it and, his eyes burned with the light of battle, for he knew well that the swift shafts should soon fly to the hearts of the doomed. Pharaoh awoke and heard it, and heard it the Lady Meriamun the Queen, and she looked on the Wanderer astonished, and looked on the bow that sang.

'The minstrel's tale was true! This is none other but the Bow of Odysseus, the sacker of cities,' said Meriamun. 'Hearken thou, Eperitus, thy great bow sings aloud. How comes it that thy bow sings?'

'For this cause, Queen,' said the Wanderer; 'because birds gather on the Bridge of War. Soon shall shafts be flying and ghosts go down to doom. Summon thy Guards, I bid thee, for foes are near.'

Terror conquered the drunkenness of Pharaoh; he bade the Guards who stood behind his chair summon all their company. They went forth, and a great hush fell again upon the hall of Banquets and upon those who sat at meat therein. The silence grew deadly still, like air before the thunder, and men's hearts sank within them, and turned to water in their breasts. Only Odysseus wondered and thought on the battle to be, though whence the foe might come he knew not, and Meriamun sat erect in her ivory chair and looked down the glorious hall.

Deeper grew the silence and deeper yet, and more and more the cloud of fear gathered in the hearts of men. Then suddenly through all the hall there was a rush like the rush of mighty wings. The deep foundations of the Palace rocked, and to the sight of men the roof above seemed to burst asunder, and lo! above them, against the distance of the sky, there swept a shape of Fear, and the stars shone through its raiment.

Then the roof closed in again, and for a moment's space once more there was silence, whilst men looked with white faces, each on each, and even the stout heart of the Wanderer stood still.

Then suddenly all adown the hall, from this place and from that, men rose up and with one great cry fell down dead, this one across the board, and that one on the floor. The Wanderer grasped his bow and counted. From among those who sat at meat twenty and one had fallen dead. Yet those who lived sat gazing emptily, for so stricken with fear were they that scarce did each one know if it was he himself who lay dead or his brother who had sat by his side.

But Meriamun looked down the hall with cold eyes, for she feared neither Death nor Life, nor God nor man.

And while she looked and while the Wanderer counted, there rose a faint murmuring sound from the city without, a sound that grew and grew, the thunder of myriad feet that run before the death of kings. Then the doors burst asunder and a woman sped through them in her night robes, and in her arms she bore the naked body of a boy.

'Pharaoh!' she cried, 'Pharaoh, and thou, O Queen, look upon thy son—thy firstborn son—dead is thy son, O Pharaoh! Dead is thy son, O Queen! In my arms he died suddenly as I lulled him to his rest,' and she laid the body of the child down on the board among the vessels of gold, among the garlands of lotus flowers and the beakers of rose-red wine.

Then Pharaoh rose and rent his purple robes and wept

aloud. Meriamun rose too, and lifting the body of her son clasped it to her breast, and her eyes were terrible with wrath and grief, but she wept not.

'See now the curse that this evil woman, this False Hathor, hath brought upon us,' she said.

But the very guests sprang up crying, 'It is not the Hathor whom we worship, it is not the Holy Hathor, it is the Gods of those dark Apura whom thou, O Queen, wilt not let go. On thy head and the head of Pharaoh be it,' and even as they cried the murmur without grew to a shriek of woe, a shriek so wild and terrible that the Palace walls rang. Again that shriek rose, and yet a third time, never was such a cry heard in Egypt. And now for the first time in all his days the face of the Wanderer grew white with fear, and in fear of heart he prayed for succour to his Goddess—to Aphrodite, the daughter of Dione.

Again the doors behind them burst open and the Guards flocked in—mighty men of many foreign lands; but now their faces were wan, their eyes stared wide, and their jaws hung down. But at the sound of the clanging of their harness the strength of the Wanderer came back to him again, for the Gods and their vengeance he feared, but not the sword of man. And now once more the bow sang aloud. He grasped it, he bent it with his mighty knee, and strung it, crying:

'Awake, Pharaoh, awake! Foes draw on. Say, be these all the men?'

Then the Captain answered, 'These be all of the Guard who are left living in the Palace. The rest are stark, smitten by the angry Gods.'

Now as the Captain spake, one came running up the hall, heeding neither the dead nor the living. It was the old priest Rei, the Commander of the Legion of Amen, who had been the Wanderer's guide, and his looks were wild with fear.

"Hearken, Pharaoh!' he cried, 'thy people lie dead by thousands in the streets—the houses are full of dead. In the Temples of Ptah and of Amen many of the priests have fallen dead also.'

'Hast thou more to tell, old man?' cried the Queen.

'The tale has not all been told, O Queen. The soldiers are mad with fear and with the sight of death, and slay their captains; barely have I escaped from those in my command of the Legion of Amen. For they swear that this death has been brought upon the land because Pharaoh will not let the Apura go. Hither, then, they come to slay Pharaoh, and thee also, O Queen, and with them come many thousands of people, catching up such arms as lie to their hands.'

Now Pharaoh sank down groaning, but the Queen spake to the Wanderer:

'Anon thy weapon sang of war, Eperitus; now war is at the gates.'

'Little I fear the rush of battle and the blows men deal in anger, Lady,' he made answer, 'though a man may fear the Gods without shame. Ho, Guards! close up, close up round me! Look not so pale-faced now death from the Gods is done with, and we have but to fear the sword of men.'

So great was his mien and so glorious his face as he cried thus, and one by one drew his long arrows forth and laid them on the board, that the trembling Guards took heart, and to the number of fifty and one ranged themselves on the edge of the daïs in a double line. Then they also made ready their bows and loosened the arrows in their quivers.

Now from without there came a roar of men, and anon, while those of the house of Pharaoh, and of the guests and nobles, who sat at the feast and yet lived, fled behind the soldiers, the brazen doors were burst in with mighty blows, and through them a great armed multitude surged along the hall. There came soldiers broken from their ranks. There came the embalmers of the Dead; their hands were overfull of work to-night, but they left their work undone; Death had smitten some even of these, and their fellows did not shrink back from them now. There came the smith, black from the forge, and the scribe bowed with endless writing; and the dyer with his purple hands, and the fisher from the stream; and the stunted weaver from the loom, and the leper from the Temple gates. They were mad with lust of life, a starveling life that the King had taxed, when he let not the Apura go. They were mad with fear of death; their women followed them with dead children in their arms. They smote down the golden furnishings, they tore the silken hangings, they cast the empty cups of the feast at the faces of trembling ladies, and cried aloud for the blood of the King.

'Where is Pharaoh?' they yelled, 'show us Pharaoh and the Queen Meriamun, that we may slay them. Dead are our firstborn, they lie in heaps as the fish lay when Sihor ran red with blood. Dead are they because of the curse that has been brought upon us by the prophets of the Apura, whom Pharaoh, and Pharaoh's Queen, yet hold in Khem.'

Now as they cried they saw Pharaoh Meneptah cowering beind the double line of Guards, and they saw the Queen Meriamun who cowered not, but stood silent above the din. Then she thrust her way through the Guards, and yet holding the body of the child to her breast, she stood before them with eyes that flashed more brightly than the uraeus crown upon her brow.

'Back!' she cried, 'back! It is not Pharaoh, it is not I, who have brought this death upon you. For we too have death here!' and she held up the body of her dead son. 'It is that False Hathor whom ye worship, that Witch of many a voice and many a face who turns your hearts faint with love. For her sake ye endure these woes, on her head is all this death. Go, tear her temple stone from stone, and rend her beauty limb from limb, and be avenged and free the land from curses.'

A moment the people stood and hearkened, muttering, as stands the lion that is about to spring, while those who pressed without cried: 'Forward! Forward! Slay them! Slay them!' Then as with one voice they screamed:

'The Hathor we love, but you we hate, for ye have brought these woes upon us, and ye shall die.'

They cried, they brawled, they cast footstools and stones at the Guards, and then a certain tall man among them drew a bow. Straight at the Queen's fair breast he aimed his arrow, and swift and true it sped toward her.

She saw the light gleam upon its shining barb, and then she did what no woman but Meriamun would have done, no, not to save herself from death—she held out the naked body of her son as a warrior holds a shield. The arrow struck through and through it, piercing the tender flesh, aye, and pricked her breast beyond, so that she let the dead boy fall.

The Wanderer saw it and wondered at the horror of the deed, for he had seen no such deed in all his days. Then shouting aloud the terrible war-cry of the Achæans he leapt upon the board before him, and as he leapt his golden armour clanged.

Glancing around, he fixed an arrow to the string and drew to his ear that great bow which none but he might so much as bend. Then as he loosed, the string sang like a swallow, and the shaft screamed through the air. Down the glorious hall it sped, and full on the breast of him who had lifted bow against the Queen the bitter arrow struck, nor might his harness avail to stay it. Through the body of him it passed and with blood-red feathers flew on, and smote another who stood behind him so that his knees also were loosened, and together they fell dead upon the floor.

Now while the people stared and wondered, again the bow-string sang like a swallow, again the arrow screamed in its flight, and he who stood before it got his death, for the shield he bore was pinned to his breast.

Then wonder turned to rage; the multitude rolled forward, and from either side the air grew dark with arrows. For the Guards at sight of the shooting of the Wanderer found heart and fought well and manfully. Boldly also the slayers came on, and behind them pressed many a hundred men. The Wanderer's golden helm flashed steadily, a beacon in the storm. Black smoke burst out in the hall, the hangings flamed and tossed in a wind from the open door. The lights were struck from the hands of the golden images, arrows stood thick in the tables and the rafters, a spear pierced through the golden cup of Pasht. But out of the darkness and smoke and dust, and the cry of battle, and through the rushing of the rain of spears, sang the swallow string of the black bow of Eurytus, and the long shafts shrieked as they sped on them who were ripe to die. In vain did the arrows of the slayers smite upon that golden harness. They were but as hail upon the temple roofs, but as driving snow upon the wild stag's horns. They struck, they rattled, and down they dropped like snow, or bounded back and lay upon the board.

The swallow string sang, the black bow twanged, and the bitter arrows shrieked as they flew.

Now the Wanderer's shafts were spent, and he judged that their case was desperate. For out of the doors of the hall that were behind them, and from the chambers of the women, armed men burst in also, taking them on the flank and rear. But the Wanderer was old in war, and without a match in all its ways. The Captain of the Guard was slain with a spear stroke, and the Wanderer took his place, calling to the men, such of them as were left alive, to form a circle on the daïs, and within the circle he set those of the house of Pharaoh and the women who were at the feast. And to Pharaoh he cast a slain man's sword, bidding him strike for life and throne if he never struck before; but the heart was out of Pharaoh because of the death of his son, and the wine about his wits, and the terrors he had seen. Then Meriamun the Queen snatched the sword from his trembling hand and stood holding it to guard her life. For she disdained to crouch upon the ground as did the other women, but stood upright behind the Wanderer, and heeded not the spears and arrows that dealt death on every hand. But Pharaoh stood, his face buried in his hands.

Now the slayers came on, shouting and clambering upon the daïs. Then the Wanderer rushed on them with sword drawn, and shield on high, and so swift he smote that men might not guard, for they saw, as it were, three blades aloft at once, and the silver-hafted sword bit deep, the gift of Phæacian Euryalus long ago. The Guards also smote and thrust; it was for their lives they fought, and back rolled the tide of foes, leaving a swathe of dead. So a second time they came on, and a second time were rolled back.

Now of the defenders few were left unhurt, and their strength was well-nigh spent. But the Wanderer cheered them with great words, though his heart grew fearful for the end; and Meriamun the Queen also bade them to be of good courage, and if need were, to die like men. Then once again the wave of War rolled in upon them, and the strife grew fierce and desperate. The iron hedge of spears was well-nigh broken, and now the Wanderer, doing such deeds as had not been known in Khem, stood alone between Meriamun the Queen and the swords that thirsted for her life and the life of Pharaoh. Then of a sudden, from far down the great hall of banquets, there came a loud cry that shrilled above the clash of swords, the groans of men, and all the din of battle.

'*Pharaoh! Pharaoh! Pharaoh!*' rose a voice. 'Now wilt thou let the people go?'

Then he who smote stayed his hand and he who guarded dropped his shield. The battle ceased and all turned to look. There at the end of the hall, among the dead and dying, there stood the two ancient men of the Apura, and in their hands were cedar rods.

'It is the Wizards—the Wizards of the Apura,' men cried, and shrunk this way and that, thinking no more on war.

The ancient men drew nigh. They took no heed of the dying or the dead: on they walked, through blood and wine and fallen tables and scattered arms, till they stood before the Pharaoh.

'*Pharaoh! Pharaoh! Pharaoh!*' they cried again. 'Dead are the first-born of Khem at the hand of Jahveh. Wilt thou let the people go?'

Then Pharaoh lifted his face and cried:

'Get you gone—you and all that is yours. Get you gone swiftly, and let Khem see your face no more.'

The people heard, and the living left the hall, and silence fell on the city, and on the dead who died of the sword, and the dead who died of the pestilence. Silence fell, and sleep, and the Gods' best gift—forgetfulness.

3. THE BATHS OF BRONZE

Even out of this night of dread the morning rose, and with it came Rei, bearing a message from the King. But he did not find the Wanderer in his chamber. The Palace eunuchs said that he had risen and had asked for Kurri, the Captain of the Sidonians who was now the Queen's Jeweller. Thither Rei went for Kurri was lodged with the servants in a court of the Royal House and as the old man came he heard the sound of hammers beating on metal. There in the shadow which the Palace wall cast into a little court, there was the Wanderer; no longer in his golden mail, but with bare arms, and dressed in such a light smock as the workmen of Khem were wont to wear.

The Wanderer was bending over a small brazier, whence a flame and a light blue smoke arose and melted into the morning light. In his hand he held a small hammer, and he had a little anvil by him, on which lay one of the golden shoulder-plates of his armour. The other pieces were heaped beside the brazier. Kurri, the Sidonian, stood beside him, with graving tools in his hands.

'Hail to thee, Eperitus,' cried Rei, calling him by the name he had chosen to give himself. 'What makest thou here with fire and anvil?'

'I am but furbishing up my armour,' said the Wanderer, smiling. 'It has more than one dint from the fight in the hall;' and he pointed to his shield, which was deeply scarred across the blazon of the White Bull, the cognizance of dead Paris, Priam's son. 'Sidonian, blow up the fire.'

Kurri crouched on his hams and blew the blaze to a white heat with a pair of leathern bellows, while the Wanderer fitted the plates and hammered at them on the anvil, making the jointures smooth and strong, talking meanwhile with Rei.

'Strange work for a prince, as thou must be in Alybas, whence thou comest,' quoth Rei, leaning on his long rod of cedar, headed with an apple of bluestone. 'In our country chiefs do not labour with their hands.'

'Different lands, different ways,' answered Eperitus. 'In my country men wed not their sisters as your kings do, though, indeed, it comes into my mind that once I met such brides in my wanderings in the isle of the King of the Winds.'

For the thought of the Æolian isle, where King Æolus gave him all the winds in a bag, came into his memory.

'My hands can serve me in every need,' he went on. 'Mowing the deep green grass in spring, or driving oxen, or cutting a clean furrow with the plough in heavy soil, or building houses and ships, or doing smith's work with gold and bronze and gray iron—they are all one to me.'

'Or the work of war,' said Rei. 'For there I have seen thee labour. Now, listen, thou Wanderer, the King Meneptah and the Queen Meriamun send me to thee with this scroll of their will,' and he drew forth a roll of papyrus, bound with golden threads, and held it on his forehead, bowing, as if he prayed.

'What is that roll of thine?' said the Wanderer, who was hammering at the bronze spear-point, that stood fast in his helm.

Rei undid the golden threads and opened the scroll, which he gave into the Wanderer's hand.

'Gods! What have we here?' said the Wanderer. 'Here are pictures, tiny and cunningly drawn, serpents in red, and little figures of men sitting or standing, axes and snakes and birds and beetles! My father, what tokens are these?' and he gave the scroll back to Rei.

'The King has made his Chief Scribe write to thee, naming thee Captain of the Legion of Pasht, the Guard of the Royal House, for last night the Captain was slain. He gives thee a high title, and he promises thee houses, lands, and a city of the South to furnish thee with wine and a city of the North to furnish thee with corn if thou wilt be his servant.'

'Never have I served any man.' said the Wanderer, flushing red, 'though I went near to being sold and to knowing the day of slavery. The King does me too much honour.'

'Thou wouldest fain begone from Khem?' asked the old man, eagerly.

'I would fain find her I came to seek, wherever she be,' said the Wanderer. 'Here or otherwhere.'

'Then, what answer shall I carry to the King?'

'Time brings thought,' said the Wanderer; 'I would see the city if thou wilt guide me. Many cities have I seen, but none so great as this. As we walk I will consider my answer to your King.'

He had been working at his helm as he spoke, for the rest of his armour was now mended. He had drawn out the sharp spear-head of bronze, and was balancing it in his hand and trying its edge.

'A good blade,' he said; 'better was never hammered. It went near to doing its work, Sidonian,' and he turned to Kurri as he spoke. 'Two things of thine I had: thy life and thy spear-point. Thy life I gave thee, they spear-point thou didst lend me. Here, take it again, and he tossed the spear-head to the Queen's Jeweller.

'I thank thee, lord,' answered the Sidonian, thrusting it in his girdle; but he muttered between his teeth, 'The gifts of enemies are gifts of evil.'

The Wanderer did on his mail set the helmet on his head and spoke to Rei. 'Come forth, friend, and show me thy city.'

But Rei was watching the smile on the face of the Sidonian, and he deemed it cruel and crafty and warlike, like the laugh of the Sardana of the sea. He said nought, but called a guard of soldiers, and with the Wanderer he passed the Palace gates and went out into the city.

The sight was strange, and it was not thus that the old man, who loved his land, would have had the Wanderer see it.

From all the wealthy houses, and from many of the poorer sort, rang the wail of the women mourners as they sang their dirges for the dead.

But in the meaner quarters many a hovel was marked with three smears of blood, dashed on each pillar of the door and on the lintel; and the sound that came from these dwellings was the cry of mirth and festival. There were two peoples; one laughed, one lamented. And in and out of the houses marked with the splashes of blood women were ever going with empty hands, or coming with hands full of jewels, of gold, of silver rings, of cups, and purple stuffs. Empty they went out, laden they came in, dark men and women with keen black eyes and the features of birds of prey. They went, they came, they clamoured with delight among the mourning of the men and women of Khem, and none laid a hand on them, none refused them.

One tall fellow snatched at the staff of Rei.

'Lend me thy staff, old man,' he said, sneering; 'lend me thy jewelled staff for my journey. I do but borrow it; when Yakûb comes from the desert thou shalt have it again.'

But the Wanderer turned on the fellow with such a glance that he fell back.

'I have seen *thee* before,' he said, and he laughed over his shoulder as he went; 'I saw thee last night at the feast, and heard thy great bow sing. Thou art not of the folk of Khem. They are a gentle folk, and Yakûb wins favour in their sight.'

'What passes now in this haunted land of thine, old man?' said the Wanderer, 'for of all the sights that I have seen, this is the strangest. None lifts a hand to save his goods from the thief.'

Rei the Priest groaned aloud.

'Evil days have come upon Khem,' he said. 'The Apura

spoil the people of Khem ere they fly into the Wilderness.'

Even as he spoke there came a great lady weeping, for her husband was dead, and her son and her brother, all were gone in the breath of the pestilence. She was of the Royal House, and richly decked with gold and jewels, and the slaves who fanned her, as she went to the Temple of Ptah to worship wore gold chains upon their necks. Two women of the Apura saw her and ran to her crying:

'Lend to us those golden ornaments thou wearest.'

Then, without a word, she took her gold bracelets and chains and rings, and let them all fall in a heap at her feet. The women of the Apura took them all and mocked her, crying:

'Where now is thy husband and thy son and thy brother, thou who art of Pharaoh's house? Now thou payest us for the labour of our hands and for the bricks that we made without straw, gathering leaves and rushes in the sun. Now thou payest for the stick in the hand of the overseers. Where now is thy husband and thy son and thy brother?' and they went still mocking, and left the lady weeping.

But of all sights the Wanderer held this the strangest, and many such there were to see. At first he would have taken back the spoil and given it to those who wore it, but Rei the Priest prayed him to forbear, lest the curse should strike them also. So they pressed on through the tumult, ever seeing new sights of greed and death and sorrow. Here a mother wept over her babe, here a bride over her husband—that night the groom of her and of death. Here the fierce-faced Apura, clamouring like gulls, tore the silver trinkets from the children of those of the baser sort, or the sacred amulets from the mummies of those who were laid out for burial, and here a water-carrier wailed over the carcass of the ass that won him his livelihood.

At length, passing through the crowd, they came to a temple that stood near to the Temple of the God Ptah. The phylons of this temple faced towards the houses of the city, but the inner courts were built against the walls of Tanis and looked out across the face of the water. Though not one of the largest temples, it was very strong and beautiful in its shape. It was built of the black stone of Syene and all the polished face of the stone was graven with images of the Holy Hathor. Here she wore a cow's head and here the face of a woman but she always bore in her hands the lotus-headed staff and the holy token of life, and her neck was encircled with the collar of the gods.

'Here dwells that Strange Hathor to whom thou didst drink last night, Eperitus,' said Rei the Priest. 'It was a wild pledge to drink before the Queen, who swears that she brings these woes on Khem. Though, indeed, she is guilt-less of this, with all the blood on her beautiful head. The Apura and their apostate sorcerer, whom we ourselves instructed, bring the plagues on us.'

'Does the Hathor manifest herself this day?' asked the Wanderer.

'That we will ask of the priests, Eperitus. Follow thou me.'

Now they passed down the avenue of sphinxes within the wall of brick, into the garden plot of the Goddess, and so on through the gates of the outer tower. A priest who watched there threw them wide at the sign that was given of Rei, the Master Builder, the beloved of Pharaoh, and they came to the outer court. Before the second tower they halted, and Rei showed to the Wanderer that place upon the pylon roof where the Hathor was wont to stand and sing till the hearers' hearts were melted like wax. Here they knocked once more, and were admitted to the Hall of Assembly where the priests were gathered, throwing dust upon their heads and mourning those among them who had died with the Firstborn. When they saw Rei, the instructed, the Prophet of Amen, and the Wanderer clad in golden armour who was with him, they ceased from their mourning, and an ancient priest of their number came forward, and greeting Rei asked him of his errand. Then Rei took the Wanderer by the hand and made him known to the priest and told him of those deeds that he had done and how he had saved the life of Pharaoh and of those of the Royal House who sat at the feast with Pharaoh.

'But when will the Lady Hathor sing upon her tower top?' said Rei, 'for the Stranger desires to see her and hear her.'

The temple priest bowed before the Wanderer, and answered gravely:

'On the third morn from now the Holy Hathor shows herself upon the temple's top,' he said; 'but thou, mighty lord, who art risen from the sea, hearken to my warning, and if, indeed, thou art no god, dare not to look upon her beauty. If thou dost look, then thy fate shall be as the fate of those who have looked before, and have loved and have died for the sake of the Hathor.'

'No god am I,' said the Wanderer, laughing, 'yet, perchance, I shall dare to look, and dare to face whatever it be that guards her, if my heart bids me see her nearer.'

'Then there shall be an end of thee and thy wanderings,' said the priest. 'Now follow me, and I will show thee those men who last sought to win the Hathor.'

He took him by the hand and led him through passages hewn in the walls till they came to a deep and gloomy cell, where the golden armour of the Wanderer shone like a lamp at eve. The cell was built against the city wall, and scarcely a thread of light came into the chink between roof and wall. All about the chamber were baths fashioned of bronze, and in the baths lay dusky shapes of dark-skinned men of Egypt. There they lay, and in the faint light their limbs were being anointed by some sad-faced attendants, as folk were anointed by merry girls in the shining baths of the Wanderer's home. When Rei and Eperitus came near the sad-faced bath-men shrank away in shame, as dogs shrink from their evil meal at night when a traveller goes past.

Marvelling at the strange sight, the bathers and the bathed, the Wanderer looked more closely and his stout heart sank within him. For all these were dead who lay in the baths of bronze, and it was not water that flowed about their limbs, but evil-smelling natron.

'Here lie those,' said the priest, 'who last strove to come near the Holy Hathor, and to pass into the shrine of the temple where night and day she sits and sings and weaves with her golden shuttle. Here they lie, the half of a score. One by one they rushed to embrace her, and one by one they were smitten down. Here they are being attired for the tomb, for we give them all rich burial.'

'Truly,' quoth the Wanderer, 'I left the world of Light behind me when I looked on the blood-red sea and sailed into the black gloom off Pharos. More evil sights have I seen in this haunted land than in all the cities where I have wandered, and on all the seas that I have sailed.'

'Then be warned,' said the priest, 'for if thou dost follow where they went, and desire what they desired, thou too shalt lie in yonder bath, and be washed of yonder waters. For whatever be false, this is true, that he who seeks love ofttimes finds doom. But here he finds it most speedily.'

The Wanderer looked again at the dead and at their ministers, and he shuddered till his harness rattled. He feared not the face of Death in war, or on the sea, but this was a new thing. Little he loved the sight of the brazen baths and those who lay there. The light of the sun and the breath of air seemed good to him, and he stepped quickly from the chamber, while the priest smiled to himself. But when he reached the outer air, his heart came back to him and he began to ask again about the Hathor— where she dwelt, and what it was that slew her lovers.

'I will show thee,' answered the priest, and brought him through the Hall of Assembly to a certain narrow way that led to a court. In the centre of the court stood the holy shrine of the Hathor. It was a great chamber, built of alabaster, lighted from the roof alone, and shut in with brazen doors, before which hung curtains of Tyrian web. From the roof of the shrine a stairway ran overhead to the roof of the temple and so to the inner pylon tower.

'Yonder, Stranger, the holy Goddess dwells within the Alabaster Shrine,' said the priest. 'By that stair she passes to the temple roof, and thence to the pylon top. There by the curtains, once in every day, we place food, and it is drawn into the sanctuary, how we know not, for none of us have set foot there, nor seen the Hathor face to face. Now, when the Goddess has stood upon the pylon and sung to the multitude below, she passes back to the shrine. Then the brazen outer doors of the temple court are thrown wide and the doomed rush on madly, one by one towards the drawn curtains. But before they pass the curtains they are thrust back, yet they strive to pass. Then we hear a sound of the clashing of weapons and the men fall dead without a word, while the song of the Hathor swells from within.

'And who are her swordsmen?' said the Wanderer.

'That we know not, Stranger; no man has lived to tell. Come, draw near to the door of the shrine and hearken, maybe thou wilt hear the Hathor singing. Have no fear; thou needst not approach the guarded space.'

Then the Wanderer drew near with a doubting heart, but Rei the Priest stood afar off, though the temple priests came close enough. At the curtains they stopped and listened. Then from within the shrine there came a sound of singing wild and sweet and shrill, and the voice of it stirred the Wanderer strangely, bringing to his mind memories of that Ithaca of which he was Lord and which he should see no more; of the happy days of youth, and of the God-built walls of windy Ilios. But he could not have told why he thought on these things, nor why his heart was thus strangely stirred within him.

'Hearken! the Hathor sings as she weaves the doom of men,' said the priest, and as he spoke the singing ended.

Then the Wanderer took counsel with himself whether he should then and there burst the doors and take his fortune, or whether he should forbear for that while. But in the end he determined to forbear and see with his own eyes what befell those who strove to win the way.

So he drew back, wondering much; and, bidding farewell to the aged priest, he went with Rei, the Master Builder, through the town of Tanis, where the Apura were still spoiling the people of Khem, and he came to the Palace where he was lodged. Here he turned over in his mind how he might see the strange woman of the temple, and yet escape the baths of bronze. There he sat and thought till at length the night drew on, and one came to summon him to sup with Pharaoh in the Hall. Then he rose up and went, and meeting Pharaoh and Meriamun the Queen in the outer chamber, passed in after them to the Hall, and on to that daïs which he had held against the rabble, for the place was clear of dead, and, save for certain stains upon the marble floor that might not be washed away, and for some few arrows that yet were fixed high up in the walls or in the lofty roof, there was nothing to tell of the great fray that had been fought but one day gone.

Heavy was the face of Pharaoh, and the few who sat with him were sad enough because of the death of so many whom they loved, and the shame and sorrow that had fallen upon Khem. But there were no tears for her one child in the eyes of Meriamun the Queen. Anger, not grief, tore her heart because Pharaoh had let the Apura go. For ever as they sat at the sad feast there came a sound of the tramping feet of armies, and of lowing cattle, and songs of triumph, sung by ten thousand voices, and thus they sang the song of the Apura:—

A lamp for our feet the Lord hath litten,
    Signs hath He shown in the Land of Khem.
The Kings of the Nations our Lord hath smitten,
    His shoe hath He cast o'er the Gods of them.
He hath made Him a mock of the heifer of Isis,
    He hath broken the chariot reins of Ra,
On Yakûb He cries, and His folk arises,
    And the knees of the Nations are loosed in awe.

He gives us their goods for a spoil to gather,
    Jewels of silver, and vessels of gold;
For Yahveh of old is our Friend and Father,
    And cherisheth Yakûb He chose of old.
The Gods of the Peoples our Lord hath chidden,
    Their courts hath He filled with His creeping things;
The light of the face of the Sun He hath hidden,
    And broken the scourge in the hands of kings.

He hath chastened His people with stripes and scourges,
    Our backs hath He burdened with grievous weights,
But His children shall rise as a sea that surges,

And flood the fields of the men He hates.
The Kings of the Nations our Lord hath smitten,
His shoe hath He cast o'er the Gods of them,
But a lamp for our feet the Lord hath litten,
Wonders hath wrought in the Land of Khem.

Thus they sang, and the singing was so wild that the Wanderer craved leave to go and stand at the Palace gate, lest the Apura should rush in and spoil the treasure-chamber.

The King nodded, but Meriamun rose, and went with the Wanderer as he took his bow and passed to the great gates.

There they stood in the shadow of the gates, and this is what they beheld. A great light of many torches was flaring along the roadway in front. Then came a body of men, rudely armed with pikes, and the torchlight shone on the glitter of bronze and on the gold helms of which they had spoiled the soldiers of Khem. Next came a troop of wild women, dancing, and beating timbrels, and singing the triumphant hymn of scorn.

Next, with a space between, tramped eight strong black-bearded men, bearing on their shoulders a great gilded coffin, covered with carven and painted signs.

'It is the body of their Prophet, who brought them hither out of their land of hunger,' whispered Meriamun. 'Slaves, ye shall hunger yet in the wilderness, and clamour for the flesh-pots of Khem!'

Then she cried in a loud voice, for her passion overcame her, and she prophesied to those who bare the coffin, 'Not one soul of you that lives shall see the land where your conjurer is leading you! Ye shall thirst, ye shall hunger, ye shall call on the Gods of Khem, and they shall not hear you; ye shall die, and your bones shall whiten the wilderness. Farewell! Set go with you. Farewell!'

So she cried and pointed down the way, and so fierce was her gaze, and so awful were her words, that the people of the Apura trembled and the women ceased to sing.

The Wanderer watched the Queen and marvelled. 'Never had woman such a hardy heart,' he mused; 'and it were ill to cross her in love or war!'

'They will sing no more at my gates,' murmured Meriamun, with a smile. 'Come, Wanderer; they await us,' and she gave him her hand that he might lead her.

So they went back to the banquet hall.

They hearkened as they sat till far in the night, and still the Apura passed, countless as the sands of the sea. At length all were gone and the sound of their feet died away in the distance. Then Meriamun the Queen turned to Pharaoh and spake bitterly:

'Thou art a coward, Meneptah, ay, a coward and a slave at heart. In thy fear of the curse that the False Hathor hath laid on us, she whom thou dost worship, to thy shame, thou hast let these slaves go. Otherwise had our father dealt with them, great Rameses Miamun, the hammer of the Khita. Now they are gone hissing curses on the land that bare them, and robbing those who nursed them up while they were yet a little people, as a mother nurses her child.'

'What then might I do?' said Pharaoh.

'There is nought to do: all is done,' answered Meriamun. 'What is thy counsel, Wanderer?'

'It is ill for a stranger to offer counsel,' said the Wandere.

'Nay, speak,' cried the Queen.

'I know not the Gods of this land,' he answered. 'If these people be favoured of the Gods, I say sit still. But if not,' then said the Wanderer, wise in war, 'let Pharaoh gather his host, follow after the people, take them unawares, and smite them utterly. It is no hard task, they are so mixed a multitude and cumbered with much baggage!

This was to speak as the Queen loved to hear. Now she clapped her hands and cried:

'Listen, listen to good counsel, Pharaoh.'

And now that the Apura were gone, his fear of them went also, and as he drank wine Pharaoh grew bold, till at last he sprang to his feet and swore by Amen, by Osiris, by Ptah, and by his father—great Rameses—that he would follow after the Apura and smite them. And instantly he sent forth messengers to summon the captains of his host in the Hall of Assembly.

Thither the captains came, and their plans were made and messengers hurried forth to the governors of other great cities, bidding them send troops to join the host of Pharaoh on its march.

Now Pharaoh turned to the Wanderer and said:

'Thou hast not yet answered my message that Rei carried to thee this morning. Wilt thou take service with me and be a captain in this war?'

The Wanderer little liked the name of service, but his warlike heart was stirred within him, for he loved the delight of battle. But before he could answer yea or nay, Meriamun the Queen, who was not minded that he should leave her, spoke hastily:

'This is my counsel, Meneptah, that the Lord Epertius should abide here in Tanis and be the Captain of my Guard while thou art gone to smite the Apura. For I may not be here unguarded in these troublous times, and if I know he watches over me, he who is so mighty a man, then I shall walk safely and sleep in peace.'

Now the Wanderer bethought him of his desire to look upon the Hathor, for to see new things and try new adventures was always his delight. So he answered that if it were pleasing to Pharaoh and the Queen he would willingly stay and command the Guard. And Pharaoh said that it should be so.

4. THE QUEEN'S CHAMBER

At midday on the morrow Pharaoh and the host of
Pharaoh marched in pomp from Tanis, taking the road
that runs across the desert country towards the Red Sea of
Weeds, the way that the Apura had gone. The Wanderer
went with the army for an hour's journey and more, in a
chariot driven by Rei the Priest, for Rei did not march
with the host. The number of the soldiers of Pharaoh
amazed the Achæan, accustomed to the levies of barren
isles and scattered tribes. But he said nothing of his wonder to Rei or any man, least it should be thought that he
came from among a little people. He even made as if he
held the army lightly, and asked the priest if this was all
the strength of Pharaoh! Then Rei told him that it was but
a fourth part, for none of the mercenaries and none of the
soldiers from the Upper Land marched with the King in
pursuit of the Apura.

Then the Wanderer knew that he was come among a
greater people than he had ever encountered yet, on land
or sea. So he went with them till the roads divided, and
there he drove his chariot to the chariot of Pharaoh and
bade him farewell. Pharaoh called to him to mount his
own chariot, and spake thus to him:

'Swear to me, thou Wanderer, who namest thyself Eperitus, though of what country thou art and what was thy
father's house none know, swear to me that thou wilt
guard Meriamun the Queen faithfully, and wilt work no

woe upon me nor upon my house while I am afar. Great thou art and beautiful to look on, ay, and strong beyond the strength of men, yet my heart misdoubts me of thee. For methinks thou art a crafty man, and that evil will come upon me through thee.'

'If this be thy mind, Pharaoh,' said the Wanderer, 'leave me not in guard of the Queen. And yet methinks I did not befriend thee so ill two nights gone, when the rabble would have put thee and all thy house to the sword because of the death of the firstborn.'

Now Pharaoh looked on him long and doubtfully, then stretched out his hand. The Wanderer took it, and swore by his own Gods, by Zeus, by Aphrodite, and Athene, and Apollo, that he would be true to the trust.

'I believe thee, Wanderer,' said Pharaoh. 'Know this, if thou keepest thine oath thou shalt have great rewards, and thou shalt be second to none in the land of Khem, but if thou failest, then thou shalt die miserably.'

'I ask no fee,' answered the Wanderer, 'and I fear no death, for in one way only shall I die, and that is known to me. Yet I will keep my oath.' And he bowed before Pharaoh, and leaping from his chariot entered again into the chariot of Rei.

Now, as he drove back through the host the soldiers called to him, saying:

'Leave us not, thou Wanderer.' For he looked so glorious in his golden armour that it seemed to them as though a god departed from their ranks.

His heart was with them, for he loved war, and he did not love the Apura. But he drove on, as so it must be, and came to the Palace at sundown.

That night he sat at the feast by the side of Meriamun the Queen. And when the feast was done she bade him follow her into her chamber where she sat when she would be alone. It was a fragrant chamber, dimly lighted with sweet-scented lamps, furnished with couches of ivory and gold, while all the walls told painted stories of strange gods and kings, and of their loves and wars. The Queen sank back upon the embroidered cushions of a couch and bade the wise Odysseus sit over against her, so near that her robes swept his golden greaves. This he did somewhat against his will, though he was no hater of fair women. But his heart misdoubted the dark-eyed Queen, and he looked upon her guardedly, for she was strangely fair to see, the fairest of all mortal women whom he had known, save the Golden Helen.

'Wanderer, we owe thee great thanks, and I would gladly know to whom we are in debt for the prices of our lives,' she said. 'Tell me of thy birth, of thy father's house, and of the lands that thou hast seen and the wars wherein thou hast fought. Tell me also of the sack of Ilios, and how thou camest by thy golden mail. The unhappy Paris wore such arms as these, if the minstrel of the North sang truth.'

Now, the Wanderer would gladly have cursed this minstrel from the North and his songs.

'Minstrels will be lying, Lady,' he said, 'and they gather old tales wherever they go. Paris may have worn my arms, or another man. I bought them from a chapman in Crete, and asked nothing of their first master. As for Ilios, I fought there in my youth, and served the Cretan Idomeneus, but I got little booty. To the King the wealth and women, to us the sword-strokes. Such is the appearance of war.

Meriamun listened to his tale, which he set forth roughly, as if he were some blunt, grumbling swordsman, and darkly she looked on him while she hearkened, and darkly she smiled as she looked.

'A strange story, Eperitus, a strange story truly. Now tell me this. How camest thou by yonder great bow, the bow of the swallow string? If my minstrel spoke truly, it was once the Bow of Eurytus of Œchalia.'

Now the Wanderer glanced round him like a man taken in ambush, who sees on every hand the sword of foes shine up into the sunlight.

'The bow, Lady?' he answered readily enough. 'I got it strangely. I was cruising with a cargo of iron on the western coast and landed on an isle, methinks the pilot called it Ithaca. There we found nothing but death; a pestilence had been in the land, but in a ruined hall this bow was lying, and I made prize of it. A good bow!'

'A strange story, truly—a very strange story,' quoth Meriamun the Queen. 'By chance thou didst buy the armour of Paris, by chance thou didst find the bow of Eurytus, that bow, methinks, with which the god-like Odysseus slew the wooers in his halls. Knowest thou, Eperitus, that when thou stoodest yonder on the board in the Place of Banquets, when the great bow twanged and the long shafts hailed down the hall and loosened the knees of many, not a little was I put in mind of the song of the slaying of the wooers at the hands of Odysseus. The fame of Odysseus has wandered far—ay, even to Khem.' And she looked straight at him.

The Wanderer darkened his face and put the matter by. He had heard something of that tale, he said, but deemed it a minstrel's feigning. One man could not fight a hundred, as the story went.

The Queen half rose from the couch where she lay curled up like a glittering snake. Like a snake she rose and watched him with her melancholy eyes.

'Strange, indeed—most strange that Odysseus, Laertes' son, Odysseus of Ithaca, should not know the tale of the slaying of the wooers by Odysseus' self. Strange, indeed, thou Eperitus, who art Odysseus.'

Now the neck of the Wanderer was in the noose, and well he knew it: yet he kept his counsel, and looked upon her vacantly.

'Men say that this Odysseus wandered years ago into the North, and that this time he will not come again. I saw him in the wars, and he was a taller man than I,' said the Wanderer.

'I have always heard,' said the Queen, 'that Odysseus was double-tongued and crafty as a fox. Look me in the eyes, thou Wanderer, look me in the eyes, and I will show thee whether or not thou art Odysseus,' and she leaned forward so that her hair well-nigh swept his brow, and gazed deep into his eyes.

Now the Wanderer was ashamed to drop his eyes before a woman's, and he could not rise and go; so he must needs gaze, and as he gazed his head grew strangely light and the blood quivered in his veins, and then seemed to stop.

'Now turn, thou Wanderer,' said the voice of the Queen, and to him it sounded far away, as if there was a wall between them, 'and tell me what thou seest.'

So he turned and looked towards the dark end of the chamber. But presently through the darkness stole a faint light, like the first gray of the dawn, and now he saw a shape like the shape of a great horse of wood, and behind the horse were black square towers of huge stones, and gates, and walls, and houses. Now he saw a door open in the side of the horse, and the helmeted head of a man looked out warily. As he looked a great white star slid down the sky so that the light of it rested on the face of the man, and that face was his own! Then he remembered how he had looked forth from the belly of the wooden horse as it stood within the walls of Ilios, and thus the star had seemed to fall upon the doomed city, an omen of the end of Troy.

'Look again,' said the voice of Meriamun from far away.

So once more he looked into the darkness, and there he saw the mouth of a cave, and beneath two palms in front of it sat a man and a woman. The yellow moon rose and its light fell upon a sleeping sea, upon tall trees, upon the cave, and the two who sat there. The woman was lovely, with braided hair, and clad in a shining robe, and her eyes were dim with tears that she might never shed: for she was a Goddess, Calypso, the daughter of Atlas. Then in the vision the man looked up, and his face was weary, and worn and sick for home, but it was his own face.

Then he remembered how he had sat thus at the side of Calypso of the braided tresses, on that last night of all his nights in her wave-girt isle, the centre of the seas.

'Look once more,' said the voice of Meriamun the Queen.

Again he looked into the darkness. There before him grew the ruins of his own hall in Ithaca, and in the courtyard before the hall was a heap of ashes, and the charred bones of men. Before the heap lay the figure of one lost in sorrow, for his limbs writhed upon the ground. Anon the man lifted his face, and behold! the Wanderer knew that it was his own face.

Then of a sudden the gloom passed away from the chamber, and once more his blood surged through his veins, and there before him sat Meriamun the Queen, smiling darkly.

'Strange sights hast thou seen, is it not so, Wanderer?' she said.

'Yea, Queen, the most strange of sights. Tell me of thy courtesy how thou didst conjure them before my eyes.'

'By the magic that I have, Eperitus, I above all wizards who dwell in Khem, the magic whereby I can read all the past of those—I love,' and again she looked upon him; 'ay, and call it forth from the storehouse of dead time and make it live again. Say, whose face was it that thou didst look upon—was it not the face of Odysseus of Ithaca, Laertes' son, and was not that face thine?'

Now the Wanderer saw that there was no escape. Therefore he spoke the truth, not because he loved it, but because he must.

'The face of Odysseus of Ithaca it was that I saw before me, Lady, and that face is mine. I avow myself to be Odysseus, Laertes' son, and no other man.'

The Queen laughed aloud. 'Great must be my strength of magic,' she said, 'for it can strip the guile from the subtlest of men. Henceforth, Odysseus, thou wilt know that the eyes of Meriamun the Queen see far. Now tell me truly: what camest thou hither to seek?'

The Wanderer took swift counsel with himself. Remembering that dream of Meriamun of which Rei the Priest had told him, and which she knew not that he had learned, the dream that showed her the vision of one whom she must love, and remembering the word of the dead Hataska, he grew afraid. For he saw well by the token of the spear point that he was the man of her dream, and that she knew it. But he could not accept her love, both because of his oath to Pharaoh and because of her whom Aphrodite had shown to him in Ithaca, her whom alone he must seek, the Heart's Desire, the Golden Helen.

The strait was desperate, between a broken oath and a woman scorned. But he feared his oath, and the anger of Zeus, the God of hosts and guests. So he sought safety beneath the wings of truth.

'Lady,' he said, 'I will tell thee all! I came to Ithaca from the white north, where a curse had driven me; I came and found my halls desolate, and my people dead, and the very ashes of my wife. But in a dream of the night I saw the Goddess whom I have worshipped little, Aphrodite of Idalia, whom in this land ye name Hathor, and she bade me go forth and do her will. And for reward she promised me that I should find one who waited me to be my deathless love.'

Meriamun heard him so far, but no further, for of this she made sure, that *she* was the woman whom Aphrodite had promised to the Wanderer. Ere he might speak another word she glided to him like a snake, and like a snake curled herself about him. Then she spoke so low that he rather knew her thought than heard her words:

'Was it indeed so, Odysseus? Did the Goddess indeed send thee to seek me out? Know, then, that not to thee alone did she speak. I also looked for thee. I also waited the coming of one whom I should love. Oh, heavy have been the days, and empty was my heart, and sorely through the years have I longed for him who should be brought to me. And now at length it is done, now at length I see him whom in my dream I saw,' and she lifted her lips to the lips of the Wanderer, and her heart, and her eyes, and her lips said 'Love.'

But it was not for nothing that he bore a stout and patient heart, and a brain unclouded by danger or by love. He had never been in a strait like this; caught with bonds that no sword could cut, and in toils that no skill could undo. On one side were love and pleasure—on the other a broken oath, and the loss for ever of the Heart's Desire. For to love another woman, as he had been warned, was to lose Helen. But again, if he scorned the Queen—nay, for all his hardihood he dared not tell her that she was not the woman of his vision, the woman he came to seek. Yet even now his cold courage and his cunning did not fail him.

'Lady,' he said, 'we both have dreamed. But if thou didst dream thou wert my love, thou didst wake to find thyself the wife of Pharaoh. And Pharaoh is my host and hath my oath.'

'I woke to find myself the wife of Pharaoh,' she echoed, wearily, and her arms uncurled from his neck and she sank back on the couch. 'I am Pharaoh's wife in word, but not in deed. Pharaoh is nothing to me, thou Wanderer—nought save a name.'

'Yet is my oath much to me, Queen Meriamun—my oath and the hospitable hearth,' the Wanderer made answer. 'I swore to Meneptah to hold thee from all ill, and there's an end.'

'And if Pharaoh comes back no more, what then Odysseus?'

'Then will we talk again. And now, Lady, thy safety calls me to visit thy Guard.' And without more words he rose and went.

The Queen looked after him.

'A strange man,' she said in her heart, 'who builds a barrier with his oath betwixt himself and her he loves and has wandered so far to win! Yet methinks I honour him the more. Pharaoh Meneptah, my husband, eat, drink, and be merry, for this I promise thee—short shall be thy days.'

5. THE CHAPEL PERILOUS

'Swift as a bird or a thought,' says the old harper of the Northern Sea. The Wanderer's thoughts in the morning were swift as night birds, flying back and brooding over the things he had seen and the words he had heard in the Queen's chamber. Again he stood between this woman and the oath which, of all oaths, was the worst to break. And, indeed, he as little tempted to break it, for though Meriamun was beautiful and wise, he feared her love and he feared her magic art no less than he feared her vengeance if she were scorned. Delay seemed the only course. Let him wait till the King returned, and it would go hard but he found some cause for leaving the city of Tanis, and seeking through new adventures the World's Desire. The mysterious river lay yonder. He would ascend the river of which so many tales were told. It flowed from the land of the blameless Æthiopians, the most just of men, at whose tables the very Gods sat as guests. There, perchance, far up the sacred stream, in a land where no wrong ever came, there, if the Fates permitted, he might find the Golden Helen.

If the Fates permitted: but all the adventure was of the Fates, who had shown him to Meriamun in a dream.

He turned it long in his mind and found little light. It seemed that as he had drifted through darkness across a blood-red sea to the shores of Khem, so he should wade through blood to that shore of Fate which the Gods appointed.

Yet after a while he shook sorrow from him, arose, bathed, anointed himself, combed his dark locks, and girdled on his golden armour. For now he remembered that this was the day when the Strange Hathor should stand upon the pylon of the temple and call the people to her, and he was minded to look upon her, and if need be to do battle with that which guarded her.

So he prayed to Aphrodite that she would help him, and he poured out wine to her and waited; he waited, but no answer came to his prayer. Yet as he turned away it chanced that he saw his countenance in the wide golden cup whence he had poured, and it seemed to him that it had grown more fair and lost the stamp of years, and that his face was smooth and young as the face of that Odysseus who, many years ago, had sailed in the black ships and looked back on the smoking ruins of windy Troy. In this he saw the hand of the Goddess, and knew that if she might not be manifest in this land of strange Gods, yet she was with him. And, knowing this, his heart grew light as the heart of a boy from whom sorrow is yet a long way off, and who has not dreamed of death.

Then he ate and drank, and when he had put from him the desire of food he arose and girded on the sword, Euryalus's gift, but the black bow he left in its case. Now he was ready and about to set forth when Rei the Priest entered the chamber.

'Whither goest thou, Eperitus?' asked Rei the instructed Priest. 'And what is it that has made thy face so fair, as though many years had been lifted from thy back?'

' 'Tis but sweet sleep, Rei,' said the Wanderer. 'Deeply I slept last night, and the weariness of my wanderings fell from me, and now I am as I was before I sailed across the blood-red sea into the night.'

'Sell thou the secret of this sleep to the ladies of Khem,' answered the aged priest, smiling, 'and little shalt thou lack of wealth for all thy days.'

Thus he spake as though he believed the Wanderer, but in his heart he knew that the thing was of the Gods.

The Wanderer answered:

'I go up to the Temple of the Hathor, for thou dost remember it is to-day that she stands upon the pylon brow and calls the people to her. Comest thou also, Rei?'

'Nay, nay, I come not, Eperitus. I am old indeed, but yet the blood creeps through these withered veins, and, perchance, if I came and looked, the madness would seize me also, and I too should rush on to my slaying. There is a way in which a man may listen to the voice of the Hathor, and that is to have his eyes blindfolded, as many do. But even then he will tear the bandage from his eyes, and look, and die with the others. Oh, go not up, Eperitus—I pray thee go not up. I love thee—I know not why—and am little minded to see thee dead. Though, perchance,' he added, as though to himself, 'it would be well for those I serve if thou wert dead, thou Wanderer, with the eyes of Fate.'

'Have no fear, Rei,' said the Wanderer, 'as it is doomed so shall I die and not otherwise. Never shall it be told,' he murmured in his heart, 'that he who stood in arms against Scylla, the Horror of the Rock, turned back from any form of fear or from any shape of Love.

Then Rei wrung his hands and went nigh to weeping, for to him it seemed a pitiful thing that so goodly a man and so great a hero should thus be done to death. But the Wanderer passed out through the city, and Rei went with him for a certain distance. At length they came to the road set on either side with sphinxes, that leads from the outer wall of brick to the garden of the Temple of Hathor, and down this road hurried a multitude of men of all races and of every age. Here the prince was borne along in his litter; here the young noble travelled in his chariot. Here came the slave bespattered with the mud of the fields; here the cripple limped upon his crutches; and here was the blind man led by a hound. And with each man came women: the wife of the man, or his mother, or his sisters, or she to whom he was vowed in marriage. Weeping they came, and with soft words and clinging arms they strove to hold back him whom they loved.

'Oh, my son! my son!' cried a woman, 'hearken to thy

mother's voice. Go not up to look upon the Goddess, for if thou dost look then shalt thou die, and thou alone art left alive to me. Two brothers of thine I bore, and behold, both are dead; and wilt thou die also, and leave me, who am old, alone and desolate? Be not mad, my son, thou art the dearest of all; ever have I loved thee and tended thee. Come back, I pray—come back.'

But her son heard not and heeded not, pressing on toward the Gates of the Heart's Desire.

'Oh, my husband, my husband!' cried another, young, of gentle birth, and fair, who bare a babe on her left arm and with the right clutched her lord's broidered robe. 'Oh, my husband, have I not loved thee and been kind to thee, and wilt thou still go up to look upon the deadly glory of the Hathor? They say she wears the beauty of the Dead. Lovest thou me not better than her who died five years agone, Merisa the daughter of Rois, though thou didst love her first? See, here is thy babe, thy babe, but one week born. Even from my bed of pain I have risen and followed after thee down these weary roads, and I am like to lose my life for it. Here is thy babe, let it plead with thee. Let me die if so it must be, but go not thou up to thy death. It is no Goddess whom thou wilt see, but an evil spirit loosed from the under-world, and that shall be thy doom. Oh, if I please thee not, take thou another wife and I will make her welcome, only go not up to thy death!'

But the man fixed his eyes upon the pylon tops, heeding her not, and at length she sank upon the road, and there with the babe would have been crushed by the chariots, had not the Wanderer borne her to one side of the way.

Now, of all sights this was the most dreadful, for on every side rose the prayers and lamentations of women, and still the multitude of men pressed on unheeding.

'Now thou seest the power of Love, and how if a woman be but beautiful enough she may drag all men to ruin,' said Rei the Priest.

'Yes,' said the Wanderer; 'a strange sight, truly. Much blood hath this Hathor of thine upon her hands.'

'And yet thou wilt give her thine, Wanderer.'

'That I am not minded to do,' he answered; 'yet I will look upon her face, so speak no more of it.'

Now they were come to the space before the bronze gates of the pylon of the outer court, and there the multitude gathered to the number of many hundreds. Presently, as they watched, a priest came to the gates, that same priest who had shown the Wanderer the bodies in the baths of bronze. He looked through the bars and cried aloud:

'Whoso would enter into the court and look upon the Holy Hathor let him draw nigh. Know ye this, all men, the Hathor is to him who can win her. But if he pass not, then shall he die and be buried within the temple, nor shall he ever look upon the sun again. Of this ye are warned. Since the Hathor came again to Khem, of men seven hundred and three have gone up to win her, and of bodies seven hundred and two lie within the vaults, for of all these men Pharaoh Meneptah alone hath gone back living. Yet there is place for more! Enter, ye who would look upon the Hathor!'

Now there arose a mighty wailing from the women. They clung madly about the necks of those who were dear to them, and some clung not in vain. For the hearts of many failed them at the last, and they shrank from entering in. But a few of those who had already looked upon the Hathor from afar, perchance a score in all, struck the women from them and rushed up to the gates.

'Surely thou wilt not enter in?' quoth Rei, clinging to the arm of the Wanderer. 'Oh, turn thy back on death and come back with me. I pray thee turn.'

'Nay, said the Wanderer, 'I will go in.'

Then Rei the Priest threw dust upon his head, wept aloud, and turned and fled, never stopping till he came to the Palace, where sat Meriamun the Queen.

Now the priest unbarred a wicket in the gates of bronze, and one by one those who were stricken of the madness entered in. For all of these had seen the Hathor many times from afar without the wall, and now they could no more withstand their longing. And as they entered two other priests took them by the hand and bound their eyes with cloths, so that unless they willed it they might not see the glory of the Hathor, but only hear the sweetness of her voice. But two there were who would not be blindfolded, and of these one was that man whose wife had fainted by the way, and the other was a man sightless from his youth. For although he might not see the beauty of the Goddess, this man was made mad by the sweetness of her voice. Now, when all had entered in, save the Wanderer, there was a stir in the crowd, and a man rushed up. He was travel-stained, he had a black beard, black eyes, and a nose hooked like a vulture's beak.

'Hold!' he cried. 'Hold! Shut not the gates! Night and day have I journeyed from the host of the Apura who fly into the wilderness. Night and day I have journeyed, leaving wife and flocks and children and the Promise of the Land, that I may once more look upon the beauty of the Hathor. Shut not the gates!'

'Pass in,' said the priest, 'pass in, so shall we be rid of one of those whom Khem nurtured up to rob her.'

He entered; then, as the priest was about to bar the wicket, the Wanderer strode forward, and his golden armour clashed beneath the portal.

'Wouldst thou indeed enter to thy doom, thou mighty lord?' asked the priest, for he knew him well again.

'Ay, I enter; but perchance not to my doom,' answered the Wanderer. Then he passed in and the brazen gate was shut behind him.

Now the two priests came forward to bind his eyes, but this he would not endure.

'Not so,' he said; 'I am come here to see what may be seen.'

'Go to, thou madman, go to! and die the death,' they answered, and led all the men to the centre of the court-yard whence they might see the pylon top. Then the priests also covered up their eyes and cast themselves at length upon the ground; so for a while they lay, and all was silence within and without the court, for they waited the coming of the Hathor. The Wanderer glanced through the bars of bronze at the multitude gathered there. Silent they stood with upturned eyes, even the women had ceased from weeping and stood in silence. He looked at those beside him. Their bandaged faces were lifted and they stared towards the pylon top as though their vision pierced the cloths. The blind man, too, stared upward, and his pale lips moved, but no sound came from them. Now at the foot of the pylon lay a little rim of shadow. Thinner and thinner it grew as the moments crept on towards the perfect noon. Now there was but a line, and now the line was gone, for the sun's red disc burned high in the blue heaven straight above the pylon brow. Then suddenly and from far there came a faint sweet sound of singing, and at the first note of the sound a great sigh went up through the quiet air, from all the multitude without. Those who were near the Wanderer sighed also, and their lips and fingers twitched, and he himself sighed, though he knew not why.

Nearer came the sweet sound of singing, and stronger it swelled, till presently those without the temple gate who were on higher ground caught sight of her who sang. Then a hoarse roar went up from every throat, and madness took them. On they rushed, dashing themselves against the gates of bronze and the steep walls on either side, and beat upon them madly with their fists and brows, and climbed on each other's shoulders, gnawing at the bars with their teeth, crying to be let in. But the women threw their arms about them and screamed curses on her whose beauty brought all men to madness.

So it went for a while, till presently the Wanderer looked up, and lo! upon the pylon's brow stood the woman's self, and at her coming all were once more silent. She was tall and straight, clad in clinging white, but on her breast there glowed a blood-red ruby stone, fashioned like a star, and from it fell red drops that stained for one moment the whiteness of her robes, and then the robe was white again. Her golden hair was tossed this way and that, and shone in the sunlight, her arms and neck were bare, and she held one hand before her eyes as though to hide the brightness of her beauty. For, indeed, she could not be called beautiful but Beauty itself.

And they who had not loved saw in her that first love

whom no man has ever won, and they who had loved saw that first love whom every man has lost. And all about her rolled a glory—like the glory of the dying day. Sweetly she sang a song of promise, and her voice was the voice of each man's desire, and the heart of the Wanderer thrilled in answer to it as thrills a harp smitten by a cunning hand; and thus she sang:

> Whom hast thou longed for most,
>   True love of mine?
> Whom hast thou loved and lost?
>   Lo, she is thine!
>
> She that another wed
>   Breaks from her vow;
> She that hath long been dead
>   Wakes for thee now.
>
> Dreams haunt the hapless bed,
>   Ghosts haunt the night,
> Life crowns her living head,
>   Love and Delight.
>
> Nay, not a dream nor ghost,
>   Nay, but Divine,
> She that was loved and lost
>   Waits to be thine!

She ceased, and a moan of desire went up from all who heard.

Then the Wanderer saw that those beside him tore at the bandages about their brows and rent them loose. Only the priests who lay upon the ground stirred not, though they also moaned.

And now again she sang, still holding her hand before her face:

> Ye that seek me, ye that sue me,
>   Ye that flock beneath my tower,
> Ye would win me, would undo me,
>   I must perish in an hour,

Dead before the Love that slew me, clasped the
    Bride and crushed the flower.

Hear the word and mark the warning,
    Beauty lives but in your sight,
Beauty fades from all men's scorning
    In the watches of the night,
Beauty wanes before the morning, and
    Love dies in his delight.

She ceased, and once more there was silence. Then
suddenly she bent forward across the pylon brow so far
that it seemed that she must fall, and stretching out her
arms as though to clasp those beneath, showed all the
glory of her loveliness.

The Wanderer looked, then dropped his eyes as one
who has seen the brightness of the noonday sun. In the
darkness of his mind the world was lost, and he could
think of naught save the clamour of the people, which
fretted his ear. They were all crying, and none were
listening.

'See! see!' shouted one. 'Look at her hair; it is dark as
the raven's wing, and her eyes—they are dark as night.
Oh, my love! my love!'

'See! see!' cried another, 'were ever skies so blue as
those eyes of hers, was ever foam so white as those white
arms?'

'Even so she looked whom once I wed many summers
gone,' murmured a third, 'even so when first I drew her
veil. Hers was that gentle smile breaking like ripples on
the water, hers that curling hair, hers that child-like
grace.'

'Was ever woman so queenly made?' said a fourth.
'Look now on the brow of pride, look on the deep, dark
eyes of storm, the arched lips, and the imperial air. Ah,
here indeed is a Goddess meet for worship.'

'Not so I see her,' cried a fifth, that man who had come
from the host of the Apura. 'Pale she is and fair, tall
indeed, but delicately shaped, brown is her hair, and
brown are her great eyes like the eyes of a stag, and ah,
sadly she looks upon me, longing for my love.'

'My eyes are opened,' screamed the blind man at the Wanderer's side. 'My eyes are opened, and I see the pylon tower and the splendid sun. Love hath touched me on the eyes and they are opened. But lo! not one shape hath she but many shapes. Oh, she is Beauty's self, and no tongue may tell her glory. Let me die! let me die, for my eyes are opened. I have looked on Beauty's self! I know what all the world journeys on to seek, and why we die and what we go to find in death.'

6. THE WARDENS OF THE GATE

The clamour swelled or sank, and the men called and cried the names of many women, some dead, some lost. Others were mute, silent in the presence of the World's Desire, silent as when we see lost faces in a dream. The Wanderer had looked once and then cast down his eyes and stood with his face hidden in his hands. He alone waited and strove to think; the rest were abandoned to the bewilderment of their passions and their amaze.

What was it that he had seen? That which he had sought his whole life long; sought by sea and land, not knowing what he sought. For this he had wandered with a hungry heart, and now was the hunger of his heart to be appeased? Between him and her was the unknown barrier and the invisible Death. Was he to pass the unmarked boundary, to force those guarded gates and achieve where all had failed? Had a magic deceived his eyes? Did he look but on a picture and a vision that some art could call again from the haunted place of Memory?

He sighed and looked again. Lo! in his charmed sight a fair girl seemed to stand upon the pylon brow, and on her head she bore a shining urn of bronze.

He knew her now. He had seen her thus at the court of King Tyndareus as he drove in his chariot through the ford of Eurotas; thus he had seen her also in the dream on the Silent Isle.

Again he sighed and again he looked. Now in his

charmed sight a woman sat, whose face was the face of the girl, grown more lovely far, but sad with grief and touched with shame.

He saw her and he knew her. So he had seen her in Troy towers when he stole thither in a beggar's guise from the camp of the Achæans. So he had seen her when she saved his life in Ilios.

Again he sighed and again he looked, and now he saw the Golden Helen.

She stood upon the pylon's brow. She stood with arms outstretched, with eyes upturned, and on her shining face there was a smile like the infinite smile of the dawn. Oh, now indeed he knew the shape that was Beauty's self—the innocent Spirit of Love sent on earth by the undying Gods to be the doom and the delight of men; to draw them through the ways of strife to the unknown end.

Awhile the Golden Helen stood thus looking up and out to the worlds beyond; to the peace beyond the strife, to the goal beyond the grave. Thus she stood while men scarce dared to breathe, summoning all to come and take that which upon the earth is guarded so invincibly.

Then once more she sang, and as she sang, slowly drew herself away, till at length nothing was left of the vision of her save the sweetness of her dying song.

> Who wins his Love shall lose her,
>   Who loses her shall gain,
> For still the spirit woos her,
>   A soul without a stain;
> And Memory still pursues her
>   With longings not in vain!
>
> He loses her who gains her,
>   Who watches day by day
> The dust of time that stains her,
>   The griefs that leave her gray,
> The flesh that yet enchains her
>   Whose grace hath passed away!
>
> Oh, happier he who gains not
>   The Love some seem to gain:
> The Joy that custom stains not

Shall still with him remain,
The loveliness that wanes not,
The Love that ne'er can wane.

In dreams she grows not older
The lands of Dream among,
Though all the world wax colder,
Though all the songs be sung,
In dreams doth he behold her
Still fair and kind and young.

Now the silence died away, and again madness came
upon those who had listened and looked. The men without
the wall once more hurled themselves against the gates,
while the women clung to them, shrieking curses on the
beauty of the Hathor, for the song meant nothing to these
women, and their arms were about those whom they loved
and who won them their bread. But most of the men who
were in the outer court rushed up to the inner gates within
which stood the alabaster shrine of the Hathor. Some
flung themselves upon the ground and clutched at it, as in
dreams men fling themselves down to be saved from falling into a pit that has no bottom. Yet as in such an evil
slumber the dreamer is drawn inch by inch to the mouth
of the pit by an unseeen hand, so these wretched men
were dragged along the ground by the might of their own
desire. In vain they set their feet against the stones to hold
themselves from going, for they thrust forward yet more
fiercely with their hands, and thus little by little drew near
the inner gates writhing forwards yet moving backwards
like a wounded snake dragged along by a rope. For of
those who thus entered the outer court and looked upon
the Hathor, few might go back alive.

Now the priests drew the cloths from their eyes, and
rising, flung wide the second gates, and there, but a little
way off, the veil of the shrine wavered as if in a wind. For
now the doors beyond the veil were thrown open, as
might be seen when the wind swayed its Tyrian web, and
through the curtain came the sound of the same sweet
singing.

'Draw near! Draw near!' cried the ancient priest. 'Let him who would win the Hathor draw near!'

Now at first the Wanderer was minded to rush on. But his desire had not wholly overcome him, nor had his wisdom left him. He took counsel with his heart and waited to let the others go, and to see how it fared with them.

The worshippers were now hurrying back and now darting onwards, as fear and longing seized them, till the man who was blind drew near, led by the hand of a priest, for his hound might not enter the second court of the temple.

'Do ye fear?' he cried. 'Cowards, I fear not. It is better to look upon the glory of the Hathor and die than to live and never see her more. Set my face straight, ye priests, set my face straight, at the worst I can but die.'

So they led him as near the curtains as they dared to go and set his face straight. Then with a great cry he rushed on. But he was caught and whirled about like a leaf in wind, so that he fell. He rose and again rushed on, again to be whirled back. A third time he rose and rushed on, smiting with his blind man's staff. The blow fell, and stayed in mid-air, and there came a hollow sound as of a smitten shield, and the staff that dealt the blow was shattered. Then there was a noise like the noise of clashing swords, and the man instantly sank down dead, though the Wanderer could see no wound upon him.

'Draw near! Draw near!' cried the priest again. 'This one is fallen. Let him who would win the Hathor draw near!'

Then the man who had fled from the host of the Apura rushed forward, crying on the Lion of his tribe. Back he was hurled, and back again, but at the third time once more there came the sound of clashing swords, and he too fell dead.

'Draw near! Draw near!' cried the priest. 'Another has fallen! Let him who would win the Hathor draw near!'

And now man after man rushed on, to be first hurled back and then slain of the clashing swords. And at length all were slain save the Wanderer alone.

Then the priest spake:

'Wilt thou indeed rush on to doom, thou glorious man? Thou hast seen the fate of many. Be warned and turn away.'

'Never did I turn from man or ghost,' said the Wanderer, and drawing his short sword he came near, warily covering his head with his broad shield, while the priests stood back to see him die. Now, the Wanderer had marked that none were touched till they stood upon the very threshold of the doorway. Therefore he uttered a prayer to Aphrodite and came on slowly till his feet were within a bow's length of the threshold, and there he stood and listened. Now he could hear the very words of the song that the Hathor sang as she wove at her loom. So dread and sweet it was that for a while he thought no more on the Guardians of the Gate, nor of how he might win the way, nor of aught save the song. For she was singing shrill and clear in his own dear tongue, the tongue of the Achæans:

Paint with threads of gold and scarlet, paint the battles fought
    for me,
All the wars for Argive Helen; storm and sack by land or sea;
All the tale of loves and sorrows that have been and are to be.

Paint her lips that like a cup have pledged the lips of heroes
    all,
Paint her golden hair unwhitened while the many winters fall,
Paint the beauty that is mistress of the wide world and its
    thrall!

Paint the storms of ships and chariots, rain of arrows flying
    far,
Paint the waves of Warfare leaping up at Beauty like a star,
Like a star that pale and trembling hangs above the waves of
    War.

Paint the ancient Ilios fallen; paint the flames that scaled the
    sky,
When the foe was in the fortress, when the trumpet and the
    cry

Rang of men in their last onset, men whose hour had dawned
    to die.

Woe for me once loved of all men, me that never yet have
    known
How to love the hearts that loved me. Woe for me, who hear
    the moan
Of my lovers' ghosts that perished in their cities overthrown.

Is there not, of Gods or mortals, oh, ye Gods, is there not
    one—
One whose heart shall mate with my heart, one to love ere
    all be done,
All the tales of wars that shall be for my love beneath the
    sun?

Now the song died away, and the Wanderer once more
bethought him of the Wardens of the Gate and of the
battle which he must fight. But as he braced himself to
rush on against the unseen foe the music of the singing
swelled forth again, and whether he willed it or willed it
not, so sweet was its magic that there he must wait till the
song was done. And now stronger and more gladly rang
the sweet shrill voice, like the voice of one who has made
moan through the livelong winter night, and now sees the
chariot of the dawn climbing the eastern sky. And thus
the Hathor sang:

Ah, within my heart a hunger for the love unfelt, unknown,
Stirs at length, and wakes and murmurs as a child that wakes
    to moan,
Left to sleep within some silent house of strangers and alone.

So my heart awakes, and waking, moans with hunger and
    with cold,
Cries in pain of dim remembrance for the joy that was of old;
For the love that was, that shall be, half forgot and half fore-
    told.

Have I dreamed it or remembered? In another world was I,

Lived and loved in alien seasons, moved beneath a golden
    sky,
In a golden clime where never came the strife of men that
    die.

But the Gods themselves were jealous, for our bliss was
    over great,
And they brought on us division, and the horror of their
    Hate,
And they set the Snake between us, and the twining coils of
    Fate.

And they said, 'Go forth and seek each other's face, and only
    find
Shadows of that face ye long for, dreams of days left far
    behind,
Love the shadows and be loved with loves that waver as the
    wind.'

Once more the sweet singing died away, but as the
Wanderer grasped his sword and fixed the broad shield
upon his arm he remembered the dream of Meriamun the
Queen, which had been told him by Rei the Priest. For in
that dream twain who had sinned were made three, and
through many deaths and lives must seek each other's
face. And now it seemed that the burden of the song was
the burden of the dream.

Then he thought no more on dreams, or songs, or
omens, but only on the deadly foe that stood before him
wrapped in darkness, and on Helen, in whose arms he yet
should lie, for so the Goddess had sworn to him in sea-girt
Ithaca. He spoke no word, he named no God, but sprang
forward as a lion springs from his bed of reeds; and, lo!
his buckler clashed against shields that barred the way,
and invisible arms seized him to hurl him back. But no
weakling was the Wanderer, thus to be pushed aside by
magic, but the stoutest man left alive in the whole world
now that Aias, Telamon's son, was dead. The priests
wondered as they saw how he gave back never a step, for
all the might of the Wardens of the Gate, but lifted his
short sword and hewed down so terribly that fire leapt

from the air where the short sword fell, the good short sword of Euryalus the Phæacian. Then came the clashing of the swords, and from all the golden armour that once the god-like Paris wore, ay, from buckler, helm, and greaves, and breastplate the sparks steamed up as they stream from the anvil of the smith when he smites great blows on swords made white with fire.

Swift as hail fell the blows of the unseen blades upon the golden armour, but he who wore it took no harm, nor was it so much as marked with the dint of the swords. So while the priests wondered at this miracle of the viewless Wardens of the Gate smote at the Wanderer, and the Wanderer smote at them again. Then of a sudden he knew this, that they who barred the path were gone, for no more blows fell, and his sword only cut the air.

Then he rushed on and passed behind the veil and stood within the shrine.

But as the curtains swung behind him the singing rose again upon the air, and he might not move, but stood fixed with his eyes gazing where, far up, a loom was set within the shrine. For the sound of the singing came from behind the great web gleaming in the loom, the sound of the song of Helen as she heard the swords clash and the ringing of the harness of those whose knees were loosened in death. It was thus she sang:

Clamour of iron on iron, and shrieking of steel upon steel,
 Hark how they echo again!
Life with the dead is at war, and the mortals are shaken and
  reel,
 The living are slain by the slain!

Clamour of iron on iron; like music that chimes with a song,
 So with my life doth it chime,
And my footsteps must fall in the dance of Erinnys, a revel
  of wrong,
 Till the day of the passing of Time!

Ghosts of the dead that have loved me, your love have been
  vanquished of death,
 But unvanquished of death is your hate;

Say, is there none that may woo me and win me of all that
    draw breath,
  Not one but is envied of Fate?

Now the song died, and the Wanderer looked up, and
before him stood three shadows of mighty men clad in
armour. He gazed upon them, and he knew the blazons
painted on their shields; he knew them for heroes long
dead—Pirithous, Theseus, and Aias.

They looked upon him, and then cried with one voice:
'Hail to thee, Odysseus of Ithaca, son of Laertes!'

'Hail to thee,' cried the Wanderer, 'Theseus, Ægeus' son!
Once before didst thou go down into the House of Hades,
and alive thou camest forth again. Hast thou crossed yet
again the stream of Ocean, and dost thou live in the
sunlight? For of old I sought thee and found thee not in
the House of Hades?'

The semblance of Theseus answered: 'In the House of
Hades I abide this day, and in the fields of asphodel. But
that thou seest is a shadow, sent forth by the Queen
Persephone, to be the guard of the beauty of Helen.'

'Hail to thee, Pirithous, Ixion's son,' cried the Wanderer
again. 'Hast thou yet won the dread Persephone to be thy
love? And why doth Hades give his rival holiday to
wander in the sunlight, for of old I sought thee, and found
thee not in the House of Hades.'

Then the semblance of Pirithous answered:

'In the House of Hades I dwell this day, and that thou
seest is but a shadow which goes with the shadow of the
hero Theseus. For where he is am I, and where he goes I
go, and our very shadows are not sundered; but we guard
the beauty of Helen.'

'Hail to thee, Aias, Telamon's son,' cried the Wanderer.
'Hast thou not forgotten thy wrath against me, for the
sake of those accursed arms that I won from thee, the
arms of Achilles, son of Peleus? For of old in the House
of Hades I spoke to thee, but thou wouldst not answer one
word, so heavy was thine anger.'

Then the semblance of Aias made answer: 'With iron
upon iron, and the stroke of bronze on bronze, would I

answer thee, if I were yet a living man and looked upon the sunlight. But I smite with a shadowy spear and slay none but men foredoomed, and I am the shade of Aias who dwells in Hades. Yet the Queen Persephone sent me forth to be the guard of the beauty of Helen.'

Then the Wanderer spake.

'Tell me, ye shadows of the sons of heroes, is the way closed, and do the Gods forbid it, or may I that am yet a living man pass forward and gaze on that ye guard, on the beauty of Helen?'

Then each of the three nodded with his head, and smote once upon his sheild, saying:

'Pass by, but look not back upon us, till thou hast seen thy desire.'

Then the Wanderer went by, into the innermost chamber of the alabaster shrine.

Now when the shadows had spoken thus, they grew dim and vanished, and the Wanderer, as they had commanded, drew slowly up on the Alabaster shrine, till at length he stood on the hither side of the web upon the loom. It was a great web, wide and high, and hid all the innermost recesses of the shrine. Here he waited, not knowing how he should break in upon the Hathor.

As he stood wondering thus his buckler slipped from his loosened hand and clashed upon the marble floor, and as it clashed the voice of Hathor took up the broken song; and thus she sang ever more sweetly:—

Ghosts of the dead that have loved me, your love has been vanquished by Death,
  But unvanquished by Death is your Hate;
Say, is there none that may woo me and win me of all that draw breath,
  Not one but is envied of Fate?

None that may pass you unwounded, unscathed of invisible spears—
  By the splendour of Zeus there is one,
And he comes, and my spirit is touched as Demeter is touched by the tears
  Of the Spring and the kiss of the sun

For he comes, and my heart that was chill as a lake in the
     season of snow,
  Is molten, and glows as with fire.
And the Love that I knew not is born and he laughs in my
     heart, and I know
  The name and the flame of Desire.

As a flame am I kindled, a flame that is blown by a wind
     from the North,
  By a wind that is deadly with cold,
And the hope that awoke in me faints, for the Love that is
     born shall go forth
  To my Love, and shall die as of old!

Now the song sobbed itself away, but the heart of the
Wanderer echoed to its sweetness as a lyre moans and
thrills when the hand of the striker is lifted from the
strings.

For a while he stood thus, hidden by the web upon the
loom, while his limbs shook the leaves of the tall poplar,
and his face turned white as turn the poplar leaves. Then
desire overcame him, and a longing he could not master,
to look upon the face of her who sang, and he seized the
web upon the loom, and rent it with a great rending noise,
so that it fell down on either side of him, and the gold
coils rippled at his feet.

7. THE SHADOW IN THE SUNLIGHT

The torn web fell—the last veil of the Strange Hathor.
It fell, and all its unravelled threads of glittering gold and
scarlet rippled and coiled about the Wanderer's feet, and
about the pillars of the loom.

The web was torn, the veil was rent, the labour was
lost, the pictured story of loves and wars was all undone.

But there, white in the silvery dusk of the alabaster
shrine, there was the visible Helen, the bride and the
daughter of Mystery, the World's Desire!

There shone that fabled loveliness of which no story
was too strange, of which all miracles seemed true. There,
her hands folded on her lap, her head bowed—there sat
she whose voice was the echo of all sweet voices, she
whose shape was the mirror of all fair forms, she whose
changeful beauty, so they said, was the child of the chang-
ful moon.

Helen sat in a chair of ivory, gleaming even through the
sunshine of her outspread hair. She was clothed in soft
folds of white; on her breast gleamed the Starstone, the
red stone of the sea-deeps that melts in the sunshine, but
that melted not on the breast of Helen. Moment by moment the red drops from the ruby heart of the star fell on
her snowy raiment, fell and vanished,—fell and vanished,
—and left no stain.

The Wanderer looked on her face, but the beauty and
the terror of it, as she raised it, were more than he could

bear, and he stood like those who saw the terror and the beauty of that face which changes men to stone.

For the lovely eyes of Helen stared wide, her lips, yet quivering with the last notes of song, were open wide in fear. She seemed like one who walks alone, and suddenly, in the noonday light, meets the hated dead; encountering the ghost of an enemy come back to earth with the instant summons of doom.

For a moment the sight of her terror made even the Wanderer afraid. What was the horror she beheld in this haunted shrine, where was none save themselves alone? What was with them in the shrine?

Then he saw that her eyes were fixed on this golden armour which Paris once had worn, on the golden shield with the blazon of the White Bull, on the golden helm, whose visor was down so that it quite hid his eyes and his face—and then at last her voice broke from her:

'Paris! Paris! Paris! Has Death lost hold of thee? Hast thou come to drag me back to thee and to shame? Paris, dead Paris! Who gave thee courage to pass the shadows of men whom on earth thou hadst not dared to face in war?'

Then she wrung her hands, and laughed aloud with the empty laugh of fear.

A thought came into that crafty mind of the Wanderer's, and he answered her, not in his own voice, but in the smooth, soft, mocking voice of the traitor Paris, whom he had heard forswear himself in the oath before Ilios.

'So, lady, thou hast not yet forgiven Paris? Thou weavest the ancient web, thou singest the ancient songs—art thou still unkind as of old?'

'Why art thou come back to taunt me?' she said, and now she spoke as if an old familiar fear and horror were laying hold of her and mastering her again, after long freedom. 'Was it not enough to betray me in the semblance of my wedded lord? Why dost thou mock?'

'In love all arts are fair,' he answered in the voice of Paris. 'Many have loved thee, Lady, and they are all dead for thy sake, and no love but mine has been more strong than death. There is none to blame us now, and none to hinder. Troy is down, the heroes are white dust; only

Love lives yet. Wilt thou not learn, Lady, how a shadow can love?'

She had listened with her head bowed, but now she leaped up with blazing eyes and face of fire.

'Begone!' she said, 'the heroes are dead for my sake, and to my shame, but the shame is living yet. Begone! Never in life or death shall my lips touch the false lips that lied away my honour, and the false face that wore the favour of my lord's.'

For it was by shape-shifting and magic art, as poets tell, that Paris first beguiled Fair Helen.

Then the Wanderer spoke again with the sweet, smooth voice of Paris, son of Priam.

'As I passed up the shrine where thy glory dwells, Helen, I heard thee sing. And thou didst sing of the waking of thy heart, of the arising of Love within thy soul, and of the coming of one for whom thou dost wait, whom thou didst love long since and shalt love for evermore. And as thou sangest, I came, I Paris, who was thy love and who am thy love and who alone of ghosts and men shall be thy love again. Wilt thou still bid me go?'

'I sang,' she answered, 'yes, as the Gods put it in my heart so I sang—for indeed it seemed to me that one came who was my love of old, and whom alone I must love, alone for ever. But thou wast not in my heart, thou false Paris! Nay, I will tell thee, and with the name will scare thee back to Hell. He was in my heart whom once as a maid I saw driving in his chariot through the ford of Eurotas while I bore water from the well. He was in my heart whom once I saw in Troy when he crept thither clad in a beggar's guise. Ay, Paris, I will name him by his name, for though he is long dead, yet him alone methinks I loved from the very first, and him alone I shall love till my deathlessness is done—Odysseus, son of Laertes, Odysseus of Ithaca, he was named among men, and Odysseus was in my heart as I sang and in my heart he shall ever be, though the Gods in their wrath have given me to others, to my shame, and against my will.'

Now when the Wanderer heard her speak, and heard his own name upon her lips, and knew that the Golden

Helen loved him alone, it seemed to him as though his heart would burst his harness. No word could he find in his heart to speak, but he raised the visor of his helm.

She looked—she saw and knew him for Odysseus—even Odysseus of Ithaca. Then in turn she hid her eyes with her hands, and speaking through them said:

'Oh, Paris! ever wast thou false, but, ghost or man, of all thy shames this is the shamefullest. Thou hast taken the likeness of a hero dead, and thou hast heard me speak such words of him as Helen never spoke before. Fie on thee, Paris! fie on thee! who wouldest trick me into shame as once before thou didst trick me in the shape of Menelaus who was my lord. Now I will call on Zeus to blast thee with his bolts. Nay, not on Zeuz will I call, but on Odysseus' self. *Odysseus! Odysseus!* Come thou from the shades and smite this Paris, this trickster, who even in death finds ways to mock thee.'

She ceased, and with eyes upturned and arms outstretched murmured, 'Odysseus! Odysseus! Come.'

Slowly the Wanderer drew near to the glory of the Golden Helen—slowly, slowly he came, till his dark eyes looked into her eyes of blue. Then at last he found his voice and spake.

'Helen! Argive Helen!' he said, 'I am no shadow come up from Hell to torment thee, and of Trojan Paris I know nothing. For I am Odysseus, Odysseus of Ithaca, a living man beneath the sunlight. Hither am I come to seek thee, hither am I come to win thee to my heart. For yonder in Ithaca Aphrodite visited me in a dream, and bade me wander out upon the seas till at length I found thee, Helen, and saw the Red Star blaze upon thy breast. And I have wandered, and I have dared, and I have heard thy song, and rent the web of Fate, and I have seen the Star, and lo! at last, at last! I find thee. Well I saw thou knewest the arms of Paris, who was thy husband, and to try thee I spoke with the voice of Paris, as of old thou didst feign the voices of our wives when we lay in the wooden horse within the walls of Troy. Thus I drew the sweetness of thy love from thy secret breast, as the sun draws out the sweetness of the flowers. But now I declare myself to be Odysseus, clad in the mail of Paris—Odysseus come on this last journey to be thy love and lord.' And he ceased.

She trembled and looked at him doubtfully, but at last she spoke:

'Well do I remember,' she said, 'that when I washed the limbs of Odysseus, in the halls of Ilios, I marked a great white scar beneath his knee. If indeed thou art Odysseus, and not a phantom from the Gods show me that great scar.'

Then the Wanderer smiled, and, resting his buckler against the pillar of the loom, drew off his golden greave, and there was the scar that the boar dealt with his tusk on the Parnassian hill when Odysseus was a boy.

'Look, Lady,' he said; 'is this the scar that once thine eyes looked on in the hills of Troy?'

'Yea,' she said, 'it is the very scar, and now I know that thou art no ghost and no lying shape, but Odysseus' self, come to be my love and lord,' and she looked most sweetly in his eyes.

Now the Wanderer wavered no more, but put out his arms to gather her to his heart. Now the Red Star was hidden on his breast, now the red drops dripped from the Star upon his mail, and the face of her who is the World's Desire grew soft in the shadow of his helm, while her eyes were melted to tears beneath his kiss. The Gods send all lovers like joy!

Softly she sighed, softly drew back from his arms, and her lips were open to speak when a change came over her face. The kind eyes were full of fear again, as she gazed where, through the window of the shrine of alabaster, the sunlight fell in gold upon the chapel floor. What was that which flickered in the sunlight? or was it only the dance of the motes in the beam? There was no shadow cast in the sunshine; why did she gaze as if she saw another watching this meeting of their loves? However it chanced, she mastered her fear; there was even a smile on her lips and mirth in her eyes as she turned and spoke again.

'Odysseus, thou art indeed the cunningest of men. Thou hast stolen my secret by thy craft; who save thee would dream of craft in such an hour? For when I thought thee Paris, and thy face was hidden by thy helm, I called on Odysseus in my terror as, a child cries to a mother. Methinks I have ever held him dear; always I have found him ready at need, though the Gods have willed that till this hour my love might not be known, nay, not to my own heart; so I called on Odysseus, and those words were wrung from me to scare false Paris back to his own place. But the words that should have driven Paris down to Hell drew Odysseus to my breast. And now it is done, and I will not go back upon my words, for we have kissed our kiss of troth, before the immortal Gods have we kissed, and those ghosts who guard the way to Helen, and whom thou alone couldst pass, as it was fated, are witnesses to our oath. And now the ghosts depart, for no more need they guard the beauty of Helen. It is given to thee to have and keep, and now is Helen once more a very woman, for at thy kiss the curse was broken. Ah, friend! since my lord died in pleasant Lacedæmon, what things have I seen and suffered by the Gods' decree! But two things I will tell thee, Odysseus, and thou shalt read them as thou mayest. Though never before in thy life-days did thy lips touch mine, yet I know that not now for the first time we kiss. And this I know also, for the Gods have set it in my heart, that though our love shall be short, and little joy shall we have one of another, yet death shall not end it. For Odysseus, I am a daughter of the Gods, and though I sleep and forget that which has been in my sleep, and though my shape change as but now it seemed to change in the eyes of those ripe to die, yet I die not. And for thee, though thou art mortal, death shall be but as the short summer nights that mark off day from day. For thou shalt live again, Odysseus, as thou hast lived before, and life by life we shall meet and love till the end is come.'

As the Wanderer listened he thought once more of that dream of Meriamun the Queen, which the priest Rei had told him. But he said nothing of it to Helen; for about the Queen and her words to him it seemed wisest not to speak.

'It will be well to live, Lady, if life by life I find thee for a love.'

'Life by life thou shalt find me, Odysseus, in this shape or in that shalt thou find me—for beauty has many forms, and love has many names—but thou shalt ever find me to lose me again. I tell thee that as but now thou wonnest thy way through the ranks of those who watch me, the cloud lifted from my mind, and I remembered, and I foresaw and I knew why I, the loved of many, might never love in turn. I knew then, Odysseus, that I am but the instrument of the Gods, who use me for their ends. And I knew that I loved thee, and thee only, but with love that began before the birth-bed, and shall not be consumed by the funeral flame.'

'So be it, Lady,' said the Wanderer, 'for this I know, that never have I loved woman or Goddess as I love thee, who art henceforth as the heart in my breast, that without which I may not live.'

'Now speak on,' she said, 'for such words as these are like music in my ears.'

'Ay, I will speak on. Short shall be our love, thou sayest, Lady, and my own heart tells me that it is born to be brief of days. I know that now I got on my last voyaging, and that death comes upon me from the water, the swiftest death that may be. This then I would dare to ask: When shall we twain be one? For if the hours of life be short, let us love while we may.'

Now Helen's golden hair fell before her eyes like the bride's veil, and she was silent for a time. Then she spoke:

'Not now, and not while I dwell in this holy place may we be wed, Odysseus, for so should we call down upon us the hate of Gods and men. Tell me, then, where thou dwellest in the city, and I will come to thee. Nay, it is not meet. Hearken, Odysseus. Tomorrow, one hour before the midnight, see that thou dost stand without the pylon gates of this my temple; then I will pass out to thee as well I may, and thou shalt know me by the jewel, the Star-stone on my breast that shines through the darkness, and by that alone, and lead me whither thou wilt. For then thou shalt be my lord, and I will be thy wife. And thereafter, as the Gods show us, so will we go. For know, it is in my mind to fly this land of Khem, where month by month the Gods have made the people die for me. So till then, farewell, Odysseus, my love, found after many days.'

'It is well, Lady,' answered the Wanderer. 'Tomorrow night I meet thee without the pylon gates. I also am minded to fly this land of witchcraft and of horror, but I may scarce depart till Pharaoh return again. For he has gone down to battle and has left me to guard his palace.'

'Of that we will talk hereafter. Go now! Go swiftly, for here we may not talk more of earthy love,' said the Golden Helen.

Then he took her hand and kissed it and passed from before her glory as a man amazed.

But in his foolish wisdom he spoke no word to her of Meriamun the Queen.

8. THE LOOSING OF THE SPIRIT OF REI

Rei the Priest had fled with what speed he might from the Gates of Death, those gates that guarded the loveliness of Helen and opened only upon men doomed to die. The old man was heavy at heart, for he loved the Wanderer. Among the dark children of Khem he had seen none like this Achaean, none so goodly, so strong, and so well versed in all arts of war. He remembered how this man had saved the life of her he loved above all women—of Meriamun, the moon-child, the fairest queen who had sat upon the throne of Egypt, the fairest and the most learned, save Taia only. He bethought him of the Wanderer's beauty as he stood upon the board while the long shafts hailed down the hall. Then he recalled the vision of Meriamun, which she told him long years ago, and the shadow in a golden helm which watched the changed Hataska. The more he thought, the more he was perplexed and lost in wonder. What did the Gods intend? Of one thing he was sure: the leaders of the host of dreams had mocked Meriamun. The man of her vision would never be her love: he had gone to meet his doom at the door of the Chapel Perilous.

So Rei hasted on, stumbling in his speed, till he came to the Palace and passed through its halls towards his chamber. At the entrance of her own place he met Meriamun the Queen. There she stood in the doorway like a picture in its sculptured frame, nor could any sight be more

135

beautiful than she was, clad in her Royal robes, and crowned with the golden snakes. Her black hair lay soft and deep on her, and her eyes looked strangely forth from beneath the ivory of her brow.

He bowed low before her and would have passed on, but she stayed him.

'Whither goest thou, Rei?' she asked, 'and why is thy face so sad?'

"I go about my business, Queen,' he answered, 'and I am sad because no tidings come of Pharaoh, nor of how it has fared with him the host of the Apura.'

'Perchance thou speakest truth, and yet not all the truth,' she answered. 'Enter I would have speech with thee.'

So he entered, and at her command seated himself before her in the very seat where the Wanderer had sat. Now, as he sat thus, of a sudden Meriamun the Queen slid to her knees before him and tears were in her eyes and her breast was shaken with sobs. And while he wondered, thinking that she wept at last for her son who was dead among the firstborn, she hid her face in her hands upon his knees, and trembled.

"What ails thee, Queen, my fosterling?" he said. But she only took his hand, and laid her own in it, and the old priest's eyes were dim with tears. So she sat for awhile, and then she looked up, but still she did not find words. And he caressed the beautiful Imperial head, that no man had seen bowed before. 'What is it, my daughter?' he said, and she answered at last:

'Hear me, old friend, who art my only friend—for if I speak not my heart will surely burst; or if it break not, my brain will burn and I shall be no more a Queen but a living darkness, where vapours creep, and wandering lights shine faintly on the ruin of my mind. Mindest thou that hour—it was the night after the hateful night that saw me Pharaoh's wife—when I crept to thee and told thee the vision that had come upon my soul, had come to mock me even at Pharaoh's side?'

'I mind it well," said Rei; 'it was a strange vision, nor might my wisdom interpret it.'

'And mindest thou what I told thee of the man of my vision—the glorious man whom I must love, he who was clad in golden armour and wore a golden helm wherein a spear-point of bronze stood fast?'

'Yes, I mind it,' said Rei.

'And how is that man named?' she asked, whispering, and staring on him with wide eyes. 'Is he not named Eperitus, the Wanderer? And hath he not come hither, the spear-point in his helm? And is not the hand of Fate upon me, Meriamun? Hearken, Rei, hearken! I love him as it was fated I should love. When first I looked on him as he came up the Hall of Audience in his glory, I knew him. I knew him for that man who shares the curse laid afore-time on him, and on the woman, and on me, when, in an unknown place, twain became three and were doomed to strive from life to life and work each other's woe upon the earth. I knew him, Rei, though he knew me not, and I say that my soul shook at the echo of his step, and my heart blossomed as the black earth blossoms when after flood Sihor seeks his banks again. A glory came upon me, Rei, and I looked back through all the mists of time and knew him for my love, and I looked forward into the depths of time to be and knew him for my love. Then I looked on the present hour, and naught could I see but darkness, and naught could I hear but the groans of dying men and a shrill sound as of a woman singing.'

'An ill tale, Queen,' said Rei.

'Ay, an ill tale, Rei, but half untold. Hearken again, I will tell thee all. Madness hath entered into me from the Hathor of Atarhechis, the Queen of Desire. I am mad with love, even I who never loved. Oh, Rei! Rei! I would win this man. Nay, look not so sternly on me, it is Fate that drives me on. Last night I spoke to him and discovered to him the name he hides from us, his own name, Odysseus, Laertes' son, Odysseus of Ithaca. Ay, thou startest, but so it is. I learned it by my magic, and wrung the truth even from the guile of the most crafty of men. But it seemed to me that he turned from me, though this much I won from him, that he had journeyed from far to seek me, the Bride that the Gods have promised him.'

The priest leaped up from his seat. 'Lady!' he cried, 'Lady! whom I serve and whom I have loved from a child, thy brain is sick, and not thy heart. Thou canst not love him. Dost thou not remember that thou art Queen of Khem and Pharoah's wife? Wilt thou throw thy honour in the mire to be trampled by a wandering stranger?'

'Ay,' she answered, 'I am Queen of Kehm and Pharaoh's wife, but never Pharaoh's love. Honour! Why dost thou prate to me of honour? Like Nile in flood, my love hath burst the bulwark of my honour, and I mark not where custom set it. For all around the waters seethe and foam, and on them, like a broken lily, floats the wreck of my lost honour. Talk not to me of honour, Rei, teach me rather how I may win my hero to my arms.'

'Thou art mad indeed,' he groaned; 'nevertheless—I had forgotten,—this must needs end in words and tears. Meriamun, I bring thee tidings. He whom thou desirest is lost to thee for ever—to thee and all the world.'

She heard, then sprang from the couch and stood over him like a lioness over a smitten stag, her fierce and lovely face alive with rage and fear.

'Is he dead?' she hissed in his ear. 'Dead! and I knew it not? Then thou hast murdered him, and thus I avenge his murder.'

With the word she snatched a dagger from her girdle—that same dagger with which she once had struck at Meneptah her brother, when he would have kissed her—and high it flashed above Rei the Priest.

'Nay,' she went on, letting the knife fall; 'after another fashion shalt thou die—more slowly, Rei, yes, more slowly. Thou knowest the torment of the palmtree? By that thou shalt die!' She paused, and stood above him with quivering limbs, and breast that heaved, and eyes that flashed like stars.

'Stay! stay!' he cried. 'It is not I who have slain this Wanderer, if he indeed is dead, but his own folly. For he is gone up to look upon the Strange Hathor, and those who look upon the Hathor do battle with the Unseen Swords, and those who do battle with the Unseen Swords must lie in the baths of bronze and seek the Under World.'

The face of Meriamun grew white at this word, as the alabaster of the walls, and she cried aloud with a great cry. Then she sank upon the couch, pressing her hand to her brow and moaning:

'How may I save him? How may I save him from that accursed witch? Alas! It is too late—but at least I will know his end, ay, and hear of the beauty of her who slays him. Rei,' she whispered, not in the speech of Khem, but in the dead tongue of a dead people, 'be not wrath with me. Oh, have pity on my weakness. Thou knowest of the Putting-forth of the Spirit—is it not so?'

'I am instructed,' he answered, in the same speech; ' 'twas I who taught thee this art, I, and that Ancient Evil which is thine.'

'True—it was thou, Rei. Thou hast ever loved me, so thou swearest, and many a deed of dread have we dared together. Lend me thy Spirit, Rei, that I may send it forth to the Temple of the False Hathor, and learn what passes in the temple, and of the death of him—whom I must love.'

'An ill deed, Meriamun, and a fearful,' he answered, 'for there shall my Spirit meet them who watch the gates, and who knows what may chance when the bodiless one that yet hath earthly life meets the bodiless ones who live no more on earth?'

'Yet wilt thou dare it, Rei, for love of me, as being instructed thou alone canst do,' she pleaded.

'Never have I refused thee aught, Meriamun, nor will I say thee nay. This only I ask of thee—that if my Spirit comes back no more, thou wilt bury me in that tomb which I have made ready by Thebes, and if it may be, by thy strength of magic wring me from the power of the strange Wardens. I am prepared—thou knowest the spell —say it.'

He sank back in the carven couch, and looked upwards. Then Meriamun drew near to him, gazed into his eyes and whispered in his ear in that dead tongue she knew. And as she whispered the face of Rei grew like the face of one dead. She drew back and spoke aloud:

'Art thou loosed, Spirit of Rei?'

Then the lips of Rei answered her, saying, 'I am loosed, Meriamun. Whither shall I go?'

'To the court of the Temple of Hathor, that is before the shrine.'

'It is done, Meriamun.'

'What seest thou?'

'I see a man clad in golden armour. He stands with buckler raised before the doorway of the shrine, and before him are the ghosts of heroes dead, though he may not see them with the eyes of the flesh. From within the shrine there comes a sound of singing, and he listens to the singing.'

'What does he hear?'

Then the loosed Spirit of Rei the Priest told Meriamun the Queen all the words of the song that Helen sang. And when she heard and knew that it was Argive Helen who sat in the halls of Hathor, the heart of the Queen grew faint within her, and her knees trembled. Yet more did she tremble when she learned those words that rang like the words she herself had heard in her vision long ago—telling of bliss that had been, of the hate of the Gods, and of the unending Quest.

Now the song ended, and the Wanderer went up against the ghosts, and the Spirit of Rei, speaking with the lips of Rei, told all that befell, while Meriamun hearkened with open ears—ay, and cried aloud with joy when the Wanderer forced his path through the invisible swords.

Then once more the sweet voice sang and the loosed Spirit of Rei told the words she sang, and to Meriamun they seemed fateful. Then he told her all the talk that passed between the Wanderer and the ghosts.

Now the ghosts being gone she bade the Spirit of Rei follow the Wanderer up the sanctuary, and from the loosed Spirit she heard how he rent the web, and of all the words of Helen and of the craft of him who feigned to be Paris. Then the web was torn and the eyes of the Spirit of Rei looked on the beauty of her who was behind it.

'Tell me of the face of the False Hathor?' said the Queen.

And the Spirit of Rei answered: 'Her face is that beauty which gathered like a mask upon the face of dead Hataska, and upon the face of the Bai, and the face of the Ka, when thou spakest with the spirit of her thou hadst slain.'

Now Meriamun groaned aloud, for she knew that doom was on her. Last of all, she heard the telling of the loves of Odysseus and of Helen, her undying foe, of their kiss, of their betrothal, and of that marriage which should be on the morrow night. Meriamun the Queen said never a word, but when all was done and the Wanderer had left the shrine again, she whispered in the ear of Rei the Priest, and drew back his Spirit to him so that he awoke as a man awakes from sleep.

He awoke and saw the Queen sitting over against him with a face white as the face of the dead, and about her deep eyes were lines of black.

'Hast thou heard, Meriamun?' he asked.

'I have heard,' she answered.

'What dreadful thing hast thou heard?' he asked again, for he knew naught of that which his Spirit had seen.

'I have heard things that may not be told,' she said, 'but this I will tell thee. He of whom we spoke hath passed the ghosts, he hath met with the False Hathor—that accursed woman—and he returns here all unharmed. Now go, Rei!'

9. THE WAKING OF THE SLEEPER

Rei departed, wondering and heavy at heart, and Meriamun the Queen passed into her bed-chamber, and there she bade the eunuchs suffer none to enter, made fast the doors, and threw herself down upon the bed, hiding her face in its woven cushions. Thus she lay for many hours as one dead—till the darkness of the evening gathered in the chamber. But though she moved not, yet in her heart there burned a fire, now white with heat as the breath of her passion fanned it, and now waning black and dull as the tears fell from her eyes. For now she knew all,—that the long foreboding, sometimes dreaded, sometimes desired, and again, like a dream, half forgotten, was indeed being fulfilled. She knew of the devouring love that must eat her life away, knew that even in the grave she should find no rest. And her foe was no longer a face beheld in a vision, but a living woman, the fairest and most devoured, Helen of Troy, Argive Helen, the False Hathor, the torch that fired great cities, the centre of all desire, whose life was the daily doom of men.

Meriamun was beautiful, but her beauty paled before the face of Helen, as a fire is slain by the sun. Magic she had also, more than any who were on the earth; but what would her spells avail against the magic of those changing eyes? And it was Helen whom the Wanderer came to seek, for *her* he had travelled the wide lands and sailed the seas. But when he told her of one whom he desired, one whom he sought, she had deemed that she herself was the one, ay, and had told him all.

At that thought she laughed out, in the madness of her anger and her shame. And he had smiled and spoken of Pharaoh her lord—and the while he spoke he had thought not on her but of the Golden Helen. Now this at least she swore, that if he might not be hers, never should he be Helen's. She would see him dead ere that hour, ay, and herself, and if it might be, Helen would she see dead also.

To what counsel should she turn? On the morrow night these two met; on the morrow night they would fly together. Then on the morrow must the Wanderer be slain. How should he be slain and leave no tale of murder? By poison he might die, and Kurri the Sidonian should be charged to give the cup. And then she would slay Kurri, saying that he had poisoned the Wanderer because of his hate and the loss of his goods and freedom; and yet how could she slay her love? If once she slew him then she, too, must die and seek her joy in the kingdom that Osiris rules, and there she might find little gladness.

What, then, should she do? No answer came into her heart. There was one that must answer in her soul.

Now she rose from the bed and stood for while staring into the dark. Then she groped her way to a place where there was a carven chest of olive-wood and ivory, and drawing a key from her girdle she opened the chest. Within were jewels, mirrors, and unguents in jars of alabaster—ay, and poisons of deadly bane; but she touched none of these. Thrusting her hand deep into the chest, she drew forth a casket of dark metal that the people deemed unholy, a casket made of 'Typhon's Bone,' for so they call gray iron. She pressed a secret spring. It opened, and feeling within she found a smaller casket. Lifting it to her lips she whispered over it words of no living speech, and in the heavy and scented dark a low flame flickered and trembled on her lips, as she murmured in the tongue of a dead people. Then slowly the lid opened, a gleam of light stole up from the box into the dusk of the chamber.

Now Meriamun looked, and shuddered as she looked. Yet she put her hand into the box, and muttering, 'Come forth——come forth, thou Ancient Evil,' drew somewhat to her and held it out from her on the palm of her hand. Behold, it glowed in the dusk of the chamber as a live ember glows among the ashes of the hearth. Red it glowed, and green, and white, and livid blue, and its shape, as it lay upon her hand, was the shape of a coiling snake, but, as it were, in opal and in emerald.

For awhile she gazed upon it, shuddering as one in doubt.

'Minded am I to let thee sleep, thou Horror,' she murmured. 'Twice have I looked on thee, and I would look no more. Nay, I will dare it, thou gift of the old wisdom, thou frozen fire, thou sleeping Sin, thou living Death of the Death of the ancient city, for thou alone hast wisdom.'

Thereon she unclasped the bosom of her robe and laid the gleaming toy, that seemed a snake of stone, upon her ivory breast, though she trembled at its icy touch, for it was more cold than death. With both her hands she clasped a pillar of the chamber, and so stood, and she was shaken with throes like the pangs of childbirth. Thus she endured awhile till that which was a-cold grew warm, watching its brightness that shone through her silken dress as the flame of a lamp shines through an alabaster vase. So she stood for an hour, then swiftly put off all her robes and ornaments of gold, and loosing the dark masses of her hair let it fall round her like a veil. Now she bent her head down to her breast, and breathed on that which lay upon her breast, for the Ancient Evil can live only in the breath of human kind. Thrice she breathed upon it, thrice she whispered, '*Awake! Awake! Awake!*'

And the first time that she breathed the Thing stirred and sparkled. The second time that she breathed it undid its shining folds and reared its head to hers. The third time that she breathed it slid from her bosom to the floor, then coiled itself about her feet and slowly grew as grows the magician's magic tree.

Greater it grew and greater yet, and as it grew it shone like a torch in a tomb, and wound itself about the body of Meriamun, wrapping her in its fiery folds till it reached her middle. Then it reared its head on high, and from its eyes there flowed a light like the light of flame, and lo! its face was the face of a fair woman—it was the face of Meriamun!

Now face looked on face, and eyes glared into eyes. Still as a white statue of the Gods stood Meriamun the Queen, and all about her form and in and out of her dark hair twined the flaming snake.

At length the Evil spoke—spoke with a human voice, with the voice of Meriamun, but in the dead speech of a dead people:

'Tell me my name,' it said.

'*Sin* is thy name,' answered Meriamun the Queen.

'Tell me whence I come,' it said again.

'From the evil that is in me,' answered Meriamun.

'Tell me whither I go.'

"Where I go there thou goest, for I have warmed thee in my breast and thou art twined about my heart.'

Then the Snake lifted up its human head and laughed horribly.

'Well art thou instructed,' it said. 'So I love thee as thou lovest me,' and it bent itself and kissed her on the lips. 'I am that Ancient Evil, that Life which endures out of the first death; I am that Death which abides in the living life. I am that which brought on thee the woe that is in division from the Heart's Desire, and the name thereof is *Hell*. From Life to Life thou hast found me at thy hand, now in this shape, now in that. I taught thee the magic which thou knowest; I showed thee how to win the Throne! Now, what wilt thou of me, Meriamun, my Mother, my Sister, and my Child? From Life to Life I have been with thee: ever thou mightest have put me from thee, ever thou fliest to the wisdom which I have, and ever from thee I draw my strength, for though without me thou mightest live, without thee I must die. Say now, what is it?—tell me, and I will name my price. No more will I ask than must be, for—ah!—I am glad to wake and live again; glad to grip thy soul within these shining folds, to be fair with thy beauty!—to be foul with thy sin!'

'Lay thy lips against my ear and thine ear against my

lips,' said Meriamun the Queen, 'and I will say what it is that I will of thee, thou Ancient Evil.'

So the human-headed Evil laid its ear against the lips of Meriamun, and Meriamun laid her lips against its ears, and they whispered each to each. There in the darkness they whispered, while the witch-light glittered down the gray snake's shining folds, beamed in its eyes, and shone through the Queen's dark hair and on her snowy breast.

At length the tale was told, and the Snake lifted its woman's head high in the air and again it laughed.

'He seeks the Good,' it said, 'and he shall find the Ill! He looks for Light, and in Darkness shall he wander! To Love he turns, in Lust he shall be lost! He would win the Golden Helen, whom he has sought through many a war, whom he has followed o'er many a sea, but first shall he find thee, Meriamun, and through thee Death! For he shall swear by the Snake who should have sworn by the Star. Far hath he wandered—further shall he wander yet, for thy sin shall be his sin! Darkness shall wear the face of Light—Evil shall shine like Good. I will give him to thee, Meriamun, but, hearken to my price. No more must I be laid cold in the gloom while thou walkest in the sunshine— nay, I must be twined about thy body. Fear not, fear not, I shall seem but a jewel in the eyes of men, a girdle fashioned cunningly for the body of a queen. But with thee henceforth I must ever go—and when thou diest, with thee must I die, and with thee pass where thou dost pass—with thee to sleep, with thee to awake again—and so, on and on, till in the end I win or thou winnest, or she wins who is our foe!'

'I give thee thy price,' said Meriamun the Queen.

'So once before thou didst give it,' answered the Evil; 'ay, far, far away, beneath a golden sky and in another clime. Happy wast thou then with him thou dost desire, but I twined myself about thy heart and of twain came three and all the sorrow that has been. So woman thou hast worked, so woman it is ordained. For thou art she in whom all woes are gathered, in whom all love is fulfilled. And I have dragged thy glory down, woman, and I have loosed thee from thy gentleness, and set it free upon the earth, and Beauty is she named. By beauty doth *she* work who is the Golden Helen, and for her beauty's sake, that all men strive to win, are wars and woes, are hopes and prayers, and longings without end. But Evil dost *thou* work who art divorced from Innocence, and evil shalt thou ever bring on him whom thou desirest. A riddle! A riddle! Read it who may—read it if thou canst, thou who are named Meriamun and Queen, but who art less than Queen and more. Who art thou? Who is she they named the Helen? Who is that Wanderer who seeks her from afar, and who, who am *I*? A riddle! a riddle! that thou mayest not read. Yet is the answer written on earth and sky and sea, and in the hearts of men.

'Now hearken! To-morrow night thou shalt take me and twine me about thy body, doing as I bid thee, and behold! for a while thy shape shall wear the shape of the Golden Helen, and thy face shall be as her face, and thine eyes as her eyes, and thy voice as her her voice. Then I leave the rest to thee, for as Helen's self thou shalt beguile the Wanderer, and once, if once only, be a wife to him whom thou desirest. Naught can I tell thee of the future, I who am but a counsellor, but hereafter it may be that woes will come, woes and wars and death. But what matter these when thou hast had thy desire, when he hath sinned, and hath sworn by the Snake who should have sworn by the Star, and when he is bound to thee by ties that may not be loosed? Choose, Meriamun, choose! Put my counsel from thee and to-morrow this man thou lovest shall be lost to thee, lost in the arms of Helen; and alone for many years shalt thou bear the burden of thy lonely love. Take it, and he shall at least be thine, let come what may come. Think on it and choose!'

Thus spake the Ancient Evil, tempting her who was named Meriamun, while she harkened to the tempting.

'I have chosen,' she said; 'I will wear the shape of Helen, and be a wife to him I love, and then let ruin fall. Sleep, thou Ancient Evil. Sleep, for no more may I endure thy face of fear that is my face, nor the light of those flaming eyes that are my eyes made mad.'

Again the Thing reared its human head and laughed

out in triumpth. Then slowly it unloosed its gleaming coils: slowly it slid to the earth and shrank and withered like a flaming scroll, till at length it seemed once more but a shining jewel of opal and amethyst.

The Wanderer, when he left the inner secret shrine, saw no more the guardians of the gates, nor heard the clash of swords unseen, for the Gods had given the beauty of Helen to Odysseus of Ithaca, as it was foretold.

Without the curtains the priests of the temple were gathered wondering—little could they understand how it came to pass that the hero who was called Eperitus had vanished through the curtains and had not been smitten down by the unseen swords. And when they saw him come forth glorious and unharmed they cried aloud with fear.

But he laughed and said, 'Fear not. Victory is to him whom the Gods appoint. I have done battle with the wardens of the shrine, and passed them, and methinks that they are gone. I have looked upon the Hathor also, and more than that seek ye not to know. Now give me food, for I am very weary.'

So they bowed before him, and leading him thence to their chamber of banquets gave him of their best, and watched him while he ate and drank and put from him the desire of food.

Then he rose and went from the temple, and again the priests bowed before him. Moreover, they gave him freedom of the temple, and keys whereby all the doors might be opened, though little, as they thought, had he any need of keys.

Now the Wanderer, walking gladly and light of heart, came to his own lodging in the courts of the Palace. At the door of the lodging stood Rei the Priest, who, when he saw him, ran to him and embraced him, so glad was he that the Wanderer had escaped alive.

'Little did I think to look upon thee again, Eperitus,' he said. 'Had it not been for that which the Queen—' and he bethought himself and stayed his speech.

'Nevertheless, here I am unhurt, of ghost or men,' the

Wanderer answered, laughing, as he passed into the lodging. 'But what of the Queen?'

'Naught, Eperitus, naught, save that she was grieved when she learned that thou hadst gone up to the Temple of the Hathor, there as she thought, to perish. Hearken, thou Eperitus, I know not if thou art God or man, but oaths are binding both on men and Gods, and thou didst swear an oath to Pharaoh—is it not so?'

'Ay, Rei. I swore an oath that I would guard the Queen well till Pharaoh came again.'

'Art thou minded to keep that oath, Eperitus?' asked Rei, looking on him strangely. 'Art thou minded to guard the fair fame of Pharaoh's Queen, that is more precious than her life? Methinks thou dost understand my meaning, Eperitus?'

'Perchance I understand,' answered the Wanderer. 'Know, Rei, that I am so minded.'

Then Rei spake again, darkly. 'Methinks some sickness hath smitten Meriamun the Queen, and she craves thee for her physician. Now things come about as they were foreshown in the portent of that vision whereof I spoke to thee. But if thou dost break thy oath to him whose salt thou eatest, then, Eperitus, God or man, thou art a dastard.'

'Have I not said that I have no mind so to break mine oath?' he answered, then sank his head upon his breast and communed with his crafty heart while Rei watched him. Presently he lifted up his head and spoke:

'Rei,' he said, 'I am minded to tell thee a strange story and a true, for this I see, that our will runs one way, and thou canst help me, and, in, helping me, thyself and Pharaoh to whom I swore an oath, and her whose honour thou holdest dear. But this I warn thee, Rei, that if thou dost betray me, not thine age, not thy office, nor the friendship thou hast shown me, shall save thee.'

'Speak on, Odysseus, Laertes' son, Odysseus of Ithaca,' said Rei; 'may my life be forfeit if I betray thy counsel, if it harm not those I serve.'

Now the Wanderer started to his feet, crying:

'How knowest thou that name?'

'I know it,' said Rei, 'and I tell thee that I know it, thou most crafty of men, to show this, that with me thy guile will not avail thee.' For he would not tell him that he had it from the lips of the Queen.

'Thou has heard a name that has been in the mouths of many,' said the Wanderer; 'perchance it is mine, perchance it is the name of another. It matters not. Now know this: I fear this Queen of thine. Hither I came to seek a woman, but the Queen I came not to seek. Yet I have not come in vain, for yonder, Rei, yonder, in the Temple of the Hathor, I found her on whose quest I came, and who awaited me there well guarded till I should come to take her. On the morrow night I go forth to the temple, and there, by the gates of the temple, I shall find her whom all men desire, but who loves me alone among men, for so it has been fated of the Gods. Thence I bring her hither that here we may be wed. Now this is my mind: if thou wilt aid me with a ship and men, that at the first light of dawn we should flee this land of thine, and that thou shouldst keep my going secret for awhile till I have gained the sea. True it is that I swore to guard the Queen till Pharaoh come again; but as thou knowest, things are so that I can best guard her by my flight, and if Pharaoh thinks ill of me—so it must be. Moreover I ask thee to meet me by the pylon of the Temple of Hathor to-morrow at one hour before midnight. There will we talk with her who is called the Hathor, and prepare our flight, and thence thou shalt go to that ship which thou hast made ready.'

Now Rei thought awhile and answered:

'Somewhat I fear to look upon this Goddess, yet I will dare it. Tell me, then, how shall I know her at the temple's gate?'

'Thou shalt know her, Rei, by the red star which burns upon her breast. But fear not, for I will be there. Say, wilt thou make the ship ready?'

'The ship shall be ready, Eperitus, and though I love thee well, I say this, that I would it rode the waves which roll around the shores of Khem and thou wert in it, and with thee she who is called the Hathor, that Goddess whom thou desirest.'

10. THE OATH OF THE WANDERER

That night the Wanderer saw not Meriamun, but on the morrow she sent a messenger to him, bidding him to her feast that night. He had little heart to go, but a Queen's courtesy is a command, and he went at sundown. Rei also went to the feast, and as he went, meeting the Wanderer in the ante-chamber, he whispered to him that all things were made ready, that a good ship awaited him in the harbor, the very ship that he had captured from the Sidonians, and that he, Rei, would be with him by the pylon gate of the temple one hour before midnight.

Presently, as he whispered, the doors were flung wide and Meriamun the Queen passed in, followed by eunuchs and waiting-women. She was royally arrayed, her face was pale and cold, but her great eyes glowed in it. Low the Wanderer bowed before her. She bent her head in answer, then gave him her hand, and he led her to the feast. They sat there side by side, but the Queen spoke little, and that little of Pharaoh and the host of the Apura, from whom no tidings came.

When at length the feast was done, Meriamun bade the Wanderer to her private chamber, and thither he went for awhile, though sorely against his will. But Rei came not in with them, and thus he was left alone with the Queen, for she dismissed the waiting ladies.

When they had gone there was silence for a space, but

ever the Wanderer felt the eyes of Meriamun watching him as though they would read his heart.

'I am weary,' she said, at length. 'Tell me of thy wanderings, Odysseus of Ithaca—nay, tell me of the seige of Ilios and of the sinful Helen, who brought all these woes about. Ay, and tell me how thou didst creep from the leaguer of the Achæans, and, wrapped in a beggar's weeds, seek speech of this evil Helen, now justly slain of the angry Gods.'

'Justly slain is she indeed,' answered the crafty Wanderer. 'An ill thing is it, truly, that the lives of so many heroes should be lost because of the beauty of a faithless woman. I had it in my own heart to slay her when I spoke with her in Troy town, but the Gods held my hand.'

'Was it so, indeed?' said the Queen, smiling darkly. 'Doubtless if yet she lived, and thou sawest her, thou wouldst slay her. Is it not so, Odysseus?'

'She lives no more, O Queen!' he answered.

'Nay, she lives no more, Odysseus. Now tell me; yesterday thou wentest up to the Temple of the Hathor; tell me what thou didst see in the temple.

'I saw a fair woman, or, perchance, an immortal Goddess, stand upon the pylon brow, and as she stood and sang those who looked were bereft of reason. And thereafter some tried to pass the ghosts who guarded the woman, and were slain of invisible swords. It was a strange sight to see.'

'A strange sight, truly. But thou didst not lose thy craft, Odysseus, nor try to break through the ghosts?'

'Nay, Meriamun. In my youth I have looked upon the beauty of Argive Helen, who was fairer than she who stood upon the pylon tower. None who have looked upon the Helen would seek to win the Hathor.'

'But, perchance, those who had looked upon the Hathor may seek to win the Helen,' she answered slowly, and he knew not what to say, for he felt the power of her magic on him.

So for awhile they spoke, and Meriamun, knowing all, wondered much at the guile of the Wanderer, but she showed no wonder in her face. At length he rose and, bowing before her, said that he must visit the guard that watched the Palace gates. She looked upon him strangely and bade him go. Then he went, and right glad he was thus to be free of her.

But when the curtains had swung behind him, Meriamun the Queen sprang to her feet, and a dreadful light of daring burned in her eyes. She clapped her hands, and bade those who came to her to seek their rest, as she would also, for she was weary and needed none to wait upon her. So the women went, leaving her alone, and she passed into her sleeping chamber,

'Now must the bride deck herself for the bridal,' she said, and straightway, pausing not, drew forth the Ancient Evil from its hiding-place and warmed it on her breast, breathing the breath of life into its nostrils. Now, as before, it grew and wound itself about her, and whispered in her ear, bidding her clothe herself in bridal white and clasp the Evil around her; then think upon the beauty she had seen gather on the face of dead Hataska in the Temple of Osiris, and on the face of the Bai, and the face of the Ka. She did its command, fearing nothing, for her heart was alight with love, and torn with jealous hate, and little did she reck of the sorrows which her sin should bring forth. So she bathed herself in perfumes, shook out her shining hair, and clad herself in white attire. Then she looked upon her beauty in the mirror of silver, and cried in the bitterness of her heart to the Evil that lay beside her like a snake alseep.

'Ah, am I not fair enow to win him whom I love? Say, thou Evil, must I indeed steal the beauty of another to win him whom I love?'

'This must thou do,' said the Evil, 'or lose him in Helen's arms. For thou art fair, yet is she Beauty's self, and her gentleness he loves, and not thy pride. Choose, choose swiftly, for presently the Wanderer goes forth to win the Golden Helen.'

Then she doubted no more, but lifting the shining Evil, held it to her. With a dreadful laugh it twined itself about her, and lo! it shrank to the shape of a girdling, double-headed snake of gold, with eyes of ruby flame. And as it shrank Meriamun the Queen thought on the beauty she had seen upon the face of dead Hataska, on the face of the Bai, and the face of the Ka, and all the while she watched her beauty in the mirror. And as she watched, behold, her face grew as the face of death, ashen and hollow, then slowly burned into life again—but all her loveliness was changed. Changed were her dark locks to locks of gold, changed were her deep eyes to eyes of blue, changed was the glory of her pride to the sweetness of the Helen's smile. Fairest among women had been her form, now it was fairer yet, and now—now she was Beauty's self, and like to swoon at the dream of her own loveliness.

'So, ah, so must the Hathor seem,' she said, and lo! her voice rang strangely in her ears. For the voice, too, was changed, it was more soft than the whispering of wind-stirred reeds; it was more sweet than the murmuring of bees at noon.

Now she must go forth, and fearful at her own loveliness, and heavy with her sin, yet glad with a strange joy, she passes from her chamber and glides like a starbeam through the still halls of her Palace. The white light of the moon creeps into them and falls upon the faces of the dreadful Gods, on the awful smile of sphinxes, and the pictures of her forefathers, kings and queens who long were dead. And as she goes she seems to hear them whisper each to each of the dreadful sin that she has sinned, and of the sorrow that shall be. But she does not heed, and never stays her foot. For her heart is alight as with a flame, and she will win the Wanderer to her arms—the Wanderer sought through many lives, found after many deaths.

Now the Wanderer is in his chamber, waiting for the hour to set forth to find the Golden Helen. His heart is alight, and strange dreams of the past go before his eyes, and strange visions of long love to be. His heart burns like a lamp in the blackness, and by that light he sees all the days of his life that have been, and all the wars he has won, and all the seas that he has sailed. And now he knows that these things are dreams indeed, illusions of the sense, for there is but one thing true in the life of men, and that is Love; there is but one thing perfect, the beauty which is Love's robe; there is but one thing which all men seek and are born to find at last, the heart of the Golden Helen, the World's Desire, that is peace and joy and rest.

He binds his armour on him, for foes may lurk in darkness, and takes the Bow of Eurytus, and the gray bolts of death; for perchance the fight is not yet done, and he must cleave his way to joy. Then he combs his locks and sets the golden helm upon them, and, praying to the Gods who hear not, he passes from his chamber.

Now the chamber opened into a great hall of pillars. As was his custom when he went alone by night, the Wanderer glanced warily down the dusky hall, but he might see little because of the shadows. Nevertheless, the moonlight poured into the centre of the hall from the clerestories in the roof, and lay there shining white as water beneath black banks of reeds. Again the Wanderer glanced with keen, quick eyes, for there was a sense in his heart that he was no more alone in the hall, though whether it were man or ghost, or, perchance, one of the immortal Gods who looked on him, he might not tell. Now it seemed to him that he saw a shape of white moving far away in the shadow. Then he grasped the black bow and laid hand upon his quiver so that the shafts rattled.

Now it would seem that the shape in the shadow heard the rattling of the shafts, or perchance saw the moonlight gleam upon the Wanderer's golden harness—at the least, it drew near till it came to the edge of the pool of light. There it paused as a bather pauses ere she steps into the fountain. The Wanderer paused also, wondering what the shape might be. Half was he minded to try it with an arrow from the bow, but he held his hand and watched.

And as he watched, the white shape glided into the space of moonlight, and he saw that it was the form of a woman draped in white, and that about her shone a gleaming girdle, and in the girdle gems which sparkled like the eyes of a snake. Tall was the shape and lovely as a statue of Aphrodite; but who or what it was he might not tell, for the head was bent and the face hidden.

Awhile the shape stood thus, and as it stood, the Wanderer passed towards it, marvelling much, till he also stood in the pool of moonlight that shimmered on his golden mail. Then suddenly the shape lifted its face so that the light fell full on it, and stretched out its arms towards him, and lo! the face was the face of Argive Helen—of her whom he went forth to seek. He looked upon its beauty, he looked upon the eyes of blue, upon the golden hair, upon the shining arms; then slowly, very slowly, and in silence—for he could find no words—the Wanderer drew near.

She did not move nor speak. So still she stood that scarce she seemed to breathe. Only the shining eyes of her snake-girdle glittered like living things. Again he stopped fearfully, for he held that this was surely a mocking ghost which stood before him, but still she neither moved nor spoke.

Then at length he found his tongue and spoke:

'Lady,' he whispered, 'is it indeed thou, is it Argive Helen whom I look upon, or is it, perchance, a ghost sent by Queen Persephone from the House of Hades to make mock of me?'

Now the voice of Helen answered him in sweet tones and low:

'Did I not tell thee, Odysseus of Ithaca, did I not tell thee, yesterday in the halls of Hathor, after thou hadst overcome the ghosts, that to-night we should be wed? Wherefore, then, dost thou deem me of the number of the bodiless?'

The Wanderer hearkened. The voice was the voice of Helen, the eyes were the eyes of Helen, and yet his heart feared guile.

'So did Argive Helen tell me of a truth, Lady, but this she said, that I should find her by the pylon of the temple, and lead her thence to be my bride. Thither I go but now to seek her. But if thou art Helen, how comest thou to these Palace halls? And where, Lady, is that Red Star which should gleam upon thy breast, that Star which weeps out the blood of men?'

'No more doth the red dew fall from the Star that was set upon my breast, Odysseus, for now that thou hast won me men die no more for my beauty's sake. Gone is the Star of War; and see, Wisdom rings me round, the symbol of the Deathless Snake that signifies love eternal. Thou dost ask how I came hither, I, who am immortal and a daughter of the Gods? Seek not to know, Odysseus, for where Fate puts it in my mind to be, there do the Gods bear me. Wouldst thou, then, that I leave thee, Odysseus?'

'Last of all things do I desire this,' he answered, for now his wisdom went a-wandering; now he forgot the word of Aphrodite, warning him that the Helen might be known by one thing only, the Red Star on her breast, whence falls the blood of men; and he no more doubted but that she was the Golden Helen.

Then she who wore the Helens' shape stretched out her arms and smiled so sweetly that the Wanderer knew nothing any more, save that she drew him to her.

Slowly she glided before him, ever smiling, and where she went he followed, as men follow beauty in a dream. She led him through halls and corridors, past the sculptured statues of the Gods, past man-headed sphinxes, and pictures of long dead kings.

And as she goes, once more it seems to her that she hears them whisper each to each of the horror of her sin and the sorrow that shall be. But naught she heeds who ever leads him on, and naught he hears who ever follows after, till at length, though he knows it not, they stand in the bed-chamber of the Queen, and by Pharaoh's golden bed.

Then once more she speaks:

'Odysseus of Ithaca, whom I have loved from the beginning, and whom I shall love till all deaths are done, before thee stands that Loveliness which the Gods predestined to thy arms. Now take thou thy Bride; but first lay thy hand upon this golden Snake, that rings me round, the new bridal gift of the Gods, and swear thy marriage oath, which may not be broken. Swear thus, Odysseus: "I love thee, Woman or Immortal, and thee alone, and by whatever name thou art called, and in whatever shape thou goest, to thee I will cleave, and to thee alone, till the day of the passing of Time. I will forgive thy sins, I will soothe thy sorrows, I will suffer none to come betwixt thee and me. This I swear to thee, Woman or Immortal, who dost stand before me. I swear it to thee, Woman, for now and for ever, for here and hereafter, in whatever shape thou goest on the earth, by whatever name thou art known among men."

'Swear thou thus, Odysseus of Ithaca, Laertes's son, or leave me and go thy ways!'

'Great is the oath,' quoth the Wanderer; for though now he feared no guile, yet his crafty heart liked it ill.

'Choose, and choose swiftly,' she answered. 'Swear the oath, or leave me and never see me more!'

'Leave thee I will not, and cannot if I would,' he said. 'Lady, I swear!' And he laid his hand upon the Snake that ringed her round, and swore the dreadful oath. Yea, he forgot the words of the Goddess, and the words of Helen, and he swore by the Snake who should have sworn by the Star. By the immortal Gods he swore it, by the Symbol of the Snake, and by the Beauty of his Bride. And as he swore the eyes of the Serpent sparkled, and the eyes of her who wore the beauty of Helen shone, and faintly the black bow of Eurytus thrilled, foreboding Death and War.

But little the Wanderer thought on guile or War or Death, for the kiss of her whom he deemed the Golden Helen was on his lips, and he went up into the golden bed of Meriamun.

11. THE WAKING OF THE WANDERER

Now Rei the Priest, as had been appointed, went to the pylon gate of the Temple of Hathor. Awhile he stood looking for the Wanderer, but though the hour had come, the Wanderer came not. Then the Priest went to the plyon and stood in the shadow of the gate. As he stood there a wicket in the gate opened, and there passed out a veiled figure of a woman upon whose breast burned a red jewel that shone in the night like a star. The woman waited awhile, looking down the moonlit road between the black rows of sphinxes, but the road lay white and empty, and she turned and hid herself in the shadow of the pylon, where Rei could see nothing of her except the red star that gleamed upon her breast.

Now a great fear came upon the old man, for he knew that he looked upon the strange and deadly Hathor. Perchance he too would perish like the rest who had looked on her to their ruin. He thought of flight, but he did not dare to fly. Then he too stared down the road seeking for the Wanderer, but no shadow crossed the moonlight. Thus things went for awhile, and still the Hathor stood silently in the shadow, and still the blood-red star shone upon her breast. And so it came to pass that the World's Desire must wait at the tryst like some foresaken village maid.

While Rei the Priest crouched thus against the pylon wall, praying for the coming of him who came not, suddenly a voice spoke to him in tones sweeter than a lute.

'Who art thou that hidest in the shadow?' said the voice.

He knew that it was the Hathor who spoke, and so afraid was he that he could not answer.

Then the voice spoke again:

'Oh, thou most crafty of men, why doth it please thee to come hither to seek me in the guise of an aged priest. Once, Odysseus, I saw thee in a beggar's weeds, and knew thee in the midst of thy foes. Shall I not know thee again in peace beneath thy folded garb and thy robes of white?'

Rei heard and knew that he could hide himself no longer. Therefore he came forward trembling, and knelt before her, saying:

'Oh, mighty Queen, I am not that man whom thou didst name, nor am I hid in any wrappings of disguise. Nay, I do avow myself to be named Rei the Chief Architect of Pharaoh, the Commander of the Legion of Amen, the chief of the Treasury of Amen, and a man of repute in this land of Khem. Now, if indeed thou art the Goddess of this temple, as I judge by that red jewel which burns upon thy breast, I pray thee be merciful to thy servant and smite me not with thy wrath, for not by my own will am I here, but by the command of that hero whom thou hast named, and for whose coming I await. Be merciful therefore, and hold thy hand.'

'Fear not thou, Rei,' said the sweet voice. 'Little am I minded to harm thee, or any man for though many men have gone down the path of darkness because of me, who am a doom to men, not by my will has it been, but by the will of the immortal Gods, who use me to their ends. Rise thou, Rei, and tell me why thou art come hither, and where is he whom I have named?'

Then Rei rose, and looking up saw the light of the Helen's eyes shining on him through her veil. But there was no anger in them, they shone mildly as stars in an evening sky, and his heart was comforted.

'I know not where the Wanderer is, O thou Immortal,' he said. 'This, I know only, that he bade me meet him here at one hour before midnight, and so I came.'

'Perchance he too will come anon,' said the sweet voice;

'but why did he, whom thou namest the Wanderer, bid thee meet him here?'

'For this reason, O Hathor. He told me that this night he should be wed to thee, and was minded thereafter to fly from Khem with thee. Therefore he bade me come, who am a friend to him, to talk with thee and him as to how thy flight should go, and yet he comes not.'

Now as Rei spake, he turned his face upward, and the Golden Helen looked upon it.

'Hearken, Rei,' she said; 'but yesterday, after I had stood upon the pylon tower as the Gods decreed, and sang to those who were ripe to die, I went to my shrine and wove my web while the doomed men fell beneath the swords of them who were set to guard my beauty, but who now are gone. And as I wove, one passed the Ghosts and rent the web and stood before me. It was he whom I await to-night, and after awhile I knew him for Odysseus of Ithaca, Odysseus, Laertes' son. But as I looked on him and spake with him, behold, I saw a spirit watching us, though he might not see it, a spirit whose face I knew not, for no such man have I known in my life days. Know then, Rei, that the face of the spirit was *thy* face, and its robes *thy* robes.'

Then once more Rei trembled in his fear.

'Now, Rei, I bid thee tell me, and speak the truth, lest evil come on thee, not at my hands indeed, for I would harm none, but at the hands of those Immortals who are akin to me. What did thy spirit yonder, in my sacred shrine? How didst thou dare to enter and look upon my beauty and hearken to my words?'

'Oh, great Queen,' said Rei, 'I will tell thee the truth, and I pray thee let not the wrath of the Gods fall upon me. Not of my own will did my spirit enter into thy Holy Place, nor do I know aught of what it saw therein, seeing that no memory of it remains in me. Nay, it was sent of her whom I serve, who is the mistress of all magic, and to her it made report, but what it said I know not.'

'And whom dost thou serve, Rei? And why did she send thy spirit forth to spy on me?'

'I serve Meriamun the Queen, and she sent my spirit

forth to learn what befell the Wanderer when he went up against the Ghosts.'

'And yet he said naught to me of this Meriamun. Say, Rei, is she fair?'

'Of all women who live upon the earth she is the very fairest.'

'Of *all*, sayest thou, Rei? Look now, and say if Merimun, whom thou dost serve, is fairer than Argive Helen, whom thou dost name the Hathor?' and she lifted her veil so that he saw the face that was beneath.

Now when he heard that name, and looked upon the glory of her who is Beauty's self, Rei shrank back till he went nigh to falling on the earth.

'Nay,' he said, covering his eyes with his hand; 'nay, thou art fairer than she.'

'Then tell me,' she said, letting fall her veil again, 'and for thine own sake tell me true, why would Meriamun the Queen, whom thou servest, know the fate of him who came up against the Ghosts?'

'Wouldst thou know, Daughter of Amen?' answered Rei; 'then I will tell thee, for through thee alone she whom I serve and love can be saved from shame. Meriamun doth also love the man whom thou wouldst wed.'

Now when the Golden Helen heard these words, she pressed her hand against her bosom.

'So I feared,' she said, 'even so. She loves him, and he comes not. Ah! if it be so! Now, Rei, I am tempted to pay this Queen of thine in her own craft, and send thy spirit forth to spy on her. Nay, that I will not do, for never shall Helen work by shameful guile of magic. Nay—but we will hence, Rei, we will to the Palace where my rival dwells, there to learn the truth. Fear not, I will bring no ill on thee, nor on her whom thou servest. Lead me to the Palace, Rei. Lead me swiftly.'

Now the Wanderer slept in the arms of Meriamun, who wore the shape of Argive Helen. His golden harness was piled by the golden bed, and by the bed stood the black bow of Eurytus. The night drew on towards the dawning, when of a sudden the Bow awoke and sung, and thus it sang:

Wake! wake! though the arms of thy Love are about thee,
        yet dearer by far
    Than her kiss is the sound of the fight;
And more sweet than her voice is the cry of the trumpet, and
        goodlier far
    Than her arms is the battle's delight:
And what eyes are so bright as the sheen of the bronze when
        the sword is aloft,
    What breast is so fair as the shield?
Or what garland of roses is dear as the helm, and what sleep
        is so soft
    As the sleep of slain men on the field?

Lo! the Snake that was twined about the form of her who wore the shape of Helen heard the magic song. It awoke, it arose. It twined itself about the body of the Wanderer and the body of her who wore the shape of Helen, knitting them together in the bond of sin. It grew, and lifting its woman's head on high, it sang in answer. And thus it sang of doom:

Sleep! be at rest for an hour; as in death men believe they
        shall rest,
    But they wake! And thou too shalt awake!
In the dark of the grave do they stir; but about them, on
        arms and on breast,
    Are the toils and the coils of the Snake:
By the tree where the first lovers lay, did I watch as I watch
        where he lies,
    Love laid on the bosom of Lust!

Then the great Bow answered the Snake, and it sang:

Of the tree where the first lovers sinned was I shapen; I bid
        thee arise,
    Thou Slayer that soon shalt be dust.

And the Snake sang reply:—

Be thou silent, my Daughter of Death, be thou silent nor
     wake him from sleep,
  With the song and the sound of thy breath.

The Bow heard the song of the Snake. The Death heard
the song of the Sin, and again its thin music thrilled upon
the air. For thus it sang:

Be thou silent, my Mother of Sin, for this watch it is given me
     to keep
  O'er the sleep of the dealer of Death!

Then the Snake sang:

Hush, hush, thou art young, and thou camest to birth when
     the making was done
  Of the world: I am older therein!

And the Bow answered:

But without me thy strength were as weakness, the prize of
     thy strength were unwon.
  I am *Death,* and thy Daughter, O Sin!

Now the song of the Snake and the song of the Bow
sunk through the depths of sleep till they reached the
Wanderer's ears. He sighed, he stretched out his mighty
arms, he opened his eyes, and lo! they looked upon the
eyes that bent above him, eyes of flame that lit the face of
a woman—the face of Meriamun that wavered on a serpent's neck and suddenly was gone. He cried aloud with
fear, and sprang from the couch. The faint light of the
dawning crept through the casements and fell upon the
bed. The faint light of the dawning fell upon the golden
bed of Pharaoh's Queen, it gleamed upon the golden armour that was piled by the bed, and on the polished surface of the great black bow. It shone upon the face of her
who lay in the bed.

Then he remembered. Surely he had slept with the
Golden Helen, who was his bride, and surely he had

dreamed an evil dream, a dream of a snake that wore the
face of Pharaoh's Queen. Yea, there lay the Golden Helen,
won at last—the Golden Helen now made a wife to him.
Now he mocked his own fears, and now he bent to wake
her with a kiss. Faintly the new-born light crept and
gathered on her face; ah! how beautiful she was in sleep.
Nay, what was this? Whose face was beneath his own?
Not so had Helen looked in the shrine of her temple,
when he tore the web. Not so had Helen seemed yonder in
the pillared hall when she stood in the moonlight space—
not so had she seemed when he sware the great oath to
love her, and her alone. Whose beauty was it then that
now he saw? By the Immortal Gods, it was the beauty of
Meriamun; it was the glory of Pharaoh's Queen!

He stared upon her lovely sleeping face, while terror
shook his soul. How could this be? What then had he
done?

Then light broke upon him. He looked around the
chamber—there on the walls were graven images of the
Gods of Khem, there above the bed the names of Meneptah and Meriamun were written side by side in the sacred
signs of Khem. Not with the Golden Helen had he slept,
but with the wife of Pharaoh! To her he had sworn the
oath, and she had worn the Helen's shape—and now the
spell was broken.

He stood amazed, and as he stood, again the great bow
thrilled, warning him of Death to come. Then his strength
came back to him, and he seized his armour and girt it
about him piece by piece till he lifted the golden helm. It
slipped from his hand; with a crash it fell upon the marble floor. With a crash it fell, and she who slept in the
bed awoke with a cry, and sprang from the bed, her dark
hair streaming down, her nightgear held to her by the
golden snake with gemmy eyes that she must wear. But
he caught his sword in his hand, and threw down the
ivory sheath.

BOOK III

1. THE VENGEANCE OF KURRI

The Wanderer and Pharaoh's Queen stood face to face in the twilight of the chamber. They stood in silence, while bitter anger and burning shame poured into his heart and shone from his eyes. But the face of Meriamun was cold as the face of the dead, and on it was a smile such as the carven sphinxes wear. Only her breast heaved tumultuously as though in triumph, and her limbs quivered like a shaken reed. At length she spoke.

'Why lookest thou so strangely on me, my Lord and Love; and why hast thou girded thy harness on thy back? Scarcely doth glorious Ra creep from the breast of Nout, and wouldst thou leave thy bridal bed, Odysseus?'

Still he spoke no word, but looked on her with burning eyes. Then she stretched out her arms and came towards him lover-like. And now he found his tongue again.

'Get thee from me!' he said, in a voice low and terrible to hear; 'get thee from me. Dare not to touch me, thou, who art a harlot and a witch, lest I forget my manhood and strike thee dead before me.'

'That thou canst not do, Odysseus,' she answered soft, 'for whatever else I be I am thy wife, and thou art bound to me for ever. What was the oath which thou didst swear not five short hours ago?'

'I swore an oath indeed, but not to thee, Meriamun. I swore an oath to Argive Helen, whom I love, and I wake to find thee sleeping at my side, thee whom I hate.'

167

'Nay,' she said, 'to me thou didst swear the oath, Odysseus, for thou, of men the most guileful, hast at length been overmastered in guile. To me, "Woman or Immortal,' thou didst swear "for now and for ever, for here and hereafter, *in whatever shape thou goest on the earth, by whatever name thou art known among men."* Oh, be not wroth my lord, but hearken. What matters the shape in which thou seest me? At least am I not fair? And what is beauty but a casket that hides the gem within? 'Tis my love which thou hast won, my love that is immortal, and not the flesh that perishes. For I have loved thee, ay, and thou hast loved me from of old and in other lives than this, and I tell thee that we shall love again and yet again when thou art no more Odysseus of Ithaca, and when I am no more Meriamun, a Queen of Khem, but while we walk in other forms upon the world and are named by other names. I am thy doom, thou Wanderer, and wherever thou dost wander through the fields of Life and Death I shall be at thy side. For I am She of whom thou art, and thou art He of whom I am, and though the Gods have severed us, yet must we float together down the river of our lives till we find that sea of which the Spirit knows. Therefore put me not from thee and raise not my wrath against thee, for if I used my magic to bring thee to my arms, yet they are thy home.' And once more she came towards him.

Now the Wanderer drew an arrow from his quiver, and set the notch against his breast and the keen barb towards the breast of Meriamun.

'Draw on,' he said. 'Thus will I take thee to my arms again. Hearken, Meriamun the witch,—Meriamun the harlot: Pharaoh's wife and Queen of Khem. To thee I swore an oath indeed, and perchance because I suffered thy guile to overcome my wisdom, because I swore upon That which circles thee about, and not by the Red Star which gleams upon the Helen's breast, it may be that I shall lose her whom I love. So indeed the Queen of Heaven told me, yonder in sea-girt Ithaca, though to my sorrow I forgot her words. But if I lost her or if I win, know this, that I love her and her only, and I hate thee like the gates of hell. For thou hast tricked me with thy magic, thou hast stolen the shape of Beauty's self and dared to wear it, thou hast drawn a dreadful oath from me, and I have taken thee to wife. And more, thou art Queen of Khem, thou art Pharaoh's wife, whom I swore to guard; but thou hast brought the last shame upon me, for now I am a man dishonoured, and I have sinned against the hospitable hearth, and the God of guests and hosts. And therefore I will do this. I will call together the guard of which I am chief, and tell them all thy shame, ay, and all my sorrow. I will shout it in the streets, I will publish it from the temple tops, and when Pharaoh comes again I will call it into his ear, till he and all who live in Khem know thee for what thou art, and see thee in thy naked shame.'

She hearkened, and her face grew terrible to see. A moment she stood as though in thought, one hand pressed to her brow and one upon her breast. Then she spoke.

'Is that thy last word, Wanderer?'

'It is my last word, Queen,' he answered, and turned to go.

Then with that hand that rested on her breast she rent her night robes and tore her perfumed hair. Past him she rushed towards the door, and as she ran sent scream on scream echoing up the painted walls.

The curtains shook, the doors were burst asunder, and through them poured guards, eunuchs, and waiting-women.

'Help,' she cried, pointing to the Wanderer. 'Help, help! oh, save mine honour from this evil man, this foreign thief whom Pharaoh set to guard me, and who guards me thus. This coward who dared to creep upon me—the Queen of Khem—even as I slept in Pharaoh's bed!' and she cast herself upon the floor and threw her hair about her, and lay there groaning and weeping as though in the last agony of shame.

Now then the guards saw how the thing was, a great cry of rage and shame went up from them, and they rushed upon the Wanderer like wolves upon a stag at bay. But he leapt backwards to the side of the bed, and even as he leapt he set the arrow in his hand upon the string of the great black bow. Then he drew it to his ear. The bow-string sang, the arrow rushed forth, and he who stood before it got his death. Again the bow-string sang, again the arrow rushed, and lo! another man was sped. A third time he drew the bow and the soul of a third went down the ways of hell. Now they rolled back from him as the waters roll from a rock, for none dared face the shafts of death. They shot at him with spears and arrows from behind the shelter of the pillars but none of these might harm him, for some fell from his mail and some he caught upon his buckler.

Now among those who had run thither at the sound of the cries of Meriamun was that same Kurri, the miserable captain of the Sidonians, whose life the Wanderer had spared, and whom he had given to the Queen to be her jeweller. And when Kurri saw the Wander's plight, he thought in his greedy heart of those treasures that he had lost, and how he who had been a captain and a rich merchant of Sidon was not nothing but a slave.

Then a great desire came upon him to work the Wanderer ill, if so he might. Now all round the edge of the chamber were shadows, for the light was yet faint, and Kurri crept into the shadows, carrying a long spear in his hand, and that spear was hafted into the bronze point which had stood in the Wanderer's helm. Little did the Wanderer glance his way, for he watched the lances and arrows that flew towards him from the portal, so the end of it was that the Sidonian passed round the chamber unseen and climbed into the golden bed of Pharaoh on the further side of the bed. Now the Wanderer stood with his back to the bed and a spear's length from it, and in the silken hangings were fixed spears and arrows. Kurri's first thought was to stab him in the back, but this he did not; first, because he feared lest he should fail to pierce the golden harness and the Wanderer should turn and slay him; and again because he hoped that the Wanderer would be put to death by torment, and he was fain to have a hand in it, for after the fashion of the Sidonians he was skilled in the tormenting of men. Therefore he waited till presently the Wanderer let fall his buckler and drew the bow. But ere the arrow reached his ear Kurri had stretched out his spear from between the hangings and touched the string with the keen bronze, so that it burst asunder and the gray shaft fell upon the marble floor. Then, as the Wanderer cast down the bow and turned with a cry to spring on him who had cut the cord, for his eye had caught the sheen of the outstretched spear, Kurri lifted the covering of purple web which lay upon the bed and deftly cast it over the hero's head so that he was immeshed. Thereon the soldiers and the eunuchs took heart, seeing what had been done, and ere ever the Wanderer could clear himself from the covering and draw his sword, they rushed upon him. Cumbered as he was, they might not easily overcome him, but in the end they bore him down and held him fast, so that he could not stir so much as a finger. Then one cried aloud to Meriamun:

'The Lion is trapped, O Queen! Say, shall we slay him?'

But Meriamun, who had watched the fray through cover of her hands, shuddered and made answer:

'Nay, but lock his tongue with a gag, strip his armour from him, and bind him with fetters of bronze, and make him fast to the dungeon walls with great chains of bronze. There shall he bide till Pharaoh come again; for against Pharaoh's honour he hath sinned and shamefully broken that oath he swore to him, and therefore shall Pharaoh make him die in such fashion as seems good to him.'

Now when Kurri heard these words, and saw the Wanderer's sorry plight, he bent over him and said:

'It was I, Kurri the Sidonian, who cut the cord of thy great bow, Eperitus; with the spear-point that thou gavest back to me I cut it, I, whose folk thou didst slay and madest me a slave. And I will crave this boon of Pharaoh, that mine shall be the hand to torment thee night and day till at last thou diest, cursing the day that thou wast born.'

The Wanderer looked upon him and answered: 'There thou liest, thou Sidonian dog, for this is written in thy face, that thou thyself shalt die within an hour and that strangely.'

Then Kurri shrank back scowling. But no more words might Odysseus speak, for at once they forced his jaws apart and gagged him with a gag of iron; and thereafter, stripping his harness from him, they bound him with fetters as the Queen had commanded.

Now while they dealt thus with the Wanderer, Meriamun passed into another chamber and swiftly threw robes upon her to hide her disarray, clasping them round her with the golden girdle which now she must always wear. But her long hair she left unbound, nor did she wash the stain of tears from her face, for she was minded to seem shamed and woe-begone in the eyes of all men till Pharaoh came again.

Rei and the Golden Helen passed through the streets of the city till they came to the Palace gates. And here they must wait till the dawn, for Rei, thinking to come thither with the Wanderer, who was Captain of the Guard, had not learned the word of entry.

'Easy would it be for me to win my way through those great gates,' said the Helen to Rei at her side, 'but it is my counsel that we wait awhile. Perchance he whom we seek will come forth.'

So they entered the porch of the Temple of Osiris that looked towards the gates, and there they waited till the dawn gathered in the eastern sky. The Helen spoke no word, but Rei, watching her, knew that she was troubled at heart, though he might not see her face because of the veil she wore; for from time to time she sighed and the Red Star rose and fell upon her breast.

At length the first arrow of the dawn fell upon the temple porch and she spoke.

'Now let us enter,' she said; 'my heart forbodes evil indeed; but much of evil I have known, and where the Gods drive me there I must go.'

They come to the gates, and the man who watched them opened to the priest Rei and the veiled woman who went with him, though he marvelled at the beauty of the woman's shape.

'Where are thy fellow-guards?' Rei asked of the soldier.

'I know not,' he answered, 'but anon a great tumult arose in the Palace, and the Captain of the Gate went thither, leaving me only to guard the gate.'

'Hast thou seen the Lord Eperitus?' Rei asked again.

'Nay, I have not seen him since supper-time last night, nor has he visited the guard as is his wont.'

Rei passed on wondering, and with him went Helen. As they trod the Palace they saw folk flying towards the hall of banquets that is near the Queen's chambers. Some bore arms in their hands and some bore none, but all fled fast towards the hall of banquets, whence came a sound of shouting. Now they drew near the hall, and there at the further end, where the doors are that lead to the Queen's chambers, a great crowd was gathered.

'Hide thee, lady—hide thee,' said Rei to her who went with him, 'for methinks that death is afoot here. See, here hangs a curtain, stand thou behind it while I learn what this tumult means.'

She stepped behind the curtain that hung between the pillars as Rei bade her, for now Helen's gentle breast was full of fears, and she was as one dazed. Even as she stepped one came flying down the hall who was of the servants of Rei the Priest.

'Stay thou,' Rei cried to him, 'and tell me what happens yonder.'

'Ill deeds, Lord,' said the servant. 'Eperitus the Wanderer, whom Pharaoh made Captain of his Guard when he went forth to slay the rebel Apura—Eperitus hath laid hands on the Queen whom he was set to guard. But she fled from him, and her cries awoke the guard, and they fell upon him in Pharaoh's very chamber. Some he slew with shafts from the great black bow, but Kurri the Sidonian cut the string of the bow, and the Wanderer was borne down by many men. Now they have bound him and drag him to the dungeons, there to await judgment from the lips of Pharaoh. See, they bring him. I must begone on my errand to the keeper of the dungeons.'

The Golden Helen heard the shameful tale, and such sorrow took her that had she been mortal she had surely died. This then was the man whom she had chosen to love, this was he whom last night she should have wed. Once more the Gods had made a mock of her. So had it ever been, so should it ever be. Loveless she had lived all her life days, now she had learned to love once and for ever—and this was the fruit of it! She clasped the curtain lest she should sink to the earth, and hearing a sound looked forth. A multitude of men came down the hall. Before them walked ten soldiers bearing a litter on their shoulders. In the litter lay a man gagged and fettered with fetters of bronze so that he might not stir, and they bore him as men bear a stag from the chase or a wild bull to the sacrifice. It was the Wanderer's self, the Wanderer overcome at last, and he seemed so mighty even in his bonds, and his eyes shone with so fierce a light, that the crowd shrank from him as though in fear. Thus did Helen see her Love and Lord again as they bore him dishonoured to his dungeon cell. She saw, and a moan and a cry burst from her heart. A moan for her own woe and a cry for the shame and faithlessness of him whom she must love.

'Oh, how fallen art thou, Odysseus, who wast of men the very first,' she cried.

He heard it and knew the voice of her who cried, and he gazed around. The great veins swelled upon his neck and forehead, and he struggled so fiercely that he fell from the litter to the ground. But he might not rise because of the fetters, nor speak because of the gag, so they lifted him again and bore him thence.

And after him went all the multitude save Rei alone. For Rei was fallen in shame and grief because of the tale that he had heard and of the deed of darkness that the man he loved had done. For not yet did he remember and learn to doubt. So he stood hiding his eyes in his hand, and as he stood Helen came forth and touched him on the shoulder, saying:

'Lead me hence, old man. Lead me back to my temple. My Love is lost indeed, but there where I found it I will abide till the Gods make their will clear to me.'

He bowed, saying no word, and following Helen stepped into the centre of the hall. There he stopped, indeed, for down it came the Queen, her hair streaming, all her robes disordered, and her face stained with tears. She was alone save for Kurri the Sidonian, who followed her, and she walked wildly as one distraught who knows not where she goes or why. Helen saw her also.

'Who is this royal lady that draws near?' she asked of Rei.

'It is Meriamun the Queen; she whom the Wanderer hath brought to shame.'

'Stay then, I would speak with her.'

'Nay, nay,' cried Rei. 'She loves thee not, Lady, and will slay thee.'

'That cannot be,' Helen answered.

2. THE COMING OF PHARAOH

Presently, as she walked, Meriamun saw Rei the Priest and the veiled woman at his side, and she saw on the woman's breast a red jewel that burnt and glowed like a heart of fire. Then like fire burned the heart of Meriamun, for she knew that this was Argive Helen who stood before her, Helen whose shape she had stolen like a thief and with the mind of a thief.

'Say,' she cried to Rei, who bowed before her, 'say, who is this woman?'

Rei looked at the Queen with terrified eyes, and spake in a voice of warning.

'This is that Goddess who dwells in the Temple of Hathor,' he said. 'Let her pass in peace, O Queen.'

'In peace she shall pass indeed,' answered Meriamun. 'What saidest thou, old dotard? That Goddess! Nay, no Goddess have we here, but an evil-working witch, who hath brought woes unnumbered upon Khem. Because of her, men die month by month till the vaults of the Temple of Hathor are full of her slain. Because of her it was that curse upon curse fell on the land—the curse of water turned to blood, of hail and of terrible darkness, ay, and the curse of the death of the firstborn among whom my own son died. And thou hast dared, Rei, to bring this witch here to my Palace halls! By Amen if I had not loved thee always thy life should pay the price. And thou,' and she stretched her hand towards the Helen, 'thou hast dared to come. It is well, no more shalt thou bring evil upon Khem. Hearken, slave,' and she turned to Kurri the Sidonian; 'draw that knife of thine and plunge it to the hilt in the breast of yonder woman. So shalt thou win freedom and all thy goods shall be given thee again.'

Then for the first time Helen spake:

'I charge thee, Lady,' she said in slow soft tones, 'bid not thy servant do this deed, for though I have little will to bring evil upon men, yet I may not lightly be affronted.'

Now Kurri hung back doubtfully fingering his dagger.

'Draw, knave, draw!' cried Meriamun, 'and do my bidding, or presently thou shalt be slain with this same knife.'

When the Sidonian heard these words he cried aloud with fear, for he well knew that as the Queen said so it would be done to him. Instantly he drew the great knife and rushed upon the veiled woman. But as he came, Helen lifted her veil so that her eyes fell upon his eyes, and the brightness of their beauty was revealed to him; and when he saw her loveliness he stopped suddenly as one who is transfixed of a spear. Then madness came upon him, and with a cry he lifted the knife, and plunging it, not into her heart, but into his own, fell down dead.

This then was the miserable end of Kurri the Sidonian, slain by the sight of Beauty.

'Thou seest, Lady,' said Helen, turning from the dead Sidonian, 'no man may harm me.'

For a moment the Queen stood astonished, while Rei the Priest muttered prayers to the protecting Gods. Then she cried:

'Begone, thou living curse, begone! Wherefore art thou come here to work more woe in this house of woe and death?'

'Fear not,' answered the Helen, 'presently I will begone and trouble thee no more. Thou askest why I am come hither. I came to seek him who was my love, and whom but last night I should have wed, but whom the Gods have brought to shame unspeakable, Odysseus of Ithaca, Odysseus, Laertes' son. For this cause I came, and I have stayed to look upon the face of her whose beauty had power to drive the thought of me from the heart of Odysseus, and bring him, who of all men was the greatest hero and the foremost left alive, to do a dastard deed and make his mighty name a byword and a scorn. Knowest thou, Meriamun, that I find the matter strange, since if all things else be false, yet is this true, that among women the fairest are the most strong. Thou are fair indeed, Meriamun, but judge if thou art more fair than Argive Helen,' and she drew the veil from her face so that the splendour of her beauty shone out upon the Queen's dark loveliness. Thus for awhile they stood each facing each, and to Rei it seemed as though the spirits of Death and Life looked one on another, as though the darkness and the daylight stood in woman's shape before him.

'Thou art fair indeed,' said the Queen, 'but in this, witch, has thy beauty failed to hold him whom thou wouldst wed from the most shameless sin. Little methinks can that man have loved thee who crept upon me like a thief to snatch my honour from me.'

Then Helen bethought her of what Rei had said, that Meriamun loved the Wanderer, and she spoke again:

'Now it comes into my heart, Egyptian, that true and false are mixed in this tale of thine. Hard it is to believe that Odysseus of Ithaca could work such a coward deed as this, or, unbidden, seek to clasp thee to his heart. Moreover, I read in thine eyes that thou thyself dost love the man whom thou namest dastard. Nay, hold thy peace, look not so wildly on me whom thou canst not harm, but hearken. Whether thy tale be true or false I know not, who use no magic and learn those things only that the Gods reveal to me. But this at least is true, that Odysseus, whom I should have wed, has looked on thee with eyes of love, even in that hour when I waited to be made his wife. Therefore the love that but two days agone bloomed in my heart, dies and withers; or if it dies not, at least I cast it from me and tread its flowers beneath my feet. For this doom the Gods have laid upon me, who am of all women the most hapless, to live beloved but loveless through many years, and at the last to love and be betrayed. And now I go hence back to my temple shrine; but fear not,

Meriamun, not for long shall I trouble thee or Khem, and men shall die no more because of my beauty, for I shall presently pass hence whither the Gods appoint; and this I say to thee—deal gently with that man who has betrayed my faith, for whatever he did was done for the love of thee. It is no mean thing to have won the heart of Odysseus of Ithaca out of the hand of Argive Helen. Fare thee well, Meriamun, who wouldst have slain me. May the Gods grant thee better days and more of joy than is given to Helen, who would look upon thy face no more.'

Thus she spake, and letting her veil fall turned to go. For awhile the Queen stood shamed to silence by these gentle words, that fell like dew upon the fires of her hate. But ere Helen had passed the length of a spear her fury burned up again. What, should she let this woman go— this woman who alone of all that breathed was more beautiful than she, by the aid of whose stolen beauty she alone had won her love, and for whose sake she had endured such bitter words of scorn? Nay, while Helen yet lived she could find nor joy nor sleep. But were Helen dead, then perchance all might yet be well, and the Wanderer yet be hers, for when the best is gone men turn them to the better.

'Close the gates and bar them,' she cried to the men, who now streamed back into the hall; and they ran to do her bidding, so that before Helen reached the Palace doors, they had been shut and the gates of bronze beyond had clashed like the shields of men.

Now Helen drew near the doors.

'Stay yon witch,' cried the Queen to those who guarded them, and in wonder they poised their spears to bar the way of Helen. But she only lifted her veil and looked upon them. Then their arms fell from their hands and they stood amazed at the sight of beauty.

'Open, I beseech you,' said the Helen gently, and straightway they opened the doors and she passed through, followed by those who guarded them, by the Queen, and by Rei. But one man there was who did not see her beauty, and he strove in vain to hold back the doors and to clasp Helen as she passed.

Now she drew near to the gates—

'Shoot the witch!' cried Meriamun the Queen; 'if she pass the gates, by my royal word I swear that ye shall die every man of you. Shoot her with arrows.'

Then three men drew their bows mightily. The string of the bow of one burst, and the bow was shattered, and the arrow of the second slipped as he drew it, and passing downwards pierced his foot; and the shaft of the third swerved ere it struck the breast of Helen, and sunk into the heart of that soldier who was next to the Queen, so that he fell down dead. It was the same man who had striven to hold to the doors and clasp the Helen.

Then Helen turned and spoke:

'Bid not thy guard to shoot again, Meriamun, lest the arrow find *thy* heart, for, know this, no man may harm me;' and once more she lifted her veil, and speaking to those at the gates said: 'Open, I beseech you, and let the Hathor pass.'

Now their weapons fell from their hands, and they looked upon her beauty, and they too made haste to open the gates. The great gates clanged upon their sockets and rolled back. She passed through them, and all who were there followed after her. But when they looked, lo! she had mingled with the people who went to and fro and was gone.

Then Meriamun grew white with rage because Helen whom she hated had escaped her, and turning to those men who had opened the doors and those who had given passage of the gates, who yet stood looking on each other with dazed eyes, she doomed them to die.

But Rei, kneeling before her, prayed for their lives:

'Ill will come of it, O Queen!' he said, 'as ill came to yonder Sidonian and to the soldier at thy feet, for none may work evil on this Goddess, or those who befriended the Goddess. Slay them not, O Queen, lest ill tidings follow on the deed!'

Then the Queen turned on him madly:

'Hearken thou, Rei!' she said; 'speak thus again, and though I have loved thee and thou hast been the chief of the servants of Pharaoh, this I swear, that thou shalt die the first. Already the count is long between thee and me, for it was thou who didst bring yon accursed witch to my Palace. Now thou hast heard, and of this be sure, as I have spoken so I will do. Get thee gone—get thee from my sight, I say, lest I slay thee now, I take back thy honours, I strip thee of thy offices, I gather thy wealth into my treasury. Go forth a beggar, and let me see thy face no more!'

Then Rei held his peace and fled, for it were better to stand before a lioness robbed of her whelps than before Meriamun in her rage. Thereon the gates were shut again, and the captain of the gates was dragged before the place where the Queen stood, and asking no mercy and taking little heed, for still his soul was filled with the beauty of Helen as a cup with wine, he suffered death, for his head was straightway smitten from him.

Rei, watching from afar, groaned aloud, then turned and left the Palace, but the Queen called to the soldiers to slay on. Even as she called there came a cry of woe without the Palace gates. Men looked each on each. Again the cry rose and a voice without called, 'Pharaoh is come again! Pharaoh is come again!' and there rose a sound of knocking at the gates.

Now for that while Meriamun thought no more of slaying the men, but bade them open the gates. They opened, and a man entered clad in raiment stained with travel. His eyes were wild, his hair was dishevelled, and scarce could his face be known for the face of Pharaoh Meneptah, it was so marred with grief and fear.

Pharaoh looked on the Queen—he looked upon the dead who lay at her feet, then laughed aloud:

'What!' he cried, 'more dead! Is there then no end to Death and the number of his slain? Nay, here he doth work but feebly. Perchance his arm grows weary. Come, where are *thy* dead, Queen? Bring forth thy dead!'

'What hath chanced, Meneptah, that thou speakest thus madly?' asked the Queen. 'She whom they name the Hathor hath passed here, and these, and another who lies yonder, do but mark her path. Speak!'

'Ay, I will speak, Queen. I have a merry tale to tell.

Thou sayest that the Hathor hath passed here and these mark her footsteps. Well, I can cap thy story. He whom the Apura name Jahveh hath passed yonder by the Sea of Weeds, and there lie many, lie to mark His footsteps.'

'Thy host! Where is thy host?' cried the Queen. 'At the least some are left.'

Yes, Queen, *all* are left—all—all—save myself alone. They drift to and fro in the Sea of Weeds—they lie by tens of thousands on its banks; the gulls tear their eyes, the lion of the desert rends their flesh; they lie unburied, their breath sighs in the sea gales, their blood sinks into the salt sands, and Osiris numbers them in the hosts of hell. Hearken! I came upon the tribes of the Apura by the banks of the Sea of Weeds. I came at eve, but I might not fall upon them because of a veil of darkness that spread between my armies and the hosts of the Apura. All night long through the veil of darkness, and through the shrieking of a great gale, I heard a sound as of the passing of a mighty people—the clangour of their arms, the voices of captains, the stamp of beasts, and the grinding of wheels. The morning came, and lo! before me the waters of the sea were built up as a wall on the right hand and the left, and between the walls of water was dry land, and the Apura passed between the walls. Then I cried to my captains to arise and follow swiftly, and they did my bidding. But the chariot wheels drew heavily in the sand, so that before all my host had entered between the waters, the Apura had passed the sea. Then of a sudden, as last of all I passed down into the path of the ocean bed, the great wind ceased, and as it ceased, lo! the walls of water that were on either side of the sea path fell together with noise like the noise of thunder. I turned my chariot wheels, and fled back, but my soldiers, my chariots, and my horses were swallowed; once more they were seen again on the crest of the black waves like a gleam of light upon a cloud, once a great cry arose to the heaven; then all was done and all was still, and of my hosts I alone was left alive of men.'

So Pharaoh spoke, and a great groan rose from those who hearkened. Only Meriamun spoke:

'So shall things go with us while that False Hathor dwells in Khem.'

Now as she spoke thus, again there came a sound of knocking at the gates and a cry of 'Open—a messenger! a messenger!'

'Open!' said Meriamun, 'though his tidings be ill, scarce can they match these that have been told.'

The gates were opened and one came through them. His eyes stared wide in fear, so dry was his throat with haste and with the sand, that he stood speechless before them all.

'Give him wine,' cried Meriamun, and wine was brought. Then he drank, and he fell upon his knees before the Queen, for he knew not Pharaoh.

'Thy tidings!' she cried. 'Be swift with thy tidings.'

'Let the Queen pardon me,' he said. 'Let her not be wrath. These are my tidings. A mighty host marches towards the city of On, a host gathered from all lands of the peoples of the North, from the lands of the Tulisha, of the Shakalishu, of the Liku, and of the Shairdana. They march swiftly and raven, they lay the country waste, naught is left behind them save the smoke of burning towns, the flight of vultures, and the corpses of men.'

'Hast done?' said Meriamun.

'Nay, O Queen! A great fleet sails with them up the eastern mouth of Sihor, and in it are twelve thousand chosen warriors of the Aquaiusha, the sons of those men who sacked Troy town.'

And now a great groan went up to heaven from the lips of those who hearkened. Only Meriamun spoke thus:

'And yet the Apura are gone, for whose sake, ye say, came the plagues. They are fled, but the curse remains, and so shall things ever be with us while yon False Hathor dwells in Khem.'

3. THE BED OF TORMENT

It was nightfall, and Pharaoh sat at meat and Meriamun sat by him. The heart of Pharaoh was very heavy. He thought of that great army which now washed to and fro on the waters of the Sea of Weeds, of whose number he alone had lived to tell the tale. He thought also of the host of the Apura, who made a mock of him in the desert. But most of all he brooded on the tidings that the messenger had brought, tidings of the march of the barbarians and of the fleet of the Aquaiusha that sailed on the eastern stream of Sihor. All that day he had sat in his council chamber, and sent forth messengers east and north and south, bidding them gather the mercenaries from every town and in every city, men to make war against the foe, for here, in his white-walled city of Tanis, there were left but five thousand soldiers. And now, wearied with toil and war, he sat at meat, and as he sat bethought him of the man whom he had left to guard the Queen.

'Where, then, is that great Wanderer, he who wore the golden harness?' he asked presently.

'I have a tale to tell thee of the man,' Meriamun answered slowly, 'a tale which I have not told because of all the evil tidings that beat about our ears like sand in a desert wind.'

'Tell on,' said Pharaoh.

Then she bent towards him, whispering in his ear.

As she whispered the face of Pharaoh grew black as the night, and ere all the tale was done he sprang to his feet.

'By Amen and by Ptah!' he cried, 'here at least we have a foe whom we may conquer. Thou and I, Meriamun, my sister and my queen, are set as far each from each as the sky is set from the temple top, and little of love is there between us. Yet I will wipe away this blot upon thy honour, which also is a blot upon my own. Sleepless shall this Wanderer lie tonight, and sorry shall he go to-morrow, but to-morrow night he shall sleep indeed.'

Thereupon he clapped his hands, summoning the guard, and bade them pass to the dungeon where the Wanderer lay, and lead him thence to the place of punishment. He bade them also call the tormentors to make ready the instruments of their craft, and await him in the place of punishment.

Then he sat for awhile, drinking sullenly, till one came to tell him that all was prepared. Then Pharaoh rose.

'Comest thou with me?' he asked.

'Nay,' said Meriamun, 'I would not look upon the man again; and this I charge thee. Go not down to him this night. Let him be bound upon the bed of torment, and let the tormentors give him food and wine, for so he shall die more hardly. Then let them light the fires at his head and at his feet and leave him till the dawn alone in the place of torment. So he shall die a hundred deaths ere ever his death begins.'

'As thou wilt,' answered Pharaoh. 'Mete out thine own punishment. To-morrow when I have slept I will look upon his torment.' And he spoke to his servants as she desired.

The Wanderer lay on the bed of torment in the place of torment. They had taken the gag from his mouth, and given him food and wine as Pharaoh commanded. He ate and drank and his strength came back to him. Then they made fast his fetters, lit the braziers at his head and foot, and left him with mocking words.

He lay upon the bed of stone and groaned in the bitterness of his heart. Here then was the end of his wanderings, and this was the breast of the Golden Helen in whose arms Aphrodite had sworn that he should lie. Oh, that he were free again and stood face to face with his foes, his harness on his back! Nay, it might not be, no mortal strength could burst these fetters, not even the strength of Odysseus, Laertes' son. Where now were those Gods whom he had served? Should he never again hear the clarion cry of Pallas? Why then had he turned him from Pallas and worshipped at the shrine of the false Idalian Queen? Thus it was that she kept her oaths; thus she repaid her votary.

So he thought in the bitterness of his heart as he lay with closed eyes upon the bed of torment whence there was no escape, and groaned: 'Would, Aphrodite, that I had never served thee, even for one little hour, then had my lot gone otherwise.'

Now he opened his eyes, and lo! a great glory rolled about the place of torment, and as he wondered at the glory, a voice spoke from its midst—the voice of the Idalian Aphrodite:

'Blame me not, Odysseus,' said the heavenly voice; 'blame me not because thou art come to this pass. Thyself, son of Laertes, art to blame. What did I tell thee? Was it not that thou shouldst know the Golden Helen by the Red Star on her breast, the jewel whence fall the red drops fast, and by the Star alone? And did she not tell thee, also, that thou shouldst know her by the Star? Yet when one came to thee wearing no Star but girdled with a Snake, my words were all forgotten, thy desires led thee whither thou wouldst not go. Thou wast blinded by desire and couldst not discern the False from the True. Beauty has many shapes, now it is that of Helen, now that of Meriamun, each sees it as he desires it. But the Star is yet the Star, and the Snake is yet the Snake, and he who, bewildered by his lusts, swears by the Snake when he should have sworn by the Star, shall have the Snake for guerdon.'

She ceased and the Wanderer spoke, groaning bitterly.

'I have sinned, O Queen!' he said. 'Is there then no forgiveness for my sin?'

'Yea, there is forgiveness, Odysseus, but first there is punishment. This is thy fate. Never now, in this space of life, shalt thou be the lord of the Golden Helen. For thou hast sworn by the Snake, and his thou art, nor mayest thou reach the Star. Yet it still shines on. Through the mists of death it shall shine for thee, and when thou wakest again, behold, thine eyes shall see it fitfully.

'And now, this for thy comfort. Here thou shalt not die, nor by torment, for thy death shall come to thee from the water as the dead seer foretold, but ere thou diest, once more thou shalt look upon the Golden Helen, and hear her words of love and know her kiss, though thine she shall not be. And learn that a great host marches upon the land of Khem, and with it sails a fleet of thine own people, the Achæans. Go down and meet them and take what comes, where the swords shine that smote Troy. And this fate is laid upon thee, that thou shalt do battle against thy own people, even against the sons of them by whose side thou didst fight beneath the walls of Ilios, and in that battle thou shalt find thy death, and in thy death, thou Wanderer, thou shalt find that which all men seek, the breast of the immortal Helen. For though here on earth she seems to live eternally, it is but the shadow of her beauty that men see—each as he desires it. In the halls of Death she dwells, and in the garden of Queen Persephone, and there she shall be won, for there no more is beauty guarded of Those that stand between men and joy, and there no more shall the Snake seem as the Star, and Sin have power to sever those that are one. Now make thy heart strong, Odysseus, and so do as thy wisdom tells thee. Farewell!'

Thus the Goddess spoke from the cloud of glory, and lo! she was gone. But the heart of the Wanderer was filled with joy because he knew that the Helen was not lost to him for ever, and he no more feared the death of shame.

Now it was midnight, and Pharaoh slept. But Meriamun the Queen slept not. She rose from her bed, she wrapped herself in a dark cloak that hid her face, and taking a lamp in her hand, glided through the empty halls till she came to a secret stair down which she passed. There was a gate at the foot of the stair, and a guard slept by it. She pushed him with her foot.

He awoke and sprang towards her, but she held a signet before his eyes, an old ring of great Queen Taia, whereon a Hathor worshipped the sun. Then he bowed and opened the gate. She swept on through many passages, deep into the bowels of the earth, till she came to the door of a little chamber where a light shone. Men talked in the chamber, and she listened to their talk. They spoke much and laughed gleefully. Then she entered the doorway and looked upon them. They were six in number, evil-eyed men of Ethiopia, and seated in a circle. In the centre of the circle lay the waxen image of a man, and they were cutting it with knives and searing it with needles of iron and pincers made of red-hot, and many instruments strange and dreadful to look upon. For these were the tormentors, and they spoke of those pains that to-morrow they should wreak upon the Wanderer, and practised them.

But Meriamun, who loved him, shivered as she looked, and muttered thus beneath her breath:

'This I promise you, black ministers of death, that in the same fashion ye shall die ere another night be sped.'

Then she passed into the chamber, holding the signet on high, and the tormentors fell upon their faces before her majesty. She passed between them, and as she went she stamped with her sandalled foot upon the waxen image and brake it. On the further side of the chamber was another passage, and this she followed till she reached a door of stone that stood ajar. Here she paused awhile, for from within the chamber there came a sound of singing, and the voice was the Wanderer's voice, and thus he sang:

Endure, my heart: not long shalt thou endure
    The shame, the smart;
The good and ill are done; the end is sure;
    Endure, my heart!
There stand two vessels by the golden throne
    Of Zeus on high,

From these he scatters mirth and scatters moan,
  To men that die.
And thou of many joys hast had thy share,
  Thy perfect part;
Battle and love, and evil things and fair;
  Endure, my heart!
Fight one last greatest battle under shield,
   Wage that war well:
Then seek thy fellows in the shadowy field
  Of asphodel,
There is the knightly Hector; there the men
  Who fought for Troy;
Shall we not fight our battles o'er again?
  Were that not joy?
Though no sun shines beyond the dusky west,
  Thy perfect part
There shalt thou have of the unbroken rest;
  Endure, my heart!

Meriamun heard and wondered at this man's hardihood, and the greatness of his heart who could sing thus as he lay upon the bed of torment. Now she pushed the door open silently and passed in. The place where she stood was dreadful. It was shaped as a lofty vault, and all the walls were painted with the torments of those who pass down to Set after living wickedly on earth. In the walls were great rings of bronze, and chains and fetters of bronze, wherein the bones of men yet hung. In the centre of the vault there was a bed of stone on which the Wanderer was fastened with fetters. He was naked, save only for a waistcloth, and at his head and feet burned polished braziers that gave light to the vault, and shone upon the instruments of torment. Beyond the further braziers grinned the cage of Sekhet, that is shaped like a woman, and the chains wherein the victim is set for the last torment by fire, were hanging from the roof.

Meriamun passed stealthily behind the head of the Wanderer, who might not see her because of the straitness of his bonds. Yet it seemed to her that he heard somewhat, for he ceased from singing and turned his ear to hearken. She stood awhile in silence looking on him she loved, who of all living men was the goodliest by far. Then at length he spoke craftily:

'Who are thou?' he said, 'If thou art of the number of the tormentors, begin thy work. I fear thee not, and no groan shall thy worst torture wring from these lips of mine. But I tell thee this, that ere I be three days dead, the Gods shall avenge me terribly, both on thee and those who sent thee. With fire and with sword they shall avenge me, for a great host gathers and draws nigh, a host of many nations gathered out of all lands, ay, and a fleet manned with the sons of my own people, of the Achæans terrible in war. They rush on like ravening wolves, and the land is black before them, but the land shall be stamped red behind their feet. Soon they shall give this city to the flames, the smoke of it shall go up to heaven, and the fires shall be quenched at last in the blood of its children—ay, in thy blood, thou who dost look on me.'

Hearing these words Meriamun bent forward to look on the face of the speaker and to see what was written there; and as she moved, her cloak slipped apart, showing the Snake's head with the eyes of flame that was set about her as a girdle. Fiercely they gleamed, and the semblance of them was shown faintly on the polished surface of the brazier wherein the fire burned at the Wanderer's feet. He saw it, and now he knew who stood behind him.

'Say, Meriamun the Queen—Pharaoh's dishonoured wife,' he said, 'say, wherefore art thou come to look upon thy work? Nay, stand not behind me, stand where I may see thee. Fear not, I am strongly bound, nor may I lift a hand against thee.'

Then Meriamun, still speaking no word, but wondering much because he knew her ere his eyes fell upon her, passed round the bed of torment, and throwing down her cloak stood before him in her dark and royal loveliness.

He looked upon her beauty, then spoke again:

'Say, wherefore art thou come hither, Meriamun? Surely, with my ears I heard thee swear that I had wronged thee. Wouldst thou then look on him who wronged thee, or art thou come, perchance, to watch my torments while thy slaves tear limb from limb, and quench yon fires with my blood? Oh, thou evil woman thou hast worked woe on me indeed, and perchance canst work more woe now that I lie helpless here. But this I tell thee, that thy torments shall outnumber mine as the stars outnumber the earth. For here, and hereafter, thou shalt be parched with such a thirst of love as never may be quenched, and in many another land, and in many another time, thou shalt endure thine agony afresh. Again, and yet again, thou shalt clasp and conquer; again, and yet again, thou shalt let slip, and in the moment of triumph lose. By the Snake's head I swore my troth to thee, I, who should have sworn by the Star; and this I tell thee Meriamun, that as the Star shall shine and be my beacon through the ages, so through the ages shall the Snake encircle thee and be thy doom.'

'Hold!' said Meriamun, 'pour no more bitter words upon me, who am distraught of love, and was maddened by thy scorn. Wouldst thou know then why I am come hither? For this cause I am come, to save thee from thy doom. Hearken, the time is short. It is true—though how thou knowest it I may not guess—it is true that the barbarians march on Khem, and with them sails a fleet laden with the warriors of thine own people. This also is true, Pharaoh has returned alone: and all his host is swallowed in the Sea of Weeds. And I, foolish that I am, I would save thee, Odysseus, thus: I will put it in the heart of Pharaoh to pardon thy great offence, and send thee forward against the foe; yes, I can do it. But this thou shalt swear to me, to be true to Pharaoh, and smite the barbarian host.'

'That I will swear,' said the Wanderer, 'ay, and keep the oath, though it is hard to do battle on my kin. Is that all thy message, Meriamun?'

'Not all, Odysseus. One more thing must thou swear, or if thou swearest it not, here thou shalt surely die. Know this, she who in Khem is named the Hathor, but who perchance has other names, hath put thee from her because last night thou wast wed to me.'

'It may well be so,' said the Wanderer.

'She hath put thee from her, and thou—thou art bound

to me by that which cannot be undone, and by an oath that may not be broken; in whatever shape I walk, or by whatever name I am known among men, still thou art bound to me, as I am bound to thee. This then thou shalt swear, that thou wilt tell naught of last night's tale to Pharaoh.'

'That I swear,' said the Wanderer.

'Also that if Pharaoh be gathered to Osiris, and it should chance that she who is named the Hathor pass with him to the Under-world, then that thou, Odysseus, wilt wed me, Meriamun, and be faithful to me for thy life days.'

Now the crafty Odysseus took counsel with his heart, and bethought him of the words of the Goddess. He saw that it was in the mind of Meriamun to slay Pharaoh and the Helen. But he cared nothing for the fate of Pharaoh, and knew well that Helen might not be harmed, and that though she change eternally, wearing now this shape, and now that, yet she dies only when the race of men is dead—then to be gathered to the number of the Gods. This he knew also, that now he must go forth on his last wandering, for Death should come upon him from the water. Therefore he answered readily:

"That oath I swear also, Meriamun, and if I break it may I perish in shame and for ever.'

Now Meriamun heard, and knelt beside him, looking upon him with eyes of love.

'It is well, Odysseus: perchance ere long I shall claim thy oath. Oh, think not so ill of me: if I have sinned, I have sinned from love of thee. Long years ago, Odysseus, thy shadow fell upon my heart and I clasped its emptiness. Now thou art come, and I, who pursued a shadow from sleep to sleep and dream to dream, saw thee a living man, and loved thee to my ruin. Then I tamed my pride and came to win thee to my heart, and the Gods set another shape upon me—so thou sayest—and in that shape, the shape of her thou seekest, thou didst make me wife to thee. Perchance she and I are *one,* Odysseus. At the least, not so readily had *I* forsaken thee. Oh, when thou didst stand in thy might holding those dogs at bay till the Sidonian knave cut thy bowstring—'

'What of him? Tell me, what of that Kurri? This would I ask thee, Queen, that he be laid where I lie, and die the death to which I am doomed.'

'Gladly would I give thee the boon,' she answered, 'but thou askest too late. The False Hathor looked upon him, and he slew himself. Now I will away—the night wanes and Pharaoh must dream dreams ere dawn. Fare the well, Odysseus. Thy bed is hard to-night, but soft is the couch of kings that waits thee,' and she went forth from him.

'Ay, Meriamun,' said the Wanderer, looking after her. 'Hard is my bed to-night, and soft is the couch of the kings of Men that waits me in the realms of Queen Persephone. But it is not thou who shalt share it. Hard is my bed to-night, harder shall thine be through all the nights of death that are to come when the Erinnyes work their will on folk forsworn.'

4. PHARAOH'S DREAM

Pharaoh slept heavily in his place, for he was wearied with grief and toil. But Meriamun passed into the chamber, and standing at the foot of the golden bed, lifted up her hands and by her art called visions down on Pharaoh, false dreams through the Ivory Gate. So Pharaoh dreamed, and thus his vision went:—

He dreamed that he slept in his bed, and that the statue of Ptah, the Creator, descended from the pedestal by the temple gate and came to him, towering over him like a giant. Then he dreamed that he awoke, and prostrating himself before the God, asked the meaning of his coming. Thereon the God spoke to him:—

'Meneptah, my son, whom I love, hearken unto me. The Nine-bow barbarians overrun the ancient land of Khem; nine nations march up against Khem and lay in waste. Hearken unto me, my son, and I will give thee victory. Awake, awake from sloth, and I will give thee victory. Thou shalt hew down the Nine-bow barbarians as a countryman hews a rotting palm; they shall fall, and thou shalt spoil them. But hearken unto me, my son, thou shalt not thyself go up against them. Low in thy dungeon there lies a mighty chief, skilled in the warfare of the barbarians, a Wanderer who hath wandered far. Thou shalt release him from his bonds and set him over thy armies, and of the sin that he has sinned thou shalt take no heed. Awake, awake, Meneptah; with this bow which I give thee shalt thou smite the Nine-bow barbarians.'

Then Meriamun laid the bow of the Wanderer, even the black bow of Eurytus, on the bed beside Pharaoh, and passed thence to her own chamber, and the deceitful dream too passed away.

Early in the morning, a waiting-woman came to the Queen saying that Pharaoh would speak with her. She went into the ante-chamber and found him there, and in his hand was the black bow of Eurytus.

'Dost thou know this weapon?' he asked.

'Yea, I know it,' she answered; 'and thou shouldst know it also, for surely it saved us from the fury of the people on the night of the death of the first-born. It is the bow of the Wanderer, who lies in the place of torment, and waits his doom because of the wrong he would have wrought upon me.'

'If he hath wronged thee, yet it is he who shall save Khem from the barbarians,' said Pharaoh. 'Listen now to the dream that I have dreamed,' and he told her all the vision.

'It is indeed evil that he who would have wrought such wickedness upon me should go forth honoured, the first of the host of Pharaoh,' quoth Meriamun.

'Yet as the God hath spoken, so let it be. Send now and bid them loose the man from the place of torment, and put his armour on him and bring him before thee.'

So Pharaoh went out, and the Wanderer was loosed from his bed of stone and clothed again in his golden harness, and came forth glorious to see, and stood before Pharaoh. But no arms were given him. Then Pharaoh told him all his dream, and why he caused him to be released from the grip of the tormentors. The Wanderer hearkened in silence, saying no word.

'Now choose, thou Wanderer,' said Pharaoh; 'choose if thou wilt be borne back to the bed of torment, there to die beneath the hands of the tormentors, or if thou wilt go forth as the captain of my host to do battle with the Nine-bow barbarians who waste the land of Khem. It seems there is little faith in thine oaths, therefore I ask no more oaths from thee. But this I swear, that if thou art false to my trust, I will yet find means to bring thee back to that chamber whence thou wast led but now.'

Then the Wanderer spoke:—

'Of that charge, Pharaoh, which is laid against me I will say nothing, though perchance if I stood upon my trial for the sin that is laid against me, I might find words to say. Thou askest no oath from me, and no oath I swear, yet I tell thee that if thou givest me ten thousand soldiers and a hundred chariots, I will smite these foes of thine so that they shall come no more of Khem, ay, though they be of my own people, yet will I smite them, and if I fail, then may those who go with me slay me and send me down to Hades.'

Thus he spoke, and as he spoke searched the hall with his eyes. For he desired to see Rei the Prest, and charge him with a message to Helen. But he sought him in vain, for Rei had fled, and was in hiding from the anger of Meriamun.

Then Pharaoh bade his officers take the Wanderer, and set him in a chariot and bear him to the city of On, where Pharaoh's host was gathering. Their charge was to watch him night and day with uplifted swords, and if he so much as turned his face from the foe toward Tanis, then they should slay him. But when the host of Pharaoh marched from On to do battle on the foe, then they should give the Wanderer his own sword and the great black bow, and obey him in everything. But if he turned his back upon the foe, then they should slay him; or if the host of Pharaoh were driven back by the foe, then they should slay him.

The Wanderer heard, and smiled as a wolf smiles, but spoke no word. Thereon the great officers of Pharaoh took him and led him forth. They set him in a chariot, and with the chariot went a thousand horsemen; and soon Meriamun, watching from the walls of Tanis, saw the long line of desert dust that marked the passing of the Wanderer from the city which he should see no more.

The Wanderer also looked back on Tanis with a heavy

heart. There, far away, he could see the shrine of Hathor gleaming like crystal above the tawny flood of water. And he must go down to death, leaving no word for Her who sat in the shrine and deemed him faithless and forsworn. Evil was the lot that the Gods had laid upon him, and bitter was his guerdon.

His thoughts were sad enough while the chariot rolled toward the city of On, where the host of Pharaoh was gathering, and the thunder of the feet of horses echoed in his ears, when, as he pondered, it chanced that he looked up. There, on a knoll of sand before him, a bow-shot from the chariot, stood a camel, and on the camel a man sat as though he waited the coming of the host. Idly the Wanderer wondered who this might be, and, as he wondered, the man urged the camel towards the chariot, and, halting before it, cried 'Hold!' in a loud voice.

'Who art thou?' cried the captain of the chariot, 'who darest cry "hold" to the host of Pharaoh?'

'I am one who have tidings of the barbarians,' the man made answer from the camel.

The Wanderer looked on him. He was wondrous little, withered and old; moreover, his skin was black as though with the heat of the sun, and his clothing was as a beggar's rags, though the trappings of the camel were of purple leather and bossed with silver. Again the Wanderer looked; he knew him not, and yet there was that in his face which seemed familiar.

Now the captain of the chariot bade the driver halt the horses, and cried, 'Draw near and tell thy tidings.'

'To none will I tell my tidings save to him who shall lead the host of Pharaoh. Let him come down from the chariot and speak with me.'

'That may not be,' said the captain, for he was charged that the Wanderer should have speech with none.

'As thou wilt,' answered the aged man upon the camel; 'go then, go on to doom! thou art not the first who hath turned aside a messenger from the Gods.'

'I am minded to bid the soldiers shoot thee with arrows,' cried the captain in anger.

'So shall my wisdom sink in the sand with my blood, and be lost with my breath. Shoot on, thou fool.'

Now the captain was perplexed, for from the aspect of the man he deemed that he was sent by the Gods. He looked at the Wanderer, who took but little heed, or so it seemed. But in his crafty heart he knew that this was the best way to win speech with the man upon the camel. Then the captain took counsel with the captain of the horsemen, and in the end they said to the Wanderer:

'Descend from the chariot, lord, and walk twelve paces forward, and there hold speech with the man. But if thou go one pace further, then we will shoot thee and the man with arrows.' And this he cried out also to him who sat upon the camel.

Then the man on the camel descended and walked twelve paces forward, and the Wanderer descended also from the chariot and walked twelve paces forward, but as one who heeds little what he does. Now the two stood face to face, but out of earshot of the host, who watched them with arrows set upon the strings.

'Greeting, Odysseus of Ithaca, son of Laertes,' he said who was clothed in the beggar's weeds.

The Wanderer looked upon him hard, and knew him through his disguise.

'Greeting, Rei the Priest, Commander of the Legion of Amen, Chief of the Treasury of Amen.'

'Rei the Priest I am indeed,' he answered, 'the rest I am no more, for Meriamun the Queen has stripped me of my wealth and offices, because of thee, thou Wanderer, and the Immortal whose love thou hast won, and by whom thou hast dealt so ill. Hearken! I learned by arts known to me of the dream of Pharaoh, and of thy sending forth to do battle with the barbarians. Then I disguised myself as thou seest, and took the swiftest camel in Tanis, and am come hither by another way to meet thee. Now I would ask thee one thing. How came it that thou didst play the Immortal false that night? Knowest thou that she waited for thee there by the pylon gate? Ay, there I found her and led her to the Palace, and for that I am stripped of my rank and goods by Meriamun, and now the Lady of

Beauty is returned to her shrine, grieving bitterly for thy faithlessness; though how she passed thither I know not.'

'Methought I heard her voice as those knaves bore me to my dungeon,' said the Wanderer. 'And she deemed me faithless! Say, Rei, dost thou know the magic of Meriamun? Dost thou know how she won me to herself in the shape of Argive Helen?'

And then, in as few words as might be, he told Rei how he had been led away by the magic of Meriamun, how he who should have sworn by the Star had sworn by the Snake.

When Rei heard that the Wanderer had sworn by the Snake, he shuddered. 'Now I know all,' he said. 'Fear not, thou Wanderer, not on thee shall all the evil fall, nor on that Immortal whom thou dost love; the Snake that beguiled thee shall avenge thee also.'

'Rei,' the Wanderer said, 'one thing I charge thee. I know that I go down to my death. Therefore I pray thee seek out her whom thou namest the Hathor and tell her all the tale of how I was betrayed. So shall I die happily. Tell her also that I crave her forgiveness and that I love her and her only.'

'This I will do if I may,' Rei answered. 'And now the soldiers murmur and I must be gone. Listen, the might of the Nine-bow barbarians rolls up the eastern branch of Sihor. But one day's march from On the mountains run down to the edge of the river, and those mountains are pierced by a rocky pass through which the foe will surely come. Set thou thy ambush there, Wanderer, there at Prosopis—so shalt thou smite them. Farewell. I will seek out the Hathor if in any way I can come at her, and tell her all. But of this I warn thee, the hour is big with Fate, and soon will spawn a monstrous birth. Strange visions of doom and death passed before mine eyes as I slept last night. Farewell!'

Then he went back to the camel and climbed it, and passing round the army vanished swiftly in a cloud of dust.

The Wanderer also went back to the host, where the captains murmured because of the halt, and mounted his chariot. But he would tell nothing of what the man had said to him, save that he was surely a messenger from the Under-world to instruct him in the waging of the war.

Then the chariot and the horsemen passed on again, till they came to the city of On, and found the host of Pharaoh gathering in the great walled space that is before the Temple of Ra. And there they pitched their camp hard by the great obelisks that stand at the inner gate, which Rei the architect fashioned by Thebes, and the divine Rameses Miamun set up to the glory of Ra for ever.

5. THE VOICE OF THE DEAD

When Meriamun the Queen had watched the chariot of the Wanderer till it was lost in the dust of the desert, she passed down from the Palace roof to the solitude of her chamber.

Here she sat in her chamber till the darkness gathered, as the evil thoughts gathered in her heart, that was rent with love of him whom she had won but to lose. Things had gone ill with her, to little purpose she had sinned after such a fashion as may not be forgiven. Yet there was hope. He had sworn that he would wed her when Pharaoh was dead, and when Argive Helen had followed Pharaoh to the Shades. Should she shrink then from the deed of blood? Nay, from evil to evil she would go. She laid her hand upon the double-headed snake that wound her about, and spake into the gloom:

'Osiris waits thee, Meneptah—Osiris waits thee! The Shades of those who have died for thy love, Helen, are gathering at the gates. It shall be done. Pharaoh, thou diest to-night. To-morrow night, thou Goddess Helen, shall all thy tale be told. *Man* may not harm thee indeed, but shall fire refuse to kiss thy loveliness? Are there no *women's* hands to light thy funeral pile?'

Then she rose, and calling her ladies, was attired in her most splendid robes, and caused the uraeus crown to be set upon her head, the snake circlet of power on her brow, the snake girdle of wisdom at her heart. And now she hid somewhat in her breast, and passed to the ante-chamber, where the Princes gathered for the feast.

Pharaoh looked up and saw her loveliness. So glorious she seemed in her royal beauty that his heart forgot its woes, and once again he loved her as he had done in years gone by, when she conquered him at the Game of Pieces, and he had cast his arms about her and she stabbed him.

She saw the look of love grow on his heavy face, and all her gathered hate rose in her breast, though she smiled gently with her lips and spake him fair.

They sat at the feast and Pharaoh drank. And ever as he drank she smiled upon him with her dark eyes and spake him words of gentlest meaning, till at length there was nothing he desired more than that they should be at one again.

Now the feast was done. They sat in the antechamber, for all were gone save Meneptah and Meriamun. Then he came to her and took her hand, looking into her eyes, nor did she say him nay.

There was a lute lying on a golden table, and there too, as it chanced, was a board for the Game of Pieces, with the dice, and the pieces themselves wrought in gold.

Pharaoh took up the gold king from the board and toyed with it in his hand. 'Meriamun,' he said, 'for these five years we have been apart, thou and I. Thy love I have lost, as a game is lost for one false move, or one throw of the dice; and our child is dead and our armies are scattered, and the barbarians come like flies when Sihor stirs within his banks. Love only is left to us, Meriamun.'

She looked at him not unkindly, as if sorrow and wrong had softened her heart also, but she did not speak.

'Can dead Love waken, Meriamun, and can angry Love forgive?'

She had lifted the lute and her fingers touched listlessly on the cords.

'Nay, I know not,' she said; 'who knows? How did Pentaur sing of Love's renewal, Pentaur the glorious minstrel of our father, Rameses Miamun?'

He laid the gold king on the board, and began listlessly to cast the dice. He threw the 'Hathor' as it chanced, the lucky cast, two sixes, and a thought of better fortune came to him.

'How did the song run, Meriamun? It is many a year since I heard thee sing.'

She touched the lute lowly and sweetly, and then she sang. Her thoughts were of the Wanderer, but the King deemed that she thought of himself.

> O joy of Love's renewing,
>   Could Love be born again;
> Relenting for thy rueing,
>   And pitying my pain:
> O joy of Love's awaking,
>   Could Love arise from sleep,
> Forgiving our forsaking
>   The fields we would not reap!
>
> Fleet, fleet we fly, pursuing
>   The Love that fled amain,
> But will he list our wooing,
>   Or call we but in vain?
> Ah! vain is all our wooing,
>   And all our prayers are vain,
> Love listeth not our suing,
>   Love will not wake again.

'Will he not wake again?' said Pharaoh. 'If two pray together, will Love refuse their prayer?'

'It might be so,' she said, 'if two prayed together; for if they prayed, he would have heard already!'

'Meriamun,' said the Pharaoh eagerly, for he thought her heart was moved by pity and sorrow, 'once thou didst win my crown at the Pieces, wilt thou play me for thy love?'

She thought for one moment, and then she said:

'Yes, I will play thee, my Lord, but my hand has lost its cunning, and it may well be that Meriamun shall lose again, as she has lost all. Let me set the Pieces, and bring wine for my lord.'

She set the Pieces, and crossing the room, she lifted a

great cup of wine, and put it by Pharaoh's hand. But he was so intent on the game that he did not drink.

He took the field, he moved, she replied, and so the game went between them, in the dark fragrant chamber where the lamp burned, and the Queen's eyes shone in the night. This way and that went the game, till she lost, and he swept the board.

Then in triumph he drained the poisoned cup of wine, and cried, 'Pharaoh is dead!'

'Pharaoh is dead!' answered Meriamun, gazing into his eyes.

'What is that look in thine eyes, Meriamun, what is that look in thine eyes?'

And the King grew pale as the dead, for he had seen that look before—when Meriamun slew Hataska.

'Pharaoh is dead!' she shrilled in the tone of women who wail the dirges. 'Pharaoh, great Pharaoh is dead! Ere a man may count a hundred thy days are numbered. Strange! but to-morrow, Meneptah, shalt thou sit where Hataska sat, dead on the knees of Death, an Osirian in the lap of the Osiris. Die, Pharaoh, die! But while thou diest, hearken. There is one I love, the Wanderer who leads thy hosts. His love I stole by arts known to me, and because I stole it he would have shamed me, and I accused him falsely in the ears of men. But he comes again, and so sure as thou shalt sit on the knees of Osiris, so surely shall he sit upon thy throne, Pharaoh. For Pharaoh is dead!'

He heard. He gathered his last strength. He rose and staggered towards her, striking at the air. Slowly she drew away, while he followed her, awful to see. At length he stood still, he threw up his hands, and fell dead.

Then Meriamun drew near and looked at him strangely.

'Behold the end of Pharaoh,' she said. 'That then was a king, upon whose breath the lives of peoples hung liked a poised feather. Well, let him go! Earth can spare him, and Death is but the richer by a weary fool. 'Tis done, and well done! Would that to-morrow's task were also done—and that Helen lay as Pharaoh lies. So—rinse the cup—

and now to sleep—if sleep will come. Ah, where hath sleep flown of late? To-morrow they'll find him dead. Well, what of it? So do kings ofttimes die. There, I will be going; never were his eyes so large and so unlovely!'

Now the light of morning gathered again on all the temple tops, and men rose from sleep to go about their labours. Meriamun watched it grow as she lay sleepless in her golden bed, waiting for the cry that presently should ring along the Palace walls. Hark! What was that? The sound of swinging doors, the rush of running feet. And now it came—long and shrill it rose.

'Pharaoh is dead! Awake! Awake, ye sleepers! Awake! awake! and look upon that which has come about. Pharaoh is dead! Pharaoh is dead!'

Then Meriamun arose, and followed by the ladies, rushed from her chamber.

'Who dreams so evilly?' she said. 'Who dreams and cries aloud in his haunted sleep?'

'O Queen, it is no dream,' said one. 'Pass into the ante-chamber and see. There lies Pharaoh dead, and with no wound upon him to tell the manner of his end.'

Then Meriamun cried aloud with a great cry, and threw her hair about her face, while tears fell from her dark eyes. She passed into the chamber, and there, fallen on his back and cold, lay Pharaoh in his royal robes. Awhile the Queen looked upon him as one who is dumb with grief. Then she lifted up her voice and cried:

'Still is the curse heavy upon Khem and the people of Khem. Pharaoh lies dead; yea, he is dead who has no wound, and this I say, that he is slain of the witchcraft of her whom men name the Hathor. Oh, my Lord, my Lord!' and kneeling, she laid her hand upon his breast; 'by this dead heart of thine I swear that I will wreak thy murder on her who wrought it. Lift him up! Lift up this poor clay, that was the first of kings. Clothe him in the robes of death, and set him on the knees of Osiris in the Temple of Osiris. Then go forth through the city and call out this, the Queen's command; call it from street to street. This is the Queen's command, that "every woman in Tanis who has lost son, or husband, or brother, or kin or lover, through the witchcraft of the False Hathor, or by the plagues that she hath wrought on Khem, or in the war with the Apura, whom she caused to fly from Khem, do meet me at sundown in the Temple of Osiris before the face of the God and of dead Pharaoh's Majesty." '

So they took Meneptah the Osirian, and wrapping him in the robes of death, bore him to the knees of Osiris, where he should sit a day and a night. And the messengers of Meriamun went forth summoning the women of the city to meet her at sunset in the Temple of Osiris. Moreover, Meriamun sent out slaves by tens and by twenties to the number of two thousand, bidding them gather up all the wood that was in Tanis, and all the oil and the bitumen, and bundles of reeds by hundreds such as are used for the thatching of houses, and lay them in piles and stacks in a certain courtyard near the Temple of Hathor. This they did, and so the day wore on, while the women wailed about the streets because of the death of Pharaoh.

Now it chanced that the camel of Rei the Priest fell down from weariness as it journeyed swiftly back to Tanis. But Rei sped forward on foot, and came to the gates of Tanis, sorely wearied, towards the evening of that day. When he heard the wailing of the women, he asked of a passer-by what new evil had fallen upon Khem, and learned the death of Pharaoh. Then Rei knew by whose hand Pharaoh was dead, and was grieved at heart, because she whom he had served and loved—Meriamun the moon-child—was a murderess. At first he was minded to go up before the Queen and put her to an open shame, and then take his death at her hands; but when he heard that Meriamun had summoned all the women of Tanis to meet her in the Temple of Osiris, he had another thought. Hurrying to that place where he hid in the city, he ate and drank. Then he put off his beggar's rags, and robed himself afresh, and over all drew the garment of an aged crone, for this was told him, that no man should be suffered to enter the Temple. Now the day was dying, and already the western sky was red, and he hurried forth and mingled with the stream of women who passed towards the Temple gates.

'Who then slew Pharaoh?' asked one; 'and why does the Queen summon us to meet her?'

'Pharaoh is slain by the witchcraft of the False Hathor,' answered another; 'and the Queen summons us that we may take counsel how to be rid of the Hathor.'

'Tell not of the accursed Hathor,' said a third; 'my husband and my brother are dead at her hands, and my son died in the death of the first-born that she called down on Khem. Ah, if I could but see her rent limb from limb I should seek Osiris happily.'

'Some there be,' quoth a fourth, 'who say that not the Hathor, but the Gods of those Apura brought the woes on Khem, and some that Pharaoh was slain by the Queen's own hand, because of the love she bears to the great Wanderer who came here a while ago.'

'Thou fool,' answered the first; 'how can the Queen love one who would have wrought outrage on her?'

'Such things have been,' said the fourth woman; 'perchance he wrought no outrage, perchance she beguiled him as women may. Yes, yes, such things have been. I am old, and I have seen such things.'

'Yea, thou art old,' said the first. 'Thou hast no child, no husband, no father, no lover, and no brother. Thou hast lost none who are dear to thee through the magic of the Hathor. Speak one more such slander on the Queen, and we will fall upon thee and tear thy lying tongue from its roots.'

'Hush,' said the second woman, 'here are the Temple gates. By Isis did any ever see such a multitude of women, and never a man to cheer them, a dreary sight, indeed! Come, push on, push on, or we shall find no place. Yea, thou soldier—we are women, all women, have no fear. No need to bare our breasts, look at our eyes blind with weeping over the dead. Push on! push on!'

So they passed by the guards and into the gates of the Temple, and with them went Rei unheeded. Already it was well-nigh filled with women. Although the sun was not yet dead, torches were set about to lighten the gloom, and by them Rei saw that the curtains before the Shrine were drawn. Presently the Temple was full to overflowing, the doors were shut and barred, and a voice from beyond the veil cried:

'Silence!'

Then all the multitude of women were silent, and the light of the torches flared strangely upon their shifting upturned faces, as fires flare over the white sea-foam. Now the curtains of the Shrine of Osiris were drawn aside slowly, and the light that burned upon the altar streamed out between them. It fell upon the foremost ranks of women, it fell upon the polished statue of the Osiris. On the knees of Osiris sat the body of Pharaoh Meneptah, his head resting against the breast of the God. Pharaoh was wrapped about with winding clothes like the marble statue of the God, and in his cold hands were bound the crook, the sceptre, and the scourge, as the crook, the sceptre, and the scourge were placed in the hands of the effigy of the God. As was the statue of the God, so was the body of Pharaoh that sat upon his knees, and cold and awful was the face of Osiris, and cold and awful was the face of Meneptah the Osirian.

At the side, and somewhat in front of the statue of the God, a throne was placed of blackest marble, and on the throne sat Meriamun the Queen. She was glorious to look on. She wore the royal robes of Khem, the double crown of Khem fashioned of gold, and wreathed with the uraeus snakes, was set upon her head; in her hand was the crystal cross of Life, and between her mantle's purple folds gleamed the eyes of her snake girdle. She sat awhile in silence speaking no word, and all the women wondered at her glory and at dead Pharaoh's awfulness. Then at length she spoke, low indeed, but so clearly that every word reached the limits of the Temple hall.

'Women of Tanis, hear me the Queen. Let each search the face of each, and if there be any man among your multitude, let him be dragged forth and torn limb from limb, for in this matter no man may hear our counsels, lest following his madness he betray them.'

Now every woman looked upon her neighbour, and she

who was next to Rei looked hard upon him so that he trembled for his life. But he crouched into the shadow and stared back on her boldly as though he doubted if she were indeed a woman, and she said no word. When all had looked, and no man had been found, Meriamun spoke again.

'Hearken, women of Tanis, hearken to your sister and your Queen. Woe upon woe is fallen on the head of Khem. Plague upon plague hath smitten the ancient land. Our first-born are dead, our slaves have spoiled us and fled away, our hosts have been swallowed in the Sea of Weeds, and barbarians swarm along our shores like locusts. Is it not so, women of Tanis?'

'It is so, O Queen,' they answered, as with one voice.

'A strange evil hath fallen on the head of Khem. A false Goddess is come to dwell within the land; her sorceries are great in the land. Month by month men go up to look upon her deadly beauty, and month by month they are slain of her sorceries. She takes the husband from his marriage bed; she draws the lover from her who waits to be a bride; the slave flies to her from the household of his lord; the priests flock to her from the altars of the Gods—ay, the very priests of Isis flock forsworn from the altars of Isis. All look upon her witch-beauty, and to each she shows an altered loveliness, and to all she gives one guerdon—Death! Is it not so, women of Tanis?'

'Alas! alas! it is so, O Queen,' answered the women, as with one voice.

'Woes are fallen on you and Khem, my sisters, but on me most of all are woes fallen. My people have been slain, my land—the land I love—has been laid waste with plagues; my child, the only one, is dead in the great death; hands have been laid on me, the Queen of Khem. Think on it, ye who are women! My slaves are fled, my armies have been swallowed in the sea; and last, O my sisters, my consort, my beloved lord, mighty Pharaoh, son of great Rameses Miamun, hath been taken from me! Look! look! ye who are wives, look on him who was your King and my most beloved lord. There he sits, and all my tears and all my prayers may not summon one single answering sigh from that stilled heart. The curse hath fallen on him also. He too hath been smitten silently with everlasting silence. Look! look! ye who are wives, and weep with me, ye who are left widowed.'

Now the women looked, and a great groan went up from all that multitude, while Meriamun hid her face with the hollow of her hand. Then again she spoke.

'I have besought the Gods, my sisters; I have dared to call down the majesty of the Gods, who speak through the lips of the dead, and I have learnt whence these woes come. And this I have won by my prayers, that ye who suffer as I suffer shall learn whence they come, not from my mortal lips, indeed, but from the lips of the dead that speak with the voice of the Gods.'

Then, while the women trembled, she turned to the body of Pharaoh, which was set upon the knees of Osiris, and spoke to it.

'Dead Pharaoh! great Osirian, ruling in the Underworld, hearken to me now! Hearken to me now, thou Osiris, Lord of the West, first of the hosts of Death. Hearken to me, Osiris, and be manifest through the lips of him who was great on earth. Speak through his cold lips, speak with mortal accents, that these people may hear and understand. By the spirit that is in me, who am yet a dweller on the earth, I charge thee speak. Who is the source of the woes of Khem? Say, Lord of the dead, who are the living evermore.'

Now the flame on the altar died away, and dreadful silence fell upon the Temple, gloom fell upon the Shrine, and through the gloom the golden crown of Meriamun, and the cold statue of the Osiris, and the white face of dead Meneptah gleamed faint and ghost-like.

Then suddenly the flame of the altar flared as flares the summer lightning. It flared full on the face of the dead, and lo! the lips of the dead moved, and from them came the sound of mortal speech. They spake in awful accents, and thus they spoke:

'*She who was the curse of Achæans, she who was the doom of Ilios; she was sits in the Temple of Hathor, the*

Fate of Man, who may not be harmed of Man, she calls down the wrath of the Gods on Khem. It is spoken!'

The echo of the awful words died away in the silence. Then fear took hold of the multitude of women because of the words of the Dead, and some fell upon their faces, and some covered their eyes with their hands.

'Arise, my sisters!' cried the voice of Meriamun. 'Ye have heard not from my lips, but from the lips of the dead. Arise, and let us forth to the Temple of the Hathor. Ye have heard who is the fountain of our woes; let us forth and seal it at its source for ever. Of men she may not be harmed who is the fate of men, from men we ask no help, for all men are her slaves, and for her beauty's sake all men forsake us. But we will play the part of men. Our woman's milk shall freeze within our breasts, we will dip our tender hands in blood, ay, scourged by a thousand wrongs we will forget our gentleness, and tear this foul fairness from its home. We will burn the Hathor's Shrine with fire, her priests shall perish at the altar, and the beauty of the false Goddess shall melt like wax in the furnace of our hate. Say, will ye follow me, my sisters, and wreak our shames upon the Shameful One, our woes upon the Spring of Woe, our dead upon their murderess?'

She ceased, and then from every woman's throat within the great Temple there went up a cry of rage, fierce and shrill.

'We will, Meriamun, we will!' they screamed. 'To the Hathor! Lead us to the Hathor's Shrine! Bring fire! Bring fire! Lead us to the Hathor's Shrine!'

6. THE BURNING OF THE SHRINE

Rei the Priest saw and heard. Then turning, he stole away through the maddened throng of women and fled with what speed he might from the Temple. His heart was filled with fear and shame, for he knew full well that Pharaoh was dead, not at the hand of Hathor, but at the hand of Meriamun the Queen, whom he had loved. He knew well that dead Meneptah spake not with the voice of the dread Gods, but with the voice of the magic of Meriamun, who, of all women that have been since the days of Taia, was the most skilled in evil magic, the lore of the Snake. He knew also that Meriamun would slay Helen for the same cause wherefore she had slain Pharaoh, that she might win the Wanderer to her arms. While Helen lived he was not to be won away.

Now Rei was a righteous man, loving the Gods and good, and hating evil, and his heart burned because of the wickedness of the woman that once he cherished. This he swore that he would do, if time was left to him. He would warn the Helen so that she might fly the fire if so she willed, ay, and would tell her all the wickedness of Meriamun her foe.

His old feet stumbled over each other as he fled till he came to the gates of the Temple of the Hathor, and knocked upon the gates.

'What wouldst thou, old crone?' asked the priest who sat in the gates.

'I would be led to the presence of the Hathor,' he answered.

'No woman hath passed up to look upon the Hathor,' said the priest. 'That women do not seek.'

Then Rei made a secret sign, and wondering greatly that a woman should have the inner wisdom, the priest let him pass.

He came to the second gates.

'What wouldst thou?' said the priest who sat in the gates.

'I would go up into the presence of the Hathor.'

'No woman hath willed to look upon the Hathor,' said the priest.

Then again Rei made the secret sign, but still the priest wavered.

'Let me pass, thou foolish warden,' said Rei. 'I am a messenger from the Gods.'

'If thou art a mortal messenger, woman, thou goest to thy doom,' said the priest.

'On my head be it,' answered Rei, and the priest let him pass wondering.

Now he stood before the doors of the Alabaster Shrine that glowed with the light within. Still Rei paused not, only uttering a prayer that he might be saved from the unseen swords; he lifted the latch of bronze, and entered fearfully. But none fell upon him, nor was he smitten of invisible spears. Before him swung the curtains of Tyrian web, but no sound of singing came from behind the curtains. All was silence in the Shrine. He passed between the curtains and looked up the Sanctuary. It was lit with many hanging lamps, and by their light he saw the Goddess Helen, seated between the pillars of her loom. But she wove no more at the loom. The web of fate was rent by the Wanderer's hands, and lay on either side, a shining cloth of gold. The Goddess Helen sat songless in her lonely Shrine, and on her breast gleamed the Red Star of light that wept the blood of men. Her head rested on her hand, and her heavenly eyes of blue gazed emptily down the empty Shrine.

Rei drew near trembling, though she seemed to see him not at all, and at last flung himself upon the earth before her. Now at length she saw him, and spoke in her voice of music.

'Who art thou that dares to break in upon my sorrow?' she said wonderingly. 'Art thou indeed a woman come to look on one who by the will of the Gods is each woman's deadliest foe?'

Then Rei raised himself, saying:

'No woman am I, immortal Lady. I am Rei, that aged priest who met thee two nights gone by the pylon gates, and led thee to the Palace of Pharaoh. And I have dared to seek thy Shrine to tell thee that thou art in danger at the hands of Meriamun the Queen, and also to give thee a certain message with which I am charged by him who is named the Wanderer.'

Now Helen looked upon him wonderingly and spoke:

'Didst thou not but now name me immortal, Rei? How then can I be in danger, who am immortal, and not to be harmed of men? Death hath no part in me. Speak not to me of dangers, who, alas! can never die till everything is done; but tell me of that faithless Wanderer, whom I must love with all the womanhood that shuts my spirit in, and all my spirit that is clothed in womanhood. For, Rei, the Gods, withholding Death, have in their wrath cursed me with love to torment my deathlessness. Oh, when I saw him standing where now thou standest, my soul knew its other part, and I learned that the curse I give to others had fallen on myself and him.'

'Yet was this Wanderer not altogether faithless to thee, Lady,' said Rei. 'Listen, and I will tell thee all.'

'Speak on,' she said. 'Oh, speak, and speak swiftly.'

Then Rei told Helen all that tale which the Wanderer had charged him to deliver in her ear, and keep no word back. He told her how Meriamun had beguiled Eperitus in her shape; how he had fallen in the snare and sworn by the Snake, he who should have sworn by the Star. He told her how the Wanderer had learned the truth, and learning it, had cursed the witch who wronged him; how he had been overcome by the guards and borne to the bed of torment; how he had been freed by the craft of Meriamun; and how he had gone forth to lead the host of Khem. All this he told her swiftly, hiding naught, while she listened with eager ears.

'Truly,' she said, when all was told, 'truly thou art a happy messenger. Now I forgive him all. Yet has he sworn by the Snake who should have sworn by the Star, and because of his fault never in this space of life shall Helen call him Lord. Yet will we follow him, Rei. Hark! what is that? Again it comes, that long shrill cry as of ghosts broke loose from Hades.'

'It is the Queen,' quoth Rei; 'the Queen who with all the women of Tanis comes hither to burn thee in thy Shrine. She hath slain Pharaoh, and now she would slay thee also, and so win the Wanderer to her arms. Fly, Lady! Fly!'

'Nay, I fly not,' said Helen. 'Let her come. But do thou, Rei, pass through the Temple gates and mingle with the crowd. There thou shalt await my coming, and when I come, draw near, fearing nothing; and together we will pass down the path of the Wanderer in such fashion as I shall show thee. Go! go swiftly, and bid those who minister to me pass out with thee.'

Then Rei turned and fled. Without the doors of the Shrine many priests were gathered.

'Fly! the women of Tanis are upon you!' he cried. 'I charge ye to fly!'

'This old crone is mad,' quoth one. 'We watch the Hathor, and, come all the women of the world, we fly not.'

'Ye are mad indeed,' said Rei, and sped on.

He passed the gates, the gates clashed behind him. He won the outer space, and hiding in the shadows of the Temple walls, looked forth. The night was dark, but from every side a thousand lights poured down towards the Shrine. On they came like lanterns on the waters of Sihor at the night of the feast of lanterns. Now he could see their host. It was the host of the women of Tanis, and every woman bore a lighted torch. They came by tens, by hundreds, and by thousands, and before them was Meriamun the Queen. Bidding certain of them stay by her asses, oxen, and camels, laden with bitumen, wood, and reeds. Now they gained the gates, and now they crashed them in with battering trees of palm. The gates fell, the women poured through them. At their head went Meriamun the Queen. Bidding certain of them stay by her chariot she passed through, and standing at the inner gates called aloud to the priests to throw them wide.

'Who art thou who darest come up with fire against the

holy Temple of the Hathor?' asked the guardian of the gates.

'I am Meriamun, the Queen of Khem,' she answered, 'come with the women of Tanis to slay the Witch thou guardest. Throw the gates wide, or die with the Witch.'

'If indeed thou art the Queen,' answered the priest, 'here there sits a greater Queen than thou. Go back! Go back, Meriamun, who art not afraid to offer violence to the immortal Gods. Go back! lest the curse smite thee.'

'Draw on! draw on! ye women,' cried Meriamun; 'draw on, smite down the gates, and tear these wicked ones limb from limb.'

Then the women screamed aloud and battered on the gates with trees, so that they fell. They fell and the women rushed in madly. They seized the priests of Hathor and tore them limb from limb as dogs tear a wolf. Now the Shrine stood before them.

'Touch not the doors,' cried Meriamun. 'Bring fire and burn the Shrine with her who dwells therein. Touch not the doors, look not in the Witch's face, but burn her where she is with fire.'

Then the women brought the reeds and the wood, and piled them around the Shrine to twice the height of a man. They brought ladders also, and piled the fuel upon the roof of the Shrine till all was covered. And they poured pitch over the fuel, and then at the word of Meriamun they cast torches on the pitch and drew back screaming. For a moment the torches smouldered, then suddenly on every side great tongues of flame leapt up to heaven. Now the Shrine was wrapped in fire, and yet they cast fuel on it till none might draw near because of the heat. Now it burned as a furnace burns, and now the fire reached the fuel on the roof. It caught, and the Shrine was but a sheet of raging flame that lit the white-walled city, and the broad face of the waters, as the sun lights the lands. The alabaster walls of the Shrine turned whiter yet with heat: they cracked and split till the fabric tottered to its fall.

'Now there is surely an end of the Witch,' cried Meriamun, and the women screamed an answer to her.

But even as they screamed a great tongue of flame shot

out through the molten doors, ten fathoms length and more, it shot like a spear of fire. Full in its path stood a group of the burners. It struck them, it licked them up, and lo! they fell in blackened heaps upon the ground.

Rei looked down the path of the flame. There, in the doorway whence it had issued, stood the Golden Helen, wrapped round with fire, and the molten metal of the doors crept about her feet. There she stood in the heart of the fire, but there was no stain of fire on her, nor on her white robes, nor on her streaming hair; and even through the glow of the furnace he saw the light of the Red Star at her breast. The flame licked her form and face, it wrapped itself around her, and curled through the masses of her hair. But still she stood unharmed, while the burners shrank back amazed, all save Meriamun the Queen. And as she stood she sang wild and sweet, and the sound of her singing came through the roar of the flames and reached the ears of the women, who, forgetting their rage, clung to one another in fear. Thus she sang—of that Beauty which men seek in all women, and never find, and of the eternal war for her sake between the women and the men, which is the great war of the world. And thus her song ended:

> Will ye bring flame to burn my Shrine
>   Who am myself a flame,
> Bring death to tame this charm of mine
>   That death can never tame?
> Will ye bring fire to harm my head
>   Who am myself a fire,
> Bring vengeance for your Lovers dead
>   Upon the World's Desire?
> Nay, women while the earth endures,
>   Your loves are not your own.
> They love you not, these loves of yours,
>   *Helen* they love alone!
> My face they seek in every face,
>   Mine eyes in yours they see,
> They do but kneel to you a space,
>   And rise and follow *me!*

Then, still singing, she stepped forward from the Shrine, and as she went the walls fell in, and the roof crashed down upon the ruin and the flames shot into the very sky. Helen heeded it not. She looked not back, but out to the gates beyond. She glanced not at the fierce blackened faces of the women, nor on the face of Meriamun, who stood before her, but slowly passed towards the gates. Nor did she go alone, for with her came a canopy of fire, hedging her round with flame that burned from nothing. The women saw the wonder and fell down in their fear, covering their eyes. Meriamun alone fell not, but she too must cover her eyes because of the glory of Helen and the fierceness of the flame that wrapped her round.

Now Helen ceased singing, but moved slowly through the courts till she came to the outer gates. Here by the gates was the chariot of Merimun. Then Helen called aloud, and the Queen, who followed, heard her words:

'Rei,' she cried, 'draw nigh and have no fear. Draw nigh that I may pass with thee down that path the Wanderer treads. Draw nigh, and let us swiftly hence, for the hero's last battle is at hand, and I would greet him ere he die.'

Rei heard her and drew near trembling, tearing from him the woman's weeds he wore, and showing the priest's garb beneath. And as he came the fire that wrapped her glory round left her, and passed upward like a cloak of flame. She stretched out her hand to him, saying:

'Lead me to yonder chariot, Rei, and let us hence.'

Then he led her to the chariot, while those who stood by fled in fear. She mounted the chariot, and he set himself beside her. Then he grasped the reins and called to the horses, and they bounded forward and were lost in the night.

But Meriamun cried in her wrath:

'The Witch is gone, gone with my own servant whom she hath led astray. Bring chariots, and let horsemen come with the chariots, for where she passes there I will follow, ay, to the end of the world and the coast of Death.'

7. THE LAST FIGHT OF ODYSSEUS, LAERTES' SON

Now the host of Pharaoh marched forth from On, to do battle with the Nine-bow barbarians. And before the host marched, the Captains came to the Wanderer, according to the command of Pharaoh, and placing their hands in his, swore to do his bidding on the march and in the battle. They brought him the great black bow of Eurytus, and his keen sword of bronze, Euryalus' gift, and many a sheaf of arrows, and his heart rejoiced when he saw the goodly weapons. He took the bow and tried it, and as he drew the string, once again and for the last time it sang shrilly of death to be. The Captains heard the Song of the Bow, though what it said the Wanderer knew alone, for to their ears it came but as a faint, keen cry, like the cry of one who drowns in the water far from the kindly earth. But they marvelled much at the wonder, and said one to another that this man was no mortal, but a God come from the Under-world.

Then the Wanderer mounted the chariot of bronze that had been made ready for him, and gave the word to march.

All night the host marched swiftly, and at daybreak they camped beneath the shelter of a long, low hill. But at the sunrise the Wanderer left the host, climbed the hill with certain of the Captains, and looked forth. Before him was a great pass in the mountains, ten furlongs or more in length, and through it ran the road. The sides of the

mountain sloped down to the road, and were strewn with
rocks split by the sun, polished by the sand, and covered
over with bush that grew sparsely, like the hair on the
limbs of a man. To the left of the mountains lay the river
Sihor, but none might pass between the mountain and the
river. The Wanderer descended from the hill, and while
the soldiers ate, drove swiftly in his chariot to the further
end of the pass and looked forth again. Here the river
curved to the left, leaving a wide plain, and on the plain
he saw the host of the Nine-bow barbarians, the mightiest
host that ever his eyes had looked upon. They were en-
camped by nations, and of each nation there were twenty
thousand men, and beyond the glittering camp of the
barbarians he saw the curved ships of the Achæans. They
were drawn up on the beach of the great river, as many a
year ago he had seen them drawn up on the shore that is
by Ilios. He looked upon plain and pass, on mountain and
river, and measured the number of the foe. Then his heart
was filled with lust of battle, and his warlike cunning
awoke. For of all leaders of men he was the most skilled
in the craft of battle, and he desired that this, his last war,
should be the greatest war of all.

Turning his horses' heads, he galloped back to the host
of Pharaoh and mustered them in battle array. It was but
a little number as against the number of the barbarians—
twelve thousand spearmen, nine thousand archers, two
thousand horsemen, and three hundred chariots. The
Wanderer passed up and down their ranks, bidding them
be of good courage for this day they should sweep the
barbarians from the land.

As he spoke a hawk flew down from the right, and fell
on a heron, and slew it in mid-air. The host shouted, for
the hawk is the Holy Bird of Ra, and the Wanderer, too,
rejoiced in the omen. 'Look, men,' he cried; 'the Bird of
Ra has slain the wandering thief from the waters. And so
shall ye smite the spoilers from the sea.'

Then he held counsel with Captains, and certain trusty
men were sent out to the camp of the barbarians. And
they were charged to give an ill report of the host of
Pharaoh, and to say that such of it as remained awaited

the barbarian onset behind the shelter of the hill on the further side of the pass.

Then the Wanderer summoned the Captains of the archers, and bade them hide all their force among the rocks and thorns on either side of the mountain pass, and there to wait till he drew the hosts of the foe into the pass. And with the archers he sent a part of the spearmen, but the chariots he hid beneath the shelter of the hill on the hither side of the pass.

Now, when the ambush was set, and all were gone save the horsemen only, his spies came in and told him that the host of the barbarians marched from their camp, but that the Achæans marched not, but stopped by the river to guard the camp and ships. Then the Wanderer bade the horsemen ride through the pass and stand in the plain beyond, and there await the foe. But when the hosts of the barbarians charged them, they must reel before the charge, and at length fly headlong down the pass as though in fear. And he himself would lead the flight in his chariot, and where he led there they should follow.

So the horsemen rode through the pass and formed their squadrons on the plain beyond. Now the foe drew nigh, and a glorious sight it was to see the midday sun sparkling on their countless spears. Of horsemen they had no great number, but there were many chariots and swordsmen, and spearmen, and slingers beyond count. They came on by nations, and in the centre of the host of each nation sat the king of the nation in a glorious chariot, with girls and eunuchs, holding fans to fan him with and awnings of silk to hide him from the sun.

Now the Wanderer hung back behind the squadrons of horsemen as though in fear. But presently he sent messengers bidding the Captains of the squadrons to charge the first nation, and fight for a while but feebly, and then when they saw him turn his horses and gallop through the pass, to follow after him as though in doubt, but in such fashion as to draw the foe upon their heels.

This the Captains of the mercenaries did. Once they charged and were beaten back, then they charged again, but the men made as though they feared the onset. Now the foe came hard after them, and the Wanderer turned his chariot and fled through the pass, followed slowly by the horsemen. And when the hosts of the barbarians saw them turn, they set up a mighty shout of laughter that rent the skies, and charged after them.

But the Wanderer looked back and laughed also. Now he was through the pass followed by the horsemen, and after them swept the hosts of the barbarians, like a river that has burst its banks. Still the Wanderer held his hand till the whole pass was choked with the thousands of the foe, ay, until the half of the first of the nations had passed into the narrow plain that lay between the hill and the mouth of the pass. Then, driving apace up the hill, he stood in his chariot and gave the signal. Lifting his golden shield on high he flashed it thrice, and all the horsemen shouted aloud. At the first flash, behold, from behind every rock and bush of the mountain sides arose the helms of armed men. At the second flash there came a rattling sound of shaken quivers, and at the third flash of the golden shield, the air was darkened with the flight of arrows. As the sea-birds on a lonely isle awake at the cry of the sailor, and wheel by thousands from their lofty cliffs, so at the third flash of the Wanderer's shield the arrows of his hidden host rushed downward on the foe, rattling like hail upon their harness. For awhile they kept their ranks, and pressed on over the bodies of those that fell. But soon the horses in the chariots, maddened with wounds, plunged this way and that, breaking their companies and trampling the soldiers down. Now some strove to fly forward, and some were fain to fly back, and many an empty chariot was dragged this way and that, but ever the pitiless rain of shafts poured down, and men fell by thousands beneath the gale of death. Now the mighty host of the Nine-bows rolled back, thinned and shattered, towards the plain, and now the Wanderer cried the word of onset to the horsemen and to the chariots that drew from behind the shelter of the hill, and following after him they charged down upon those barbarians who had passed the ambush, singing the song of Pentaur as they charged. Among those nigh the mouth of the pass was the king of the nation of the Libu, a great man, black and terrible to see. The Wanderer drew his bow, the arrow rushed forth and pierced the king, and he fell dead in his chariot. Then those of his host who had passed the ambush turned to fly, but the chariot of the Wanderer dashed into them, an after the chariot came the horsemen, and after the horsemen the chariots of Pharaoh.

Now all who were left of the broken host rolled back, mad with fear, while the spearmen of Pharaoh galled them as hunters gall a flying bull, and the horsemen of Pharaoh trampled them beneath their feet. Red slaughter raged all down the pass, helms, banners, arrow-points shone and fell in the stream of the tide of war, but at length the stony way was clear save for the dead alone. Beyond the pass the plain was black with flying men, and the fragments of the broken nations were mixed together as clay and sand are mixed of the potter. Where now were the hosts of the Nine-bow barbarians? Where now were their glory and their pride?

The Wanderer gathered his footmen and his chariots and set them in array again, but the horsemen he sent out to smite the flying nations and wait his coming by the camp; for there were mustering those who were left of the nations, perchance twenty thousand men, and before their ships were ranged the dense ranks of the Achæans, shield to shield, every man in his place.

The Wanderer led his host slowly across the sandy plain, till at length he halted it two bow-shots from the camp of the barbarians. The camp was shaped like a bow, and the river Sihor formed its string, and round it was a deep ditch, and beyond the ditch a wall of clay. Moreover, within the camp and nearer to the shore there was a second ditch and wall, and behind it were the beaks of the ships and the host of Aquaiusha, even of his own dear people the Achæans. There were the old blazons, and the spears that had fought below Troy town. There were the two lions of Mycenæ, the Centaur of the son of Polypaetas, son of Pirithous; there were the Swan of Lacedæmon, and the Bull of the Kings of Crete, the Rose of Rhodes, the Serpent of Athens, and many another knightly bearing of old friends and kindred dear. And now they were the blazons of foemen, and the Wanderer warred for a strange king, and for his own hand, beneath the wings of the Hawk of the Legion of Ra.

The Wanderer sent heralds forward, calling to those barbarians who swarmed behind the wall to surrender to the host of Pharaoh, but this, being entrenched by the river Sihor, they would in nowise do. For they were mad because of their slaughtered thousands, and moreover they knew that it is better to die than to live as slaves. This they saw also, that their host was still as strong as the host of Pharaoh, which was without the wall, and weary with the heat and stress of battle and the toil of marching through the desert sands. Now the Captains of the host of Pharaoh came to the Wanderer, praying him that he would do no more battle on that day, because the men were weary, and the horses neighed for food and water.

But he answered them: 'I swore to Pharaoh that I would utterly smite the people of the Nine-bows and drive them down to death, so that the coasts of Khem may be free of them. Here I may not camp the host, without food or pasture for the horses, and if I go back, the foe will gather heart and come on, and with them the fleet of the Achæans, and no more shall we lure them into ambush, for therein they have learned a lesson. Nay, get you to your companies. I will go up against the camp.'

Then they bowed and went, for having seen his deeds and his skill and craft in war, they held him the first of Captains, and dared not say him nay.

So the Wanderer divided his host into three parts, set it in order of battle, and moved up against the camp. But he himself went with the centre part against the gate of the camp, for here there was an earthen way for chariots, if but the great gates might be passed. And at a word the threefold host rushed on to the charge. But those within the walls shot them with spears and arrows, so that many were slain, and they were rolled back from the wall as a wave is rolled from the cliff. Again the Wanderer bade them charge on the right and left, bearing the dead before them as shields, and hurling corpses into the ditch to fill it. But he himself hung back awhile with the middle army, watching how the battle went, and waiting till the foe at the gate should be drawn away.

Now the mercenaries of Pharaoh forced a passage on the right, and thither went many of the barbarians who watched the gate, that they might drive them back.

Then the Wanderer bade men take out the poles of chariots and follow him and beat down the gates with the poles. This with much toil and loss they did, for the archers poured their arrows on the assailants of the gate. Now at length the gates were down, and the Wanderer rushed through them with his chariot. But even as he passed the mercenaries of Pharaoh were driven out from the camp on the right, and those who led the left attack fled also. The soldiers who should have followed the Wanderer saw and wavered a little moment, and while they wavered the companies of the barbarians poured into the gateway and held it so that none might pass. Now the Wanderer was left alone within the camp, and back he might not go. But fear came not nigh him, nay, the joy of battle filled his mighty heart. He cast his shield upon the brazen floor of the chariot, and cried aloud to the charioteer, as he loosened the long gray shafts in his quiver.

'Drive on, thou charioteer! Drive on! The jackals leave the lion in the toils. Drive on! Drive on! and win a glorious death, for thus should Odysseus die.'

So the charioteer, praying to his Gods, lashed the horses with his scourge, and they sprang forward madly among the foe. And as they rushed, the great bow rang and sang the swallow string—rung the bow and sung the string, and the lean shaft drank the blood of a leader of men. Again the string sang, again the shaft sped forth, and a barbarian king fell from his chariot as a diver plunges into the sea, and his teeth bit the sand.

'Dive deep, thou sea-thief!' cried the Wanderer, 'thou mayest find treasures there! Drive on, thou charioteer, so should lions die while jackals watch.'

Now the barbarians looked on the Wanderer and were amazed. For ever his chariot rushed to and fro, across the mustering ground of the camp, and ever his gray shafts carried death before them, and ever the foemen's arrows fell blunted from his golden harness. They looked on him amazed, they cried aloud that this was the God of War come down to do battle for Khem, that it was Sutek the Splendid, that it was Baal in his strength; they fled amain before his glory and his might. For the Wanderer raged among them like great Rameses Miamun among the tribes of the Khita; like Monthu, the Lord of Battles, and lo! they fled before him, their knees gave way, their hearts were turned to water, he drove them as a herdsman drives the yearling calves.

But now at length a stone from a sling smote the charioteer who directed the chariot, and sunk in between his eyes, so that he fell down dead from the chariot. Then the reins flew wide, and the horses rushed this way and that, having no master. And now a spear pierced the heart of the horse on the right, so that he fell, and the pole of the chariot snapped in two. Then the barbarians took heart and turned, and some of them set on to seize the body of the charioteer, and spoil his arms. But the Wanderer leaped down and bestrode the corpse with shield up and spear aloft.

Now among the press of the barbarians there was a stir, as of one thrusting his way through them to the front. And above the plumes of their helmets and the tossing of their shields the Wanderer saw the golden head, unhelmeted, of a man, taller than the tallest there from the shoulders upwards. Unhelmeted he came and unshielded, with no body armour. His flesh was very fair and white, and on it were figures pricked in blue, figures of men and horses, snakes and sea-beasts. The skin of a white bear was buckled above his shoulder with a golden clasp, fashioned in the semblance of a boar. His eyes were blue, fierce and shining, and in his hand he held for a weapon the trunk of a young pine-tree, in which was hafted a weighty axe-head of rough unpolished stone.

'Give way!' he cried. 'Give place, ye dusky dwarfs, and let a man see this champion!'

So the barbarians made a circle about the Wanderer and the giant, and stood silently to watch a great fight.

'Who art thou?' said the mighty man disdainfully, 'and whence? Where is thy city, and thy parents who begat thee?'

'Now I will avow that men call me Odysseus, Sacker of Cities, Laertes' son, a Prince of the Achæans,' said the Wanderer. 'And who art thou, I pray thee, and where is thy native place, for city, I wot, thou hast none?'

Then the mighty man, swinging his great stone axe in a rhythmic motion, began to chant a rude lay, and this was the manner of the singing—

> Laestrygons men
> And Cimmerians call us
> Born of the land
> Of the sunless winter,
> Born of the land
> Of the nightless summer:
> Cityless we,
> Beneath dark pine boughs,
> By the sea abiding
> Sail o'er the swan's bath.
> *Wolf* am I hight,
> The son of Signy,
> Son of the were-wolf.
> Southwards I sailed,
> Sailed with the amber,
> Sailed with the foam-wealth.
> Among strange peoples,
> Winning me wave-flame,[1]
> Winning me war-fame,
> Winning me women.
> Soon shall I slay thee,
> Sacker of Cities!

With that, and with a cry, he rushed on the Wanderer, his great axe swung aloft, to fell him at a blow.

But while the giant had been singing, the Wanderer had shifted his place a little, so that the red blaze of the setting sun was in his face. And as the mighty man came on, the Wanderer lifted up his golden shield and caught the sun-

[1] Gold.

light on it, and flashed it full in the giant's eyes, so that he was dazzled, and could not see to strike. Then the Wanderer smote at his naked right arm, and struck it on the joint of the elbow; with all his force he smote, and the short sword of Euryalus bit deep, and the arm fell, with the axe in the hand-grip. But so terrible was the stroke that bronze might not abide it, and the blade was shattered from the ivory handle.

'Did'st thou feel aught, thou Man-eater?' cried Odysseus, jeering, for he knew from the song of the giant that he was face to face with a wanderer from an evil race, that of old had smitten his ships and devoured his men—the Laestrygons of the land of the Midnight Sun, the Man-eaters.

But the giant caught up his club of pine-tree in his left hand, the severed right arm yet clinging to it. And he gnawed on the handle of the stone axe with his teeth, and bit the very stone, and his lips foamed, for a fury came upon him. Roaring aloud, suddenly he smote at the Wanderer's head, and beat down his shield, and crushed his golden helm so that he fell on one knee, and all was darkness around him. But his hands lit on a great stone, for the place where they fought was the holy place of an ancient temple, old and ruined before King Mena's day. He grasped the stone with both hands; it was the basalt head of a fallen statue of a God or a man, of a king long nameless, or of a forgotten God. With a mighty strain the Wanderer lifted it as he rose, it was a weight of a chariot's burden and poising it, he hurled it straight at the breast of the Laestrygon, who had drawn back, whirling his axe, before he smote another blow. But ere ever the stroke fell, the huge stone struck him full and broke in his breast-bone, and he staggered long, and fell like a tree, and the black blood came up through his bearded lips, and his life left him.

Then the multitude of the barbarians that stood gazing at the fray drew yet further back in fear, and the Wanderer laughed like a God at that old score paid, and at the last great stroke of the hands of the City-sacker, Odysseus.

8. 'TILL ODYSSEUS COMES!'

The Wanderer laughed like a God, though he deemed that the end was near, and the foes within the camp and the friends without looked on him and wondered.

'Slay him!' cried the foes within, speaking in many tongues. 'Slay him!' they cried, and yet they feared the task, but circled round like hounds about a mighty boar at bay.

'Spare him!' shouted the host of the Achæans, watching the fray from far, as they stood behind their inner wall, for as yet they had not mingled in the battle but stayed by their ships to guard them.

'Rescue him!' cried the Captains of Pharaoh without, but none came on to force the way.

Then of a sudden, as Fate hung upon the turn, a great cry of fear and wonder rose from the ranks of Pharaoh's host beyond the wall. It swelled and swelled till at length the cry took the sound of a name—the sound of the name of *Hathor*.

'The Hathor! the Hathor! See, the Hathor comes!'

The Wanderer turned his head and looked swiftly. A golden chariot sped down the slope of sand towards the gate of the camp. The milk-white horses were stained with sweat and splashed with blood. They thundered on towards the gate down the way that was red with blood, as the horses of the dawn rush through the blood-red sky. A little man, withered and old, drove the chariot, leaning forward as he drove, and by his side stood the Golden Helen. The Red Star blazed upon her breast, her hair and filmy robes floated on the wind.

She looked up and forth. Now she saw him, Odysseus of Ithaca, her love, alone, beset with foes, and a cry broke from her. She tore away the veil that hid her face, and her beauty flashed out upon the sight of men as the moon flashes from the evening mists. She pointed to the gate, she stretched out her arms towards the host of Pharaoh, bidding them look upon her and follow her. Then a shout went up from the host, and they rushed onwards in the path of the chariot, for where the Helen leads there men must follow through Life to Death through War to Peace.

On the chariot rushed to the camp, and after it the host of Pharaoh followed. The holders of the gate saw the beauty of her who rode in the chariot; they cried aloud in many tongues that the Goddess of Love had come to save the God of War. They fled this way and that, or stood drunken with the sight of beauty, and were dashed down by the horses and crushed of the chariot wheels. Now she had passed the gates, and after her poured the host of Pharaoh. Now Rei reined up the horses by the broken chariot of the Wanderer, and now the Wanderer, with a shout of joy, had sprung into the chariot of Helen.

'And art thou come to be with me in my last battle?" he whispered in her ear. 'Art thou indeed that Argive Helen whom I love, or am I drunk with the blood of men and blind with the sheen of spears, and is this the vision of a man doomed to die?'

'It is no vision, Odysseus, for I am Helen's self,' she answered gently. 'I have learned all the truth, and knowing thy fault, count it but a little thing. Yet because thou didst forget the words of the immortal Goddess, who, being my foe now and for ever, set this cunning snare for thee, the doom is on thee, that Helen shall not be thine in this space of life. For thou fightest in thy last battle, Odysseus. On! see thy hosts clamour to be led, and there the foe hangs black as storm and shoots out the lightning of his spears. On, Odysseus, on! that the doom may be accomplished, and the word of the Ghost fufilled!'

Then the Wanderer turned and called to the Captains, and the Captains called to the soldiers and set them in array, and following the blood-red Star they rolled down upon the gathered foe as the tide rolls upon the rocks when the breath of the gale is strong; and as the waters leap and gather till the rocks are lost in the surge, so the host of Pharaoh leapt upon the foe and swallowed them up. And ever in the forefront of the war blazed the Red Star on Helen's breast, and ever the sound of her singing pierced the din of death.

Now the host of the Nine-bow barbarians was utterly destroyed, and the host of Pharaoh came up against the wall that was set about the camp of the Achæans to guard their ships, and at its head came the golden chariot wherein were the Wanderer and Helen. The Captains of the Achæans looked wondering from their wall, watching the slaughter of their allies.

'Now, who is this,' cried a Captain, 'who is this clad in golden armour fashioned like our own, who leads the host of Pharaoh to victory?'

Then a certain aged leader of men looked forth and answered:

'Such armour I have known indeed, and such a man once wore it. The armour is fashioned like the armour of Paris, Priam's son—Paris of Ilios; but Paris hath long been dead.'

'And who is she,' cried the Captain, 'she on whose breast a Red Star burns, who rides in the chariot of him with the golden armour, whose shape is the shape of Beauty, and who sings aloud while men go down to death?'

Then the aged leader of men looked forth again and answered:

'Such a one I have known, indeed; so she was wont to sing, and hers was such a shape of beauty, and such a Star shone ever on her breast. Helen of Ilios—Argive Helen it was who wore it—Helen, because of whose loveliness the world grew dark with death; but long is Helen dead.'

Now the Wanderer glanced from his chariot and saw the crests of the Achæans and the devices on the shields of men with whose fathers he had fought beneath the walls of Ilios. He saw and his heart was stirred within him, so that he wept there in the chariot.

'Alas! for the fate that is on me,' he cried, 'that I must make my last battle in the service of a stranger against my own people and the children of my own dear friends.'

'Weep not, Odysseus', said Helen, 'for Fate drives thee on—Fate that is cruel and changeless, and heeds not the loves or hates of men. Weep not, Odysseus, but go on up against the Achæans, for from among them thy death comes.'

So the Wanderer went on, sick at heart, shooting no shafts and striking no blow, and after him came the remnant of the host of Pharaoh. Then he halted the host, and at his bidding Rei drove slowly down the wall seeking a place to storm it, and as he drove they shot at the chariot from the wall with spears and slings and arrows. But not yet was the Wanderer doomed. He took no hurt, nor did any hurt come to Rei nor to the horses that drew the chariot, and as for Helen, the shafts of Death knew her and turned aside. Now while they drove thus Rei told the Wanderer of the death of Pharaoh, of the burning of the Temple of Hathor, and of the flight of Helen. The Wanderer hearkened and said but one thing, for in all this he saw the hand of Fate.

'It is time to make an end, Rei, for soon will Meriamun be seeking us, and methinks that I have left a trail that she can follow,' and he nodded at the piled-up dead that stretched further than the eye could reach.

Now they were come over against that spot in the wall where stood the aged Captain of the Achæans, who had likened the armour of the Wanderer to the armour of Paris, and the beauty of her at his side to the beauty of Argive Helen.

The Captain loosed his bow at the chariot, and leaning forward watched the flight of the shaft. It rushed straight at Helen's breast, then of a sudden turned aside, harming her not. And as he marvelled she lifted her face and looked towards him. Then he saw and knew her for that Helen whom he had seen while he served with Cretan Idomeneus in the Argive ships, when the leaguer was done and the smoke went up from burning Ilios.

Again he looked, and lo! on the Wanderer's golden shield he saw the White Bull, the device of Paris, son of Priam, as ofttimes he had seen it glitter on the walls of Troy. Then great fear took him, and he lifted up his hands and cried aloud:

'Fly, ye Achæans! Fly! Back to your curved ships and away from this accursed land. For yonder in the chariot stands Argive Helen, who is long dead, and with her Paris, son of Priam, come to wreak the woes of Ilios on the sons of those who wasted her. Fly, ere the curse smite you.'

Then a great cry of fear rose from the host of the Achæans, as company called to company that the ghosts of Paris of Ilios and Argive Helen led the armies of Pharaoh on to victory. A moment they gazed as frightened sheep gaze upon the creeping wolves, then turning from the wall, they rushed headlong to their ships.

Behind them came the soldiers of Pharaoh, storming the walls and tearing at their flanks as wolves tear the flying sheep. Then the Archæans turned at bay, and a mighty fray raged round the ships, and the knees of many were loosened. And of the ships, some were burned and some were left upon the bank. But a remnant of them were pushed off into the deep water, and hung there on their oars waiting the end of the fray.

Now the sun was gone down, so that men could scarce see to slay each other. The Wanderer stood in his chariot on the bank, watching the battle, for he was weary, and had little mind to swell the slaughter of the people of his own land.

Now the last ship was pushed off, and at length the great battle was done. But among those on the ship was a man still young, and the goodliest and mightiest among all the host of the Achæans. By his own strength and valour he had held the Egyptians back while his comrades ran the curved ship down the beach, and the Wanderer, looking on him, deemed him their hardiest warrior and most worthy of the Achæans.

He stood upon the poop of the ship, and saw the light from the burning vessels gleam on the Wanderer's golden helm. Then of a sudden he drew a mighty bow and loosed an arrow charged with death.

'This gift to the Ghost of Paris from Telegonus, son of Circe and of Odysseus, who was Paris' foe,' he cried with a loud voice.

And as he cried it, and as the fateful words struck on the ears of Odysseus and the ears of Helen, the shaft, pointed by the Gods, rushed on. It rushed on, it smote the Wanderer with a deadly wound where the golden body-plate of his harness joined the taslets, and pierced him through. Then he knew that his fate was accomplished, and that death came upon him from the water, as the ghost of Tiresias in Hades had foretold. In his pain, for the last time of all, he let fall his shield and the black bow of Eurytus. With one hand he clasped the rail of the chariot and the other he threw about the neck of the Golden Helen, who bent beneath his weight like a lily before the storm. Then he also cried aloud in answer:

'Oh, Telegonus, son of Circe, what wickedness hast thou wrought before the awful Gods that this curse should have been laid upon thee to slay him who begat thee? Hearken, thou son of Circe, I am not Paris, I am Odysseus of Ithaca, who begat thee, and thou hast brought my death upon me from the water, as the Ghost foretold.'

When Telegonus heard these words, and knew that he had slain his father, the famed Odysseus, whom he had sought the whole world through, he would have cast himself into the river there to drown, but those with him held him by strength, and the stream took the curved ship and floated it away. And thus for the first and last time did the Gods give it to Telegonus to look upon the face and hear the voice of his father, Odysseus.

But when the Achæans knew that it was the lost Odysseus who had led the host of Pharaoh against the armies of the Nine Nations, they wondered no more at the skill of the ambush and the greatness of the victory of Pharaoh.

Now the chariots of Meriamun were pursuing, and they splashed through the blood of men in the pass, and rolled over the bodies of men in the plain beyond the pass. They came to the camps and found them peopled with dead, and lit with the lamps of the blazing ships of the Aquaiusha. Then Meriamun cried aloud:

'Surely Pharaoh grew wise before he died, for there is but one man on the earth who with so small a force could have won so great a fray. He hath saved the crown of Khem, and by Osiris he shall wear it.'

Now the chariots of Meriamun had passed the camp of the barbarians, and were come to the inner camp of the Achæans, and the soldiers shouted as she came driving furiously.

The Wanderer lay dying on the ground, there by the river-bank, and the light of the burning ships flamed on his golden armour, and on the Star at Helen's breast.

'Why do the soldiers shout?' he asked, lifting his head from Helen's breast.

'They shout because Meriamun the Queen is come,' Rei answered.

'Let her come,' said the Wanderer.

Now Meriamun sprang from her chariot and walked, through the soldiers who made way, bowing before her royalty, to where the Wanderer lay, and stood speechless looking on him.

But the Wanderer lifting his head spake faintly:

'Hail! O Queen!' he said. 'I have accomplished the charge that Pharaoh laid upon me. The host of the Nine-bow barbarians is utterly destroyed, the fleet of the Aquaiusha is burned, or fled, the land of Khem is free from foes. Where is Pharaoh, that I may make report to him ere I die?'

'Pharaoh is dead, Odysseus,' she answered. 'Oh, live on! live on! and thyself thou shalt be Pharaoh.'

'Ay, Meriamun the Queen,' answered the Wanderer, 'I know all. Pharaoh is dead! Thou didst slay Pharaoh, thinking thus to win me for thy Lord, me, who am won of Death. Heavily shall the blood of Pharaoh lie upon thee in that land whither I go, Meriamun, and whither thou must follow swiftly. Thou didst slay Pharaoh, and Helen, who through thy guile is lost to me, thou wouldst have slain also, but thou couldst not harm her immortality. And now I die, and this is the end of all these Loves and Wars and Wanderings. My death has come upon me from the water.'

Meriamun stood speechless, for her heart was torn in two, so that in her grief she forgot even her rage against Helen and Rei the Priest.

Then Helen spoke. 'Thou diest indeed, Odysseus, yet it is but for a little time, for thou shalt come again and find me waiting.'

'Ay, Odysseus,' said the Queen, 'and I also will come again, and thou shalt love me then. Oh, now the future opens, and I know the things that are to be. Beneath the Wings of Truth shall we meet again, Odysseus.'

'There shall we meet again, Odysseus, and there thou shalt draw the Veil of Truth,' said the Helen.

'Yea,' quoth the dying Wanderer; 'there or otherwhere shall we meet again, and there and otherwhere love and hate shall lose and win, and die to arise again. But not yet is the struggle ended that began in other worlds than this, and shall endure till evil is lost in good, and darkness swallowed up in light. Bethink thee, Meriamun, of that vision of thy bridal night, and read its riddle. Lo! I will answer it with my last breath as the Gods have given me wisdom. When we three are once more twain, then shall our sin be purged and peace be won, and the veil be drawn from the face of Truth. Oh, Helen, fare thee well! I have sinned against thee, I have sworn by the Snake who should have sworn by the Star, and therefore I have lost thee.'

'Thou hast but lost to find again beyond the Gateways of the West,' she answered low.

Then she bent down, and taking him in her arms, kissed him, whispering in his ear, and the blood of men that fell ever from the Star upon her breast, dropped like dew upon his brow, and vanished as it dropped.

And as she whispered of joy to be, and things too holy

to be written, the face of the Wanderer grew bright, like the face of a God.

Then suddenly his head fell back, and he was dead, dead upon the heart of the World's Desire. For thus was fulfilled the oath of Idalian Aphrodite, and thus at the last did Odysseus lie in the arms of the Golden Helen.

Now Meriamun clasped her breast, and her lips turned white with pain. But Helen rose, and standing at the Wanderer's head looked on Meriamun, who stood at his feet.

'My sister,' said Helen to the Queen; 'see now the end of all. He whom we loved is lost to us, and what hast thou gained? Nay, look not so fiercely on me. I may not be harmed of thee, as thou hast seen, and thou mayest not be harmed of me, who would harm none, though ever thou wilt hate me who hate thee not, and till thou learnest to love me, Sin shall be thy portion and Bitterness thy comfort.'

But Meriamun spoke no word.

Then Helen beckoned to Rei and spake to him, and Rei went weeping to do her bidding.

Presently he returned again, and with him were soldiers bearing torches. The soldiers lifted up the body of the Wanderer, and bore it to a mighty pyre that was built up of the wealth of the barbarians, of chariots, spears, and the oars of ships, of wondrous fabrics, and costly furniture. And they laid the Wanderer on the pyre, and on his breast they laid the black bow of Eurytus.

Then Helen spoke to Rei once more, and Rei took a torch and fired the pyre so that smoke and flame burst from it. And all the while Meriamun stood by as one who dreams.

Now the great pyre was a mass of flame, and the golden armour of the Wanderer shone through the flame, and the black bow twisted and crumbled in the heat. Then of a sudden Meriamun gave a great cry, and tearing the snake girdle from her middle hurled it on the flames.

'From fire thou camest, thou Ancient Evil,' she said in

a dead tongue; 'to fire get thee back again, false counsellor.'

But Rei the Priest called aloud in the same tongue:

'An ill deed thou hast done, O Queen, for thou hast taken the Snake to thy bosom, and where the Snake passes there thou must follow.'

Even as he spoke, the face of Meriamun grew fixed, and she was drawn slowly toward the fire, as though by invisible hands. Now she stood on its very brink, and now with one loud wail she plunged into it and cast herself at length on the body of the Wanderer.

And as she lay there on the body, behold the Snake awoke in the fire. It awoke, it grew, it twined itself about the body of Meriamun and the body of the Wanderer, and lifting its head, it laughed.

Then the fire fell in, and the Wanderer and Meriamun the Queen, and the Snake that wrapped them round, vanished in the heart of the flames.

For awhile the Golden Helen stood still, looking on the dying fire. Then she let her veil fall, and turning, wandered forth into the desert and the night, singing as she passed.

And so she goes, wandering, wandering, till Odysseus comes again.

Now this is the tale that I, Rei the Priest, have been bidden to set forth before I lay me down to sleep in my splendid tomb that I have made ready by Thebes. Let every man read it as he will, and every woman as the Gods have given her wit.

PALINODE

Thou that of old didst blind Stesichorus,
If e'er, sweet Helen, such a thing befell,
We pray thee of thy grace, be good to us,
Though little in our tale accordeth well
With that thine ancient minstrel had to tell,
Who saw, with sightless eyes grown luminous,
These Ilian sorrows, and who heard the swell
Of ocean round the world ring thunderous,
And thy voice break when knightly Hector fell!

And thou who all these many years hast borne
To see the great webs of thy weaving torn
By puny hands of dull, o'er-learned men,
Homer, forgive us that thy hero's star
Once more above sea waves and waves of war,
Must rise, must triumph, and must set again!